MARCH ON

BOOKS IN THE TUCKER SERIES

MARCH ON

David Johnson

This book is a work of fiction. Names, characters, businesses,
organizations, places, events, and incidents either are the product of
the author's imagination or are used fictitiously. Any resemblance to
actual persons, living or dead, or locales is entirely coincidental.

March On is a new release of a previously published edition.
This new edition has been updated and edited.
Text copyright © 2014 David Johnson

Published by Lake Union Publishing, Seattle

www.apub.com

Amazon, the Amazon logo, and Lake Union Publishing
are trademarks of Amazon.com, Inc., or its affiliates.

ISBN-13: 9781477827031
ISBN-10: 147782703X

Cover design by Jason Blackburn

Library of Congress Control Number: 2014943975

Printed in the United States of America

This book is dedicated to anyone who has experienced a violent trauma perpetrated by another person. Please remember that what happened to you does not define you. You are much more than that. If you are reading this, you are indeed a survivor. Never give up on your journey of recovering your life. Healing will come. Allow your fear to give way to trust, your doubt to faith, and your resentment to forgiveness.

CHAPTER ONE

April's eyes shine with excitement as she says, "Now remember, everyone joins in on the chorus. March, you and Debbie sing 'like a fox' with me, then Smiley, you and August sing the next 'like a fox,' and finally, Tucker, you and Shady Green sing that highest harmony note on the third 'like a fox.' Okay, everybody, 'Fox on the Run' in the key of G. 1, 2, 3, 4."

April attacks her Autoharp with the energy of a rabbit running from a pack of beagles. Shady Green and Smiley Carter only miss the first beat before they jump on board her fast-moving musical train right in tempo with her, Shady strumming his battered guitar and Smiley his five-string banjo. A short instrumental introduction gives way to April leading the group who sings first, and then nodding at each pair when it's time for them to sing their line. After three verses and a chorus each time, April, Smiley, and Shady all finish the song on the same stroke.

Shady spins his guitar in the air. However, he miscalculates its rotation and it clatters to the floor, one of the strings breaking with a loud twang.

Debbie gasps and claps her hand over her mouth in shock and dismay.

August and Smiley laugh.

Tucker says, "It ain't no wonder yore git-tar looks like it was drug behind Smiley's tractor."

Shady snatches his guitar off the floor by its neck. "Ah pwak-ticed that las' nigh' an' caugh' it jus' fine." He mumbles something else under his breath as he sits down and starts removing the broken string.

This triggers a short burst of laughter from April. "Shady still wants to be one of those guitar players who used to break their guitars after a song. Only trouble is, he can't afford the replacement."

Shady blushes and looks at April. "May-ee un day ah catch it."

"Fair enough," April says, "maybe one day you will."

There is a lull and, as if everyone notices it at the same time, there is a realization that March hasn't said anything. Everyone looks at him.

As if someone had sprinkled it with glitter, the front of March's beard sparkles with the light shining through the prisms of his scattered tears. When Debbie sees his tears, she lays her head on his shoulder and puts her arm across his back. He leans his head over and touches it to hers. He sniffs loudly and says, "I don't know when I'm going to be able to come back home for a visit and not end up crying. It's for sure not my intent to bring anybody down, because the tears you see are tears of joy, contentment, and peace. All those years I was gone from here, lost in the world, I never dreamed I could come back home. I don't know who it was that said you can't go home again, or what he meant when he said it, but for me it's not true. I say you can go home again if it means finding the place that you're loved and accepted for who you are, if that's the kind of family you came from. I can't tell you all enough times that I love you. I wish I could see you, look in your eyes, so you would know I really mean it."

March's emotional declaration holds everyone spellbound. Silence hangs in the air like tinsel on a Christmas tree, adorning March's words with honor and respect.

Suddenly the loud honk of Smiley blowing his nose breaks the intensity of the moment and everyone laughs.

"My gosh," August says, "I've told you that you need to warn people before you blow that air horn of yours!"

Smiley folds his blue bandanna and stuffs it in his back pocket. "Well I can't help it that every time I cry, some of the tears find their way down the inside of my nose and make it drip like a leaky roof."

Tucker rattles the ice in her tea glass as she takes a drink. Setting it on the end table beside her chair, she says, "Even though it's been two years since we got y' back, March, I don't never git tired of hearin' y' talk like that. It's th' sweetest music this ol' woman's ears ever heard."

April puts her Autoharp on the floor and rushes to Tucker. Throwing her arms around her, she says, "Oh Tuckuh, you ah the best, most wooonderful, most unbelievable, grandmothuh that ever graced God's earth. You know that nobody loves you like April does. Tell everyone that I'm your favorite. Go ahead, tell them, tell them!" She finishes by peppering Tucker's face with a flurry of kisses.

"Oh my lord, child," Tucker exclaims, "you're gonna smother me! And quit actin' like Scarlett O'Hara. Y' know good an' well they ain't nobody what could replace y'." She rolls her eyes at everyone else and says, "Though goodness knows I've tried to, but won't nobody take y'."

Grabbing her chest with both hands, April falls to the floor. "Oh the pain of being rejected by one's own grandmothuh! I fear this wound may be the end of me!"

March laughs heartily. Clapping his hands, he says loudly, "Let's give a round of applause for this year's Academy Award winner, April Tucker!"

Everyone joins him in clapping and laughing. April tries to maintain a pouting expression, but finally her facade breaks and she laughs, too.

"When I start practicing law and have to persuade a jury to rule in favor of my client," August says, "I may have to take drama lessons from you, April. Or maybe I could just hire you to come in and do the summations for me." He snaps his fingers and adds, "That's a good idea!"

Tucker looks over her shoulder at the dining table, "I'll tell y', them dishes ain't gittin' no cleaner just sittin' on th' table. I'm guessin' we girls better see what we can do with 'em." Grunting, she pushes herself out of her recliner.

Debbie quickly gets up and walks toward the dining room.

"Tucker," April says from her position on the floor, "that is such a sexist attitude. Who says women are always supposed to do all the domestic duties in a house? It's 1992, not 1952. Men should do their fair share of work in the home, too."

Tucker folds her arms across her chest and looks around the room. "Well let's just think 'bout that fer a minute. What we have t' choose from are an old man who can barely get around anymore, a man who can't even hold his git-tar without droppin' it, a blind man, and a man who wouldn't know nothin' 'bout how t' clean a cast-iron skillet without ruinin' it. I'm sure all yore teachers up at UT fills yore head with lots of good ideas, but they ain't got no idea what th' crop of men 'round here looks like."

Standing up, August says, "Gentlemen, I do believe our integrity has been called into question this day. I say it's time for us to rise up and show these women that we are comfortable enough in our manhood to take care of a job as simple as cleaning some dishes."

March stands up, waving his hands in front of him. "I'll do the washing. Take me to the sink!"

Smiley's eyes are wide and his mouth open. "Now wait just a minute, son. I think we need to think this through or at least take a vote on it. Isn't that how these things are supposed to be decided?"

Shady Green jumps up, having forgotten his guitar was across his lap. It bounces across the floor and another string breaks. "Shhh—!" he hisses loudly.

Tucker makes a sweeping gesture with her arm. "I rest m' case."

Huffing loudly, April gets up off the floor and says, "I suppose you're right, Tucker, but it's still not fair."

Once the three women are out of the living room, Smiley gives the men an exaggerated wink and a thumbs-up gesture.

Oblivious to Smiley, March says loudly, "Well I still think I could have washed. I'm not some kind of helpless female—oops! I mean, person." He covers his face and laughs as verbal insults hail upon him from the dining room.

"I don't know about you boys, August and Shady," Smiley says, "but this ol' fella is about ready to head to the house. That Thanksgiving turkey we ate is just about to put me to sleep."

"Whatever you say, Pop," August says. "I'll be back here in the morning to pick you guys up and we'll head back to Knoxville."

"Sure thing," March says.

"Don't get here too early," April says. "Me and Debbie need our beauty sleep, don't we, Debbie?"

Winking at April, Debbie says, "Well I really don't see how I could be much more beautiful, but if a few extra hours will add to this perfect package, then I'm all for it."

"Ain't she the most humble thing?" March says. "That's just one of the things I love about her." He laughs.

"How come ya'll gotta head back s' soon?" Tucker asks. "Seems like ya'll barely got here an' now you're headin' back."

"I've got to get back to work at Patricia Neal," Debbie says. "And March hasn't been working long enough at the Voc Rehab

Center to get much time off. I'm really sorry. I would love to stay longer."

"And I've got to get back for classes," April says.

"Yeah, me too," August chimes in.

"Tucker," Smiley says, "it looks like we done got us a bunch of hardworking, high-achieving children here. Let's be thankful for it. Lord knows they's lots of kids out there ain't trying to do nothing to better themselves. Yes sir, this is a fine bunch of young people right here."

Tucker stops scraping a plate and looks from Debbie to March. "Well I just got me one question: When is it that you two is gonna fin'lly git married? Ever' time y' come home I expect y' t' make a big announcement. What's takin' y' so long t' make up yore mind?"

March's beard covers his blushing cheeks but can't hide the crimson glow of his nose and ears. "Good grief, Tucker," he says. "Don't you ever run any thought through a filter before it comes out your mouth?"

Looking nonplussed, Tucker says, "What's th' matter with askin' th' kid that y' raised when he's gonna get married? What's wrong with that?"

"Well, maybe that's between me and Debbie," March replies.

Turning back to scraping dishes, Tucker mutters, "Well I still don't see no harm in askin'."

April endeavors to insert herself into the awkwardness of the moment by drawing attention away from March and Debbie. "Okay, August, so you'll be here in the morning, right?"

"For sure, sis."

"We'll be packed and ready then." She gives her brother a hug and kisses Smiley on the cheek. "It's always good to see you, Smiley. And I sure enjoyed making music with you, Shady Green."

"'ank oo," Shady replies with a snaggletooth grin.

Putting on his cap, Smiley says, "Tucker, that was your usual top-of-the-line Thanksgiving meal. Much obliged."

"I'll see y' 'round," Tucker replies.

Lying in bed in the spare bedroom of Tucker's mobile home, Debbie Cooper stares at the ceiling. Turning her head to look at the digital clock on the bedside table, she sees 1:15 a.m. glowing in the darkness. Sleep has proved as elusive to her as the answer to Tucker's question earlier that night about when she and March are going to get married.

It seems to her that everyone is eager for them to marry. Even April expressed bewilderment when she helped Debbie make her bed.

"I have no idea why you and March don't sleep in here together instead of him sleeping on the couch in the living room," April had said. "People do it all the time, Debbie. Marriage isn't looked at like it used to be. People are more casual about it. It's not like you and March aren't spending nights together back in Knoxville, is it?"

Debbie had paused before answering April, unsure how much trust and confidence she could place in her. For certain she loved April and enjoyed her company, too, but April enjoyed living life too close to the edge and didn't always make smart choices. Debbie thought about letting April believe what she wanted to about her and March, but conscience dictated to her that perhaps hearing and seeing a different view of marriage was what April needed.

"Actually," she'd said to April, "that's not how it is with me and your brother. Sure, there's been a few times we've spent the night at each other's apartment, but we've always slept in separate beds. It's not something we've said out loud, but we've more or less agreed that we aren't going to let sex decide for us which direction our lives are going to take."

7

April stopped in the middle of putting a pillowcase on the bed pillow. "You're kidding, aren't you? That's absurd. You two love each other, even I can see that. You sound like you're living in the 1950s or something like that. I just don't get it."

Lying now in the darkness and quiet, Debbie chastises herself for her own duplicity in her conversation with April. A part of her agrees with April's assertions. And while Debbie tried to play it off as her and March's moral standards that are keeping them chaste, the larger truth is that it is more about March than Debbie. For while everyone around them seems eager for them to marry, March does not. In spite of their many intimate conversations, it is the one topic that has never crossed his lips.

Though April's comments seem to indicate she would have no problem if March and Debbie were sexually active, and Debbie finds herself sexually attracted to March, he gives no indication that he's eager to return her overtures of passion. He is the one who usually puts on the brakes when things heat up between them after they've kissed for a while.

Debbie catches herself unconsciously rubbing the stump of her amputated arm. "This is what it's about," she says to herself. "Who could find a woman attractive whose body is so terribly disfigured? I can't hold his face in my hands. Even when he wants to hold hands, he has to stop and think about whether he's on the side where my hand is. That kills the spontaneity and probably turns him off, too."

Turning away from the clock so she won't be reminded of the passing minutes without sleep, she continues musing. "So where is this relationship going? Why doesn't he break up with me and move on with his life? Pity?" The thought is so detestable to her that she actually gags and sits up coughing. "He better not pity me! I despise pity! It's a wasted emotion."

She gets out of bed and goes to the bathroom to get a drink of water. "So maybe I need to be the one who breaks up with him," she thinks. "He's too decent a man to walk away from me if he feels sorry for me. He's the kind who would stay with me forever, even if his heart wasn't in it. That's the kind of loyal friend he is."

Arriving back at her bed, she grabs her pillow and throws it against the headboard, then she punches it. "March Tucker, if you pity me and I find out about it, then I pity you for what I will do to you." Tears sting her eyes at the potential pain she is facing, the pain of losing the most important person in her life.

CHAPTER TWO

B ye, Tucker!" August, March, April, and Debbie yell simultane- ously as they pile into August's car, giving a final wave to Tucker, standing on her front porch.

Waving back, Tucker yells, "Ya'll be careful! I'll see y' at Christmas!"

August turns the key and his 1985 Toyota Corolla's engine spins to life. Letting out the clutch, he eases the car away from their childhood home. "Man, I don't know about you guys," August says, "but I never get tired of coming home here. I know Tucker was rough on us—it might even be called abuse today—but I still love her for what she did for us. She didn't have to take us in to raise."

From the back seat, March says, "I know what you mean. You all probably get tired of hearing me talk about it, but those eight years I was gone, sometimes homeless and stealing food just to stay alive, all I wanted was to get back home to you all and Tucker. There was one night in particular I was sleeping in the tall grass alongside the interstate in Arkansas. It was January and I felt like I was freez- ing to death. I started thinking about that old wood-burning stove in the old house. Remember that thing?"

"Do I ever!" August replies. "I've seen it get so hot it would be glowing red during the night."

"Exactly," March agrees. "And that's what I focused my mind on, how warm it felt to lie on the floor next to it, or to back up to it with your hands behind your back. It would warm you all the way to your core. Just thinking about that old wood stove was what saved me from frostbite and hypothermia. At least that's what I believe."

"I'll tell you what I've learned," April says. "Sometimes it takes leaving something to appreciate how much it means to you. It wasn't until I went away to Spirit Lake that I began to have an appreciation for the life I had with Tucker. And now that I'm at UT Knoxville, I think of more and more things that were so unique about how we grew up. When I tell classmates about using an outhouse as a little girl, they look at me like I'm making it up."

"I've just got to chime in here," Debbie interjects. "When March's memory came back to him and he began telling me stories about growing up, I really thought they were things he'd read about, and that he'd somehow come to believe they were about him. The first one was telling me about him and you, August, playing a game of throwing dirt clods at each other."

August and March both erupt into laughter.

"We called it war," August says. "March was a deadeye when it came to throwing dirt clods. It didn't matter that he was smaller and younger. He still would have me running from him sometimes."

"I'll bet I could still beat you today," March says, "even if I was blindfolded."

Everyone falls silent at the awkward comment.

"Oh, wait," March continues, grinning broadly, "I don't have to be blindfolded anymore."

April wheels around to slap him on the knee while Debbie punches his arm.

"That's cruel," Debbie exclaims. "You've got to stop doing that."

"Owww!" March howls. "August, pull over and help me. These women are beating up on a blind man. There's got to be some kind of law against that."

Peals of laughter ring out within the tiny confines of the car.

Once they all catch their breath, they settle in for the six-hour drive.

March relaxes back into the seat beside Debbie, expecting her to rest against him as she usually does. Even though they are close enough that he can feel the heat from her body, it is the distance between them that he notices most. And she seemed unusually quiet at breakfast this morning. He wants to ask her if anything is wrong, but the cramped quarters of the car don't allow for any intimate conversation. He's left with his imagination, especially the fear-induced part, to start listing possible reasons for the change in Debbie.

He begins by retracing everything he's said or done since they left Knoxville to come to Dresden.

Did I tell her goodnight last night? I know I was going to, but then April was in the bedroom with her and I didn't want to interrupt. But I thought I went back and did tell her goodnight. Didn't I? And why does she have to get upset about a little thing like that? I just got busy and forgot. Can't it be that simple? How am I going to apologize while we're all riding together in the car? Maybe at the first rest stop I can do it.

Just as he thinks he's resolved his dilemma, his mind turns a page.

That's not it. She's tired of me, that's what it is. Initially it was the fascination of this new patient at the hospital that attracted her to me. I was all mystery, and that intrigued her. But now she's learned that I grew up dirt-poor, that there is nothing special or intriguing about me. She probably is ready to move on to someone who is more multidimensional than me and represents more of a challenge to her.

12

Like a beagle jumping a rabbit out of a brush pile, this musing flushes out another thought.

Of course! It's that I'm not intellectually stimulating enough for her. I never even finished high school. Debbie is a very intelligent woman. Sometimes she brings up topics that I've never even heard of. How embarrassed she must be at times to be with me in group settings and I have nothing to contribute to the conversation. I must look and sound mentally slow at times.

Suddenly his insecurities hurl a dart that pricks his heart.

Pity! It's about pity! She probably felt sorry for me from the very start; the poor blind amnesiac. Then I latched onto her like a shipwrecked sailor onto a piece of driftwood and that just made her pity me even more. She looked at me like some kind of abandoned puppy that needed rescuing. Now her pity tank has run out and she's ready to let someone else have their turn trying to raise me. She's probably trying to find a people pound she can drop me off at and have me euthanized. I despise pity!

With both his blood pressure and his pulse elevated because of his anxiety-induced adrenaline rush, his palms are sweating and his breathing is rapid. He tugs at his shirt collar, hoping that will make his breathing easier. He flinches when Debbie lays her hand on his thigh.

"Are you okay?" she whispers. "You look like you're about to jump out of your skin. What's the matter?"

March doesn't trust his voice to maintain a whisper, so he answers Debbie by holding up his hand and shaking his head.

She immediately removes her hand from his thigh, and March feels her scoot toward the door of the car.

March suddenly feels like he's back lying in the grass by the interstate on that cold January night, except that this time the chill is caused by the emptiness in his heart and the abandonment he feels. He knows that Debbie misinterpreted his nonverbal messages, believing he wanted her to leave him alone, but he can't talk to her and explain himself without August and April hearing him.

"Hey, August," March says. "I'm sorry, but I've got to use the bathroom. I forgot to go pee before we left Tucker's."

"What?" August replies. "We haven't even got to McKenzie yet."

"I know, I know, but I've got to get rid of this coffee. Find a service station in McKenzie."

August lets off the accelerator and turns on his blinker. "Okay, but we'll never get to Knoxville at this rate."

August locates a service station and pulls in. "How do you want to do this?" he asks.

"If Debbie will just walk me to the door of the restroom, I can manage things from there."

Looking out the window beside her, Debbie says, "I think it would be better if August took you."

Before March can think of something else to say that will let Debbie know he really wants her to take him, August opens his door and says, "Sure thing. No problem."

CHAPTER THREE

Once August and March return to the car, April adjusts the makeup mirror on her sun visor so she can see both March and Debbie. Clearly something is going on between them because normally Debbie would have escorted March to the bathroom without hesitation. April could hear the chill in Debbie's voice when she suggested August accompany him.

She watches Debbie turn her head away from March when he slides into the backseat. April can practically see the frost on her shoulder. March turns his unseeing gaze toward Debbie. When Debbie remains frozen, March slumps back in the seat and faces the front, apparently lost in the emotional blizzard.

April feels a bow playing a sympathetic note on her heartstrings as she tries to imagine how difficult it must be for March to interpret his blind world. At the same time she wonders, as she has several times since meeting Debbie, how it must be for her to be in a relationship with a blind man, much less what it must be like to have a prosthetic hand. Tying shoestrings, fastening jeans, putting on earrings, and especially fastening a bra must require a level of dexterity that April can only imagine.

Maybe it's the commonality they have in being handicapped that brought them together in the first place, April thinks to herself. *But that might not be enough to hold them together. Even though they're doing a really good job of covering it up, something has happened that has put a wedge between them.*

Weary of trying to figure out her brother and his girlfriend, April raises the sun visor back in place and rests her head on the headrest as she closes her eyes. Almost immediately her thoughts drift to her life in Knoxville, especially the part-time job she has, a job she is certain was placed in her path by God.

She was scanning the want ads in the *Knoxville News Sentinel* two months ago and saw someone was looking for help providing care for two young boys plus doing some light housekeeping. Even though it wasn't the kind of job she was looking for, she called the number. A man answered the phone almost immediately. Though he didn't identify himself by name, there was something about the man that seemed familiar to her.

Her phone call was perfect timing, he'd told her, and he'd asked if she could come on over right away for the interview. Looking back now she admits to herself that it was not the safest move on her part, but she agreed to go and borrowed her roommate's car without telling her where she was going.

She found the house with little trouble. It looked much like all the other houses in the subdivision, a two-story brick structure with white trim. But even in September, it was evident that the yard to this house received much more attention than its neighbors'. There were large azaleas, with rhododendrons rising above them. At each corner of the house were neatly trimmed holly trees that just touched the edge of the soffit. As she climbed the steps to the front door she noticed pansies and mums planted in the flowerbeds. Lying in the front yard were two small bicycles, no doubt belonging to the boys who lived there.

Just as she was about to knock on the front door, it flew open and two young boys ran into her. It was so unexpected and they were running with such reckless abandon that they all tumbled onto the landing in front of the door. A small cry of pain escaped from April as her ankle twisted under her.

Trying to untangle herself from the two boys, April suddenly heard the voice of the man from the phone.

"Oh my gosh! What happened?! Boys, what have you done now?!"

And it was at that moment that April realized why he seemed so familiar to her. Looking up into the doorway, she said, "James, from Spirit Lake, is that really you?"

Though he was in the motion of reaching down to help her up, the man stopped and, furrowing his brow, peered closely at her face. It was a few seconds before recognition spread across his face and he smiled. "April, can it be?"

Thankful that their dad was distracted by recognizing the woman they'd just bowled over, the two boys scampered toward their bicycles, jumped on them, and pedaled furiously to outdistance their dad's voice, which might call them back for punishment.

Squatting beside April, James had said, "Are you hurt? And what are you doing here?"

"I think I just twisted my ankle a little bit, but I'm fine. Actually, I'm the one who called you a little bit ago about the job in the paper."

His arms under her armpits, he lifted April to her feet. "That is unbelievable. What a small world this is. Come on in the house and I'll get some ice to put on your ankle."

Not only did April have difficulty getting her balance when she started following him into the house, but her mind felt like it was being pulled apart like the wedges of a peeled orange. Even though it had been two years since they were together at Spirit Lake, upon seeing James she immediately felt all those old feelings of insecurity that plagued her when she first arrived there. However, meeting him in a totally different context, she felt more like an adult, almost like a peer.

But the strangest thing to her was the attraction she felt upon first seeing him in the doorway. He was never what she would have called unattractive while they were at Spirit Lake, but she never noticed how handsome he really was, until now. His square jawline, full lips, Roman nose, and soft, gray eyes were all the traits she found attractive in a guy. When he'd slipped his arms around her to help her up, she actually felt her nipples tingle and grow hard. And the last wedge of her brain that she grappled with was the one that said all her attraction to him was gross!

Once in the house, he helped her to a loveseat in the living room, then rushed to the kitchen to get some ice. While he was in the kitchen, she looked at the artwork on the walls. There was a print of Norman Rockwell's famous barbershop scene. Over the mantle of the fireplace there was what had to be a family portrait of James, his two boys, and, April surmised, his wife. Based on the brief look she got at the boys when they crashed into her, she guessed the portrait was two to three years old. James's dark features created quite a contrast to his wife's blonde hair and pale complexion. She had a small nose, a relaxed smile accented by deep dimples on both cheeks, and eyes that even from this distance April could tell were emerald green, the same color as the jade broach around her neck.

When James returned to the living room, he handed her the icepack and sat in the chair across from her. "So how are you, April? And what are you doing in Knoxville?"

"I'm doing really good. I graduated high school once I returned home with Tucker and now I'm starting my second year here at UT."

"That is fantastic. I'm so proud of you. What's your major?"

"I haven't really decided yet. Maybe social work, maybe psychology. I think I want to be a therapist like you and Mary. I might even go back to Spirit Lake and try to get hired there as a therapist." James holds her for a moment with his unblinking eyes, the same way he used to when she was in his office at Spirit Lake. Back then she was eager to look away, but being with him in his living room she found herself returning his gaze and trying to look deeper into his eyes. Finally he blinked and said, "I can see you working there. You've got a lot of traits a good therapist needs."

His words of praise had given her chills and she could feel a blush creeping up from her chest to her neck. She felt like a puppy must feel when it gets its belly rubbed. In an attempt to keep her face from blushing red, she turned the conversation to the ad in the paper and asked what kind of help he was needing.

It was then that his eyes had turned sad and the lines in his face deepened. "It's my wife, Susan. Her cancer miraculously went into remission two years ago. She had a good eighteen months. Her hair grew back, she regained her strength, and she even went back to working at the art gallery part-time." He delivered his words with energy, and his face brightened. But when he finished speaking, the cloud returned and his eyes grew red. "It's a cruel disease, April. Cancer—I hate it!"

"You probably don't remember this," April said, "but my grandmother, Ella, died of cancer even after she'd beaten breast cancer. It's one of the things that turned my life upside down."

"Oh, I'm sorry, April. I do remember that now. I should have thought before speaking."

"It's okay. I'm okay with it now." She took the icepack off her ankle and turned so she could face him. "How is Susan now?"

James's expression told April everything she needed to know. She didn't want him to have to say it out loud. But before she could cut in, he said, "The end is coming. It won't be long now, maybe a month. The doctors can't say for sure."

"So how can I help?" she asked.

"We need someone who can help with the boys some, do some house cleaning and some laundry, maybe cook a meal occasionally. I guess what we really need is a nanny who can live with us, for a while anyway. But you're busy with school and studies, so it might not be something you can commit to. It's a lot to take on."

April knew immediately that she was going to accept the position but was afraid he would think her rash and immature, so she told him she would think about it and call him tomorrow.

"What in the world are you smiling about?" August's voice cuts into her reverie and startles her.

Sitting up, she says, "What?"

"To use one of Smiley Carter's expressions, you were grinning like a possum eating grapes, whatever that means."

"Do you have a problem with someone having a pleasant thought and smiling about it?" April snaps.

August holds up both his hands briefly then puts them back on the steering wheel. "Whoa there, sister. Don't bite my head off. I was just asking a question, trying to make some conversation. Apparently the customers in the back of my limousine are having some kind of lovers' quarrel and are not currently predisposed to engaging in stimulating conversation with each other or with me."

April slaps August's arm. "Shhh!" she says, as she squints at him.

"Keep your high-dollar lawyer words to yourself," March growls from the backseat. "I don't even understand what you just said."

Debbie acts as if there is no one in the car except her and continues looking out the window.

The cold front from the backseat sweeps over August and April, too. They look at each other with raised eyebrows. April shrugs and August shakes his head as they continue traveling toward Knoxville.

CHAPTER FOUR

"He's waking up, boss."

"Throw some water in his face."

The cold water would normally have made Buzzard gasp, but in his addled state it only confuses him. With one eye swollen shut, he manages to open his other eye into a slit. He sees blood on the concrete floor and pieces of something he can't distinguish lying in it. Ropes have him tightly bound to a chair. The only thing he can move is his right arm. Slowly he raises it and looks at his hand. With the force of a freight train, pain and recognition hit him at the same time.

Blood is dripping from his hand, and where his pinky and ring finger should be, there are only bloody stumps. Fear and pain jerk his head up and he stares at the man standing in front of him. "What have you done to me?!" he cries out. "You're insane!"

Pushing his red hair out of his sweating face, the man grins and says, "You're the one who's insane, Buzzard. You thought ol' Red wouldn't be able to find you, didn't you? While I was sitting in prison for ten years, the only thing that kept me going was knowing I would get out one day and I would find the people who set me up and make them pay."

Through his swollen face Buzzard says, "I've told you and told you that I don't know what you're talking about! I heard the feds busted you, but that's all I know." Looking again at his hand, he yells, "You cut my fingers off! What am I going to do?!"

Red grips the two-foot piece of garden hose in his lap and strikes Buzzard across the face. "You're going to tell me where my money is, that's what you're going to do! Or you're going to sit in this chair and I'll start cutting fingers off your other hand."

Buzzard begins sobbing. "I've told you, I don't know what you're talking about. You've got to believe me!"

Red scoots his chair closer to Buzzard and puts his face inches from his face. In a calm, low, malevolent tone, he says, "I'll give it to you again, slowly, so you don't miss any of it. Ten years ago, someone broke into my hideaway in the mountains and stole all my money out of the safe and all the drugs I was holding for another big sale. They only left one brick of heroin. As soon as I walked in the cabin and discovered what had happened, the feds busted through every door and window with an assault team. Somebody," he taps Buzzard on the forehead for emphasis, "somebody told the feds about my hideaway and then stole everything before they staked it out. You and Roan and Big Country were the only three people who knew about that cabin, so one of you or all of you set me up."

Red stands up quickly, kicking his chair across the floor. "It's judgment time for you, Buzzard! Tell me what I want to know or prepare to feel more pain. I want you to tell me who did it and where Roan and Big Country are. And I want to hear it now!"

Red motions to his right, and a large black man steps into Buzzard's field of vision and hands a pair of lopping shears to Red. The blades are crimson with Buzzard's blood. Working the action of the shears, Red says, "You know there's not much difference in trimming limbs off a tree and trimming fingers off a man, except that the tree doesn't howl and scream as much." He throws back his head and laughs loudly.

Then, as if he flipped a switch, his expression turns grim and he approaches Buzzard. "Hold him," he says, and someone from behind him grabs his arm with the good hand while the black man grips his wrist.

Buzzard jerks and twists, trying to wrench his arm and hand free, but his bonds are so tight he's unable to get any leverage.

"I believe I'll start with the pinky again," Red says as he moves in with the shears.

Buzzard makes his hand into a fist to protect his fingers.

"Now, Buzzard, we've already been through this. That won't keep me from doing what I want to do." Red forces the point of one of the blades in between Buzzard's pinky and his palm, then rams it further, until the middle joints of all four of his fingers are lying on one blade and the other blade is poised above them. Gripping the handles of the shears, he presses them together.

One by one the ends of Buzzard's fingers pop off and fall to the floor. A four-faucet fountain of blood shoots into the air as Buzzard screams, "Nooo!" Then he passes out.

The two men holding Buzzard release their grip on him. The black man turns to Red and says, "We're wasting our time with him, boss. I don't think he knows nothing."

Dropping the shears on the floor, Red says, "I believe you're right." He reaches inside his pants pocket and pulls out a small caliber pistol.

The other man chuckles and says, "What kind of cap pistol is that? I've got a nine millimeter in my truck. Let me go get it for you."

"Here's a lesson for you two," Red says. "Never use more force than is necessary to get what you want, no matter what the situation is. This little twenty-five caliber pistol will actually do better than your cannon. When you shoot someone in the head with a nine millimeter, the bullet goes straight through and blows a hole out the other side. Sometimes that kills a person, but sometimes it doesn't. When I shoot this tiny bullet into someone's head, the bullet actually ricochets around and damages more parts of the brain. That way you're more certain to kill them."

Red lets off the safety of his pistol, cocks the hammer, puts the barrel on Buzzard's hairline, and fires. Within seconds, Buzzard exhales one last time, his body goes limp, and his bowels and bladder empty.

"Phew!" Red exclaims. "What a stench! That's one thing all these movies and TV shows don't show when a person dies. The disgusting side of death." Turning to the two men with him, Red says, "Do like I showed you. Use the fillet knives and handsaws and cut him up into parts and bag all the parts separately, then throw each bag in a different Dumpster in and around Knoxville. I'm going to try and locate Roan. When I do, I'll contact you."

The third accomplice in the grizzly scene cackles. "Man, this is the craziest thing I've ever done! Where in the world did you get the idea to get rid of a body this way?"

"I grew up in a place called Reelfoot Lake," Red answers. "When I was growing up my daddy and granddaddy was part of a secret organization called the Night Riders. It was sort of a redneck version of the mafia. The law pretty much stayed out of their way, mainly because some of them were Night Riders, too. Me and my half brother used to lay awake at night and listen to some of the men telling tales while they sat at the fireplace drinking. One night we listened to them telling about this man who had gotten mad at my daddy and burned his duck blind, which was one of the sorriest things anybody could do. Daddy rounded up two or three of his buddies and they took matters into their own hands. That man was never heard from again because his body was scattered all over the lake."

The black man asks, "What about the other man, Big Country?" Red shakes his head. "It can't be him. I treated that boy like a son. I don't believe he would ever turn against me."

"But what if it turns out it was him?"

Red's eyes close to slits and the scar on the side of his face flares crimson. "Then he'll face judgment just like Buzzard did."

CHAPTER FIVE

As the group enters Knoxville traffic, August says, "Okay, folks, where am I dropping everyone off? You'll go to James's, right April?"

April looks at him with raised eyebrows, confused that he would even ask the question. "Well of course. That's where I live, isn't it?" Then it hits her that the question is really for March and Debbie. Will they be spending the night together at one of their apartments? Or will they each go to their separate places?

"I know, I know," August replies to her. "I just thought I'd ask. You might have had some other plans, that's all I was asking."

March turns his face toward Debbie. "Why don't we—"

Debbie cuts him off. "Just take me to my apartment, please."

Trying to keep the air light, August smiles and says, "Yes, ma'am, milady. Your chariot will carry you with quick dispatch to the place of your abode."

But the cold atmosphere in the car turns August's warm words into icicles. They fall to the floorboard and shatter like glass.

Thirty minutes later, August slows to a stop in front of March's apartment. He shuts off the engine and gets out to open the trunk.

In the car, April says, "I'll be talking to you, March." She places her hand on his knee and squeezes it. "I love you."

"Love you, too, sis," March replies. He turns toward Debbie, holding his anxious and hopeful heart in his hand. "I guess we can talk later? Maybe?"

Debbie looks at March. The fearful tone in March's voice pangs her, especially realizing she's the one who fired the arrow that wounded him. But because of her confused heart, she doesn't trust her words to be an honest reflection of her feelings. So she says as little as she can. "Sure."

His hope now dashed on the rocky shores of love lost, March says, "I'll wait for you to call me." He opens his car door, gets out, and unfolds his cane.

Carrying March's small suitcase, August walks to his side and says, "Come on, bro, I've got your luggage. Let me walk you to the door and help you inside."

March finds August's arm and takes the suitcase from him. "I've got it. You guys go on. I'm fine."

August steps closer to his brother. "Listen," he says in a low tone, "I don't know what's going on with you and Debbie, but don't worry about it. These things have a way of working themselves out and people end up not even knowing what they were fighting about. Hey, she may just be PMSing. You know, all those hormones racing around make girls crazy sometimes."

Nothing in August's words or tone of voice can lighten March's heavy heart. He puts his arms around his brother and gives him a brief hug. "Thanks for driving us all home." Then he turns and walks up the sidewalk, tapping his way as he goes.

Once he's in his dark apartment, March sits down in his recliner and taps the clock beside his chair. "The time is 8:56 p.m.," a mechanical voice tells him. He listens to the sounds of his apartment—the compressor in the refrigerator kicking on, the low hum of his central heating unit, the occasional creak and pop of the floor in the apartment above him. "So is this it, God?" he says aloud. "You bring the prodigal son home, delivering him from his lostness, and put someone in his life who awakens love, and now you're going to take her away from me? Was she just one of your angels like Clarence was for George Bailey, and now her job is done? She's earned her wings? What kind of cruel joke is that?!"

His cathartic outburst pulls the plug from his tear ducts and the briny solution mixed with emotions begins flowing. Deep sobs rack his body and he cries out in the darkness, "Oh, Debbie, don't leave me!"

He cries until exhaustion overtakes his sadness and he falls asleep.

After his mind has had a respite, March awakes. He immediately picks up the receiver of his phone, listens for the dial tone, and begins to punch in Debbie's phone number. Just before he punches the last number, he taps his clock. "The time is 11:14 p.m."

What am I doing? Do I really want to wake her up and make her even madder at me?

He slowly lowers the receiver back into its cradle. Getting up, he goes to the bathroom. After taking a shower, he makes his way into the kitchen, fixes himself a glass of iced tea, and returns to his chair.

"The time is 11:42 p.m.," his clock says in response to his touch.

The phone rings. He is so startled that he spills some tea on his lap. He picks up the receiver, puts it to his ear, and says, "Hello?"

The person on the other end is crying. "March?" Debbie's broken voice speaks to him. "I know it's late, but I can't sleep. Can I come over so we can talk?"

Like a lit match, Debbie's voice lights the candle of hope in March's heart. "Please come," he answers her.

Sniffling, Debbie says, "I'll be there as soon as I can."

The phone clicks in March's ear as Debbie hangs up.

Like a thundering herd of panicked wildebeests, March's imagination runs pell-mell in every direction, searching for a reason for Debbie's late-night visit. The brief flicker of hope turns into panic.

She's going to tell me she met someone else!

This is the end. She's going to break up with me.

She has an incurable disease and is going to do the "brave thing" and break off our relationship in order to spare my feelings.

She's tired of feeling sorry for me and has realized she doesn't really love me.

She's sick of the awkwardness of dating someone who is blind.

She's transferring to Montana and doesn't want to try to maintain a long-distance relationship.

Hoping he can shake off his fears, March shakes his head like a dog after a swim. But, much like a cocklebur, his fears can't be flung off.

To distract himself, he decides to make a pot of coffee. He is in the middle of preparing it when a thought strikes him. *The lights! I've got to turn on some lights before Debbie gets here.*

More than once Debbie has chastised him for not having any lights burning when she's come for a visit. "I understand that you don't have need of them," she said, "but you have to remember that the majority of people do have their vision and need lights on to help them. It's about you being sensitive to other folks."

As quickly as he can, March negotiates the path to each room in his apartment and turns on some lights. As a last thought, he turns on the stereo and George Strait's album *Pure Country* begins playing.

Just as he sits down, the doorbell rings. He listens as the lock on the door turns and the door opens. The breeze outside his apartment sweeps through the open door and carries Debbie's scent to

March. He stands and turns to face the doorway she'll be coming through.

A weak place in the subflooring creaks just as she steps in the room where March is waiting.

Smiling, March says, "I'm hoping you are my girlfriend and not just a burglar who smells like her."

Debbie laughs tentatively and says, "Hello, March. Is that coffee I smell?"

"Freshly made," March replies. "Want me to fix you a cup? We can sit in the living room and talk."

"Let's both go in the kitchen. I'd rather sit together at your dinette table."

"Uh, sure," March says. But he doesn't like leaving the comfort and warmth of his living room.

As they enter the small kitchen, Debbie says, "You go ahead and sit down. I'll fix our coffee for us."

March dutifully takes a seat and waits silently for Debbie to take the lead in this delicate dance of hearts.

After she sets their coffee mugs on the table, they both take careful sips of the hot brew and set the mugs down simultaneously. Apprehension fills the air like a thick fog.

Grabbing March's hands, Debbie says, "Put your hands on my face so you can see me. I want you to get both my tone of voice and my facial expressions while we talk because this may be the most important conversation we've ever had."

As he places his trembling hands on the sides of Debbie's face, in a distant corner of his mind he hears his former therapist, Dr. Sydney, saying, "Always remember, March, fear of abandonment will forever be close by, nipping at the edges of your heart and mind. Don't run from it. Go to it and learn from it."

Using his index and middle fingers, he searches for a frown crease between her eyes. Then gently runs his fingers along her eyebrows to see if they are relaxed. His thumbs travel across her lips but can't find the smile dimples in her cheeks. A chill runs up his spine.

Placing her hands on his wrists, Debbie says, "What do you see?"

"You're very serious, but you're not angry. I don't believe you're tense, but I do believe you're a little nervous."

"Is that all?"

"No. I also see a beautiful woman; a woman I love."

"Stop right there. Don't even go there until you hear what I've got to say."

March slowly takes his hands from her face, breaking contact with the thing that has brought him the most security he's felt since he ran away from home as a child. Folding his hands, he rests them on the table.

"If you want to blame someone for what I'm about to say to you," Debbie begins, "then blame Tucker. It was her question after we ate dinner the other night that started my mind spinning."

Immediately March's mind flips through the pages of his memory, searching for any record of a question from Tucker. In milliseconds he scans the conversation at the dining table, then goes quickly to the singing session afterward. Nowhere does he find a question from Tucker. But suddenly his mind is arrested by the conversation that occurred when the dishes were being cleaned up. As if it was underlined in red, Tucker's question leaps from the page.

"Do you remember what she asked?" Debbie says. Not waiting for March's reply, she continues, "She asked when we were going to get married and what was taking us so long to make up our minds. I don't know why, but it wasn't until then that I realized it was a topic you and I have never discussed. And I also realized that I had made some assumptions about our future without ever having talked with you about it. That's a pretty foolish thing for a girl to do.

"I've been left alone with my imagination to try and figure things out. The problem with that is I have a very active imagination, so it came up with multiple theories, none of which I could prove or disprove.

"I went back to the first time we met. Do you remember that?"

"Like it was yesterday," March answers truthfully. "Remember me thinking you were married?"

"Yes. You thought the sound of my prosthesis on your wheelchair was a wedding ring. And I thought you were a jerk because of the chip you carried on your shoulder."

Nodding his head, March says, "And you were correct in your assessment of me. I was a first-class jerk. But it was because I was afraid."

"Afraid of what?"

"Afraid of being alone for the rest of my life. One surefire way of not getting hurt by someone leaving you is to never let anyone get close to you. My way of doing that was by being a bully, having a smart mouth, and by saying hurtful things to people. Even though I had amnesia when we first met, those insensitive and cruel parts of my personality were still present." March pauses before saying his next line, unsure if Debbie, as director of this scene, will edit it out. He decides to risk it and says, "But all of that changed because of you."

"Well you know what?!" Debbie says angrily. "All that was then and this is now and I'm getting tired of being pushed away."

If Debbie had slapped March across the face, it wouldn't have been any more painful and surprising than her sharp-edged words. Before he can recover and respond, she continues.

"I feel us get close and I get excited about the future, but then you take a step back and put distance between us. I need you to be honest with me. If you're tired of me, just tell me. I'm a big girl and I'll get over you. If there is someone else who you are interested in, let me know and I'll step out of the way. But if it's pity you feel for me . . ." She gnashes her teeth at the utterance of the despised word.

March raises his right hand and touches the corners of Debbie's eyes, searching for tears or creases that might tell him how she is feeling.

As if his touch broke the surface tension of her pent-up tears, Debbie's voice breaks and tears spring up in her eyes and roll down her cheeks.

March feels the warm moisture and, taking his thumb, he tries to rub her tears away. Putting his tearstained thumb to his lips, he kisses it and then carefully touches each of her closed eyelids.

Overwhelming sadness fills March's chest at the pain he is causing this person he loves so much. "Debbie, I am not tired of you. I am not interested in seeing someone else. And I do not now, nor have I ever, pitied you. The plain and simple truth is, and I know you don't want me to say this, I love you. It's a kind of love I've never felt before and it has continued to grow over the course of our time together. It's a beautiful thing."

"I expected you to say something like this," Debbie says. "So if all that is true, what I need is for you to tell me where you see our relationship going."

It is Tucker's question repackaged, but still it's the question that cuts to the quick of things. March feels sweat begin beading on the small of his back and on his upper lip. He's stood here many times facing his three accusers: his mind, his heart, and his memories. Thus far he hasn't been able to sort out which is telling him the truth. But now, choose he must or risk losing Debbie. He picks the door of his heart and opening it says, "I want us to spend the rest of our lives together, if you will have me."

"Oh, March," Debbie says, her voice thick with emotion.

March hears her chair scoot and suddenly she is at his side, wrapping her arms around him and kissing him. He turns his chair and lifts her onto his lap. Embracing her tightly he returns her kisses. Their tongues touch, tentatively at first. Then March kisses her deeply, plunging his tongue into her mouth. Debbie responds hungrily as she grabs his beard and pulls him deeper into her.

Keeping her lips locked to his, Debbie shifts herself and straddles March.

He pulls her closer and feels the pressure of her breasts on his chest. His hands go to the small of her back and he massages it as she groans with pleasure. The unbelievable heat of her vagina resting on top of his lap sends blood surging into his groin. He feels his erection swelling.

Suddenly a vicious flashback grabs March by the back of his shirt collar, dragging him backward and depositing him into a scene from his dark, disgusting past.

CHAPTER SIX

Standing huddled in a dark alleyway a couple blocks off the Las Vegas Strip, March watches the cars pull over to the curb and the women lining the sidewalk taking turns leaning into the rolled-down windows. He has never seen women wear as much makeup as these women. Their dresses are shorter than some shirts he's seen other women wear. He's amazed at how they can maintain their balance on the ridiculously high and skinny heels of their shoes.

Some of the women get inside the cars and the drivers speed away with them, while other women stay leaned over in the window, their heads bobbing up and down. After a few minutes they extract themselves from the window and straighten up. A hand comes from inside the car and the green flash of cash passes into the woman's hand. After the car drives away, some of the women take a small bottle of something out of their purses, turn it up to drink, but then spit it out on the sidewalk.

March can make no sense out of any of it. All he knows is that the last time he ate anything was three days ago when Marge, the truck driver he got a ride from at the rest area on Interstate 15 out of Utah, bought him a sandwich and said this was as far as he could ride with her. Hanging around the back doors of restaurants in Las Vegas to see if there might be some scraps has thus far been a fruitless quest. It seems every door in this city, front and back, has guards, guards with bulging biceps and permanent scowls on their faces. They look like they could—and would—rip a young boy's head off just for the fun of it.

Some of the women he is watching are drinking hot coffee, the steam rising up in white clouds from the cups cradled in their hands. The aroma of the coffee eases its way into March's nostrils and his stomach responds with a growl.

Periodically a man walks up to the women and some of them gather around him while he hands out sandwiches. March's mouth waters and his stomach growls even louder, like an angry lion demanding to be fed. His fear of the unknown is no match for the feeling of desperation that has a grip on him, and so he forces himself out of the shadows and walks toward the man with the sandwiches.

When March is about twenty feet away, one of the women steps directly into his path. March stops but doesn't look up at her. His eyes are locked on the man with the sandwiches.

"Are you hungry?" the woman asks.

When March doesn't answer, she shoves a sandwich at him. "Here, take mine."

Finally March's trance is broken and he looks at the sandwich, then up at the woman. Her lipstick is blood red and her eyes look like she's made up for Halloween. There is a ring in her nose and four earrings in each ear. But she is smiling and that takes the edge off of an otherwise frightening visage. March looks at the sandwich but doesn't move.

Shoving it at him again, the woman says, "Here. I said, take it."

March grabs the sandwich out of her hand and bites into it without removing the outside paper wrapper. He's taken another bite before she can intervene and pull back the paper.

"How old are you, kid? Thirteen maybe?"

March ignores her.

"Listen to me, kid." Anxiety tints the edges of her voice. "Whatever you do, don't talk to that man handing out the sandwiches. No matter what it looks like to you, he is not a nice man. You need to find a policeman and let him help you get back home, wherever that is. If you stay around here, you will get hurt."

The warning in her earnest voice begins to soak into March's consciousness. Now that his brain is satisfied death is not imminent, it begins taking stock of the environment.

Without warning, March's angel of mercy is shoved to the side, stumbles, and falls to the ground. Standing in front of March is the man who delivered the sandwiches. His hair is fiery red and a crimson, jagged scar runs from the corner of his left ear down to his tattoo-covered neck. There is a black teardrop tattooed at the corner of one eye. "Well, who do we have here?" he says loudly. "Is this Pip? Or perhaps a future Artful Dodger?" He throws back his head and laughs.

March's angel has recovered from her fall and steps between March and this frightening man. "Come on, Red," she says. "It's just a kid. Leave him alone and let him find some help and get back home again."

Red grabs the woman's hair and jerks her head to one side. "Did I ask your opinion about any of this? Are you paid to tell me what to do?" He jerks her hair until she cries out, then says, "The answer to both questions is no. So get back to work."

Rubbing her head, the woman gives March one last look, her face now etched with sadness, and returns to take her place with the other women lined up on the curb.

Red puts his hand on March's shoulder. "You look hungry and tired. Well, tonight is your lucky night because you fell into the hands of Red, the most generous man on the streets of Las Vegas.

Come along with me. Let's get you some more food and something to drink. Then I've got a place you can stay, with a warm bath and a clean bed. Just what you look like you need."

Everything has happened so quickly that March feels like he is in a dream, a dream reminiscent of *Alice in Wonderland*, with characters that seem unreal and where knowing who and what you can trust is impossible to figure out. But *food, drink, warm bath*, and *clean bed* are all terms he understands, so he goes willingly with Red. As they near a street corner where the lights burn more brightly, a car drives past them and March's temporary angel of mercy looks out of the passenger window at him. Her tear-streaked makeup mottles her face and there is blood at the corner of her mouth.

March looks up at Red to see his reaction, but even though March is certain Red saw the woman, his expression registers no emotion.

Red buys March a bag of takeout from McDonald's and they take a cab to a hotel. March is so ravenous the Big Mac and fries have practically disappeared by the time they get there, even though the cab ride was brief. The hotel is the largest building March has ever seen and the lobby is dazzling with all its lights and mirrors. Riding the glass elevator gives March the sense that he is Aladdin on a dizzying magic carpet ride.

When they get to the room, Red shows March the shower and tells him to get all the grime of the road scrubbed off and then put on the bathrobe on the back of the door. "We'll throw your old clothes away, and I'll buy you some new ones."

The combination of the hot shower and all the carbohydrates he recently ate have an intoxicating effect on March. With drooping eyes, he towels off and puts on the bathrobe. All he wants now is to go to sleep.

When he steps out of the bathroom, there is another man in the room with Red. He is an older man, dressed in a suit and tie. He smiles at March.

"This is my friend, Thomas," Red says to March. "Come shake his hand."

March does as he's told, but he feels uneasy.

Thomas excuses himself and goes to the bathroom.

When the door is shut, Red grabs March's face in one hand and tilts it upward. "Here's the way this is going to go down, kid. I've treated you fair, haven't I? Thirty minutes ago you were almost dead from starvation and exposure. And now your belly is full, you've had a hot shower, and you've got a nice place to stay tonight. So it's your turn to do ol' Red a favor. I do you a favor and you do Red a favor. That's how life works, right?

"Thomas in there likes boys, not girls or women. He likes boys. I'm going to leave you and him alone together for a little bit. You are to do whatever he tells you he wants you to do." Squeezing March's face harder and giving his head a shake for emphasis, Red continues, "I mean whatever he wants you to do. It's very important that he is happy with what you do. That's how I make my money and that's how I'm able to take care of you by feeding you and giving you a place to live. If anything goes wrong, if Thomas is dissatisfied in any way, you will be punished and I'll take you out in the desert to die. Do you understand everything I've said?"

Hopelessness and despair, the twin killers of the survival instinct, and March's constant companions since he ran away from home years ago, make him nod his head in silent acceptance of his fate.

Thomas steps out of the bathroom and Red says, "I'll be back in a bit. You two enjoy yourselves." Then he leaves the room.

Thirty minutes later, March watches Thomas stuff his shirt into his pants, zip them up, and fasten his belt. Leaving his necktie off, he slips on his jacket and exits the room without another word or glance at March.

When the door shuts behind Thomas, March lunges into the bathroom and falls to his knees beside the toilet. With the force of a tsunami, half-digested hamburger, french fries, and Coke mingled with semen spew out of March's mouth.

"March? March!"

He hears a woman's voice.

"What happened? Are you okay?"

It is Debbie's voice. Debbie's voice! He pulls himself on board the ship *Present* and out of the Sea of the Past by means of the lifeline of Debbie's voice. With the cry of a lost boy who's finally been found, March cries, "Oh, Debbie!" He buries his face into the crook of her neck. His body shakes with his sobs. "Oh, Debbie, oh, Debbie," he says over and over.

"Talk to me, March, please. Tell me what just happened. It's like you suddenly left your body and I was here alone. I was afraid you had had a stroke." She runs her fingers gently through the hair on the back of his head, and his sobs begin to subside.

"Hold me," March says. "Please don't let me go."

"I've got you, March. I've got you. I'm right here with you, and I'm not going anywhere."

CHAPTER SEVEN

As April approaches James's house, the dimness of the interior tells her that the boys are already asleep. She imagines James is sitting by Susan's bedside, keeping vigil, as he does every night. In April's eyes his devotion to his wife is nothing short of amazing. To witness a man with that level of kindness and tenderness has been a revelation, and it has drawn her to him. It's the kind of love that she craves.

Letting herself in with her house key, she pauses and takes in the now-familiar smells of the house—the kiss of lavender (Susan's favorite scent) and laundry detergent (indicating James has had to take care of some of the laundry), while underneath these scents is a sweet, musky smell that is the result of the mixture of James's soap and aftershave plus his own unique manly scent. April smiles at the thought of James showering.

She makes her way first to the boys' room to check on them. The evidence of her being gone for a few days is scattered across the floor of the bedroom. Toys of every description are lying exactly in the places they were last used, even though the boys know the rule about putting things where they belong.

Her first impulse is to flip on the light switch and make them get up and clean their room. But then she notices that the boys are sleeping together instead of separately in their twin beds. Christopher, the smaller of the twins rests his head on the shoulder of his brother, Michael. Michael's left arms lies across Christopher's chest, no doubt placed there in an effort to comfort his brother.

Having never babysat back home, April was unsure if she would be able to manage the two boys. But it has been easier than she expected, and the unexpected bonus has been how much she cares for the boys. A true maternal instinct has been unearthed in her.

Approaching the bed, April thinks, *If I had a camera, I would take a picture of this and title it "A Brother's Love."* She adjusts the covers so that Michael's arm is no longer exposed to the coolness of the room. Leaning down, she touches the boys' foreheads with her lips.

Christopher stirs and, with his eyes still closed, says, "Mommy?"

April places her hand on the side of his face and whispers, "Shhh, go back to sleep. Everything's fine." Her gentle touch and soft voice work as well as the Sandman. Christopher nestles closer to his brother and returns to his dreams.

She leaves the boys' room, walks down the hallway, and looks into James and Susan's room. The focal point of the room is the hospital bed. A small-watt lamp beside the bed casts yellow light on Susan's jaundiced skin and draws sharp shadows on her gaunt features. She is so thin that she barely causes a ripple on the blanket covering her.

Every time April sees her, memories are stirred of Ella's last days. And April has to force down the regret that rises in her throat that she wasn't more attentive to her grandmother during those final hours of her life.

As he is every night, James is asleep in an armchair in the corner of the room; a reading lamp burns faithfully behind him and an open book lies on his stomach. April walks quietly to his chair. With the fingernail of her index finger, she slowly traces his jawline from his earlobe to his chin. The stubble of his beard creates drag on her finger.

When I saw you two months ago, I had an immediate attraction to you, but I knew better than to trust it. Now that I've lived in your house for two months I'm certain of my feelings. I love you, James Washington. And even if you won't admit it, I know you have feelings for me, too. Your loyalty to Susan is what stands in the way of us. But she won't be here much longer, and then we can build a new life together.

It takes all her willpower to refrain from bending down and kissing him. She looks over her shoulder at Susan, half expecting her to be pointing a bony, accusing finger at her. But Susan lies in the exact same position she has lain in for the past three weeks, except—except something seems different.

There are wrinkles in April's forehead and a crease between her eyes as she steps to the bedside in order to give Susan a closer look. *I think she's dead!* April places the first two fingers of her right hand on Susan's neck, searching for a pulse. The pressure of her fingers finds no rhythmic response. *Oh my god, she is dead!*

A mixture of disparate emotions expands in her chest—panic, sadness, relief, and excitement. She pushes to the side the chastising tongue of her conscience for feeling relief and excitement in response to the death of someone James loves. Turning around, she looks at James. *Now you're all mine. There will need to be an appropriate period of grieving, but then we can begin building a new life together.* A chill of pleasure travels slowly down her back and ends up between her legs. She slowly closes her eyes in response and squeezes her legs together.

Kneeling beside James's chair, she puts her hand on his thigh and gently squeezes. "James, wake up," she says softly.

James's eyes open slowly and he seems briefly disoriented. He looks down at April and recognition dawns. Taking the book off his stomach and closing it, he says sleepily, "What time is it? How long have you been back?"

She puts on a mask of concern and sadness and says, "James, it's Susan. She's gone."

James immediately jerks upright in his chair and stares at the hospital bed.

April notices the road map of red lines in the sclera of his eyes becomes more pronounced and his tear ducts release an emotional, saline-tinged flood.

He blinks and tears begin running from both corners of his eyes. Turning to look at April, he says, "Are you sure?"

She nods sympathetically and takes one of his hands in hers. "I'm so sorry, James." Standing, she gently pulls on his hand. "Do you want to see her?"

Keeping his eyes on Susan, James allows April to provide him leverage to dislodge himself from the mourner's chair he's practically lived in for the past few months. Side by side they approach the pyre that has held the body of his wife while cancer slowly took her from him. He bends down and kisses the cooling skin of her forehead while his tears bathe her cheeks—a preburial washing. Placing his hands on both sides of her face, he whispers, "Rest now, my love. All of your suffering is finished. I will see you again one day." His lips rest briefly on hers and then he stands up.

April is surprised to taste her own tears and swipes at her cheeks. Processing her memories of Ella, her feelings of empathy for how Michael and Christopher are going to feel about losing their mother, plus her feelings toward James is proving to be a balancing act she can't quite manage. She stands close enough to James that their arms are touching but waits for him to give her some kind of hint as to what he wants from her.

James begins crying and softly sobbing. He turns toward April and says, "Oh, April, what am I going to do?"

April steps into his open arms as he wraps them around her and rests the side of his face on top of her head. She puts her arms around his waist and, squeezing, pushes her body tightly into his. *Yes! I knew he would turn to me after she died. It'll just be me and you now, James.*

CHAPTER EIGHT

Before pulling into the parking lot of the Budget Inn, Roan gives another furtive glance in his rearview mirror, trying to make sure he hasn't been followed. What has him on edge is that he hasn't heard from his friend Buzzard for five days. They had been planning to rob a 7-Eleven store tomorrow. Each passing hour that Roan hears nothing from Buzzard increases his anxiety and apprehension that something has gone wrong.

Seeing no one, he drives into the parking lot, stopping in the space in front of his room. He grabs the bag of takeout from KFC and gets out of his car. His eyes flitting left and right, he walks the few feet to his door and lets himself in.

As soon as he steps inside, someone grabs him and shoves him forward. His shins strike the edge of the bed, causing him to topple to the floor. He hears the door slamming shut behind him and the deadbolt being thrown as the fluorescent lights over the two double beds flicker to life. Swearing, he jumps to his feet to face the intruder.

Just as his eyes fall on a muscle-bound black man standing in front of his door, Roan hears the toilet in the bathroom being flushed. Confused, he makes a half-turn so he can keep an eye on the black man and also see the bathroom door.

When the man in the bathroom comes out, Roan relaxes and smiles. "Hey Red, am I glad to see you. You scared me to death. I wasn't sure who had broken into my room." He extends his hand, "How long have you been out of prison?"

Red ignores Roan's hand and brushes past him, taking a seat in the chair by the window. He takes out a cigarette and lights it. He exhales and speaks through the veil of smoke, "So you heard about me going to prison, huh?"

"Man, I sure did. I heard the feds busted up everything and put you away on hard time. That's bad luck, man, bad luck."

Smiling, Red says, "Luck? Let me tell you what luck is, Roan. Luck is finding a coin on the sidewalk that has the year of your birth on it." He rubs out his cigarette. The smile has evaporated and a lean, hard look takes its place. "But when the feds find my secret hideaway and know exactly where the money and drugs are hidden and there are only three other people in the world that know that information, that is not luck. No sir, Roan, that may be lots of things but luck is not one of them. You know what I call it?"

Sweat starts beading on Roan's face at the sinister tone in Red's voice. Feeling less certain of the intent of his visitors, he glances at the black man at the door. There is nothing to be read in his body language because he appears to be an ebony statue. Looking at Red, Roan says, "I'm not sure what you're getting at. Me and Buzzard and Big Country was the only ones who knew about your hideaway."

"I'm glad you remember it the same way I do," Red replies. "The only conclusion I can come up with about getting busted and sent to prison is that one of you—or all of you—set me up."

Roan takes a step toward Red, holding his hands out, and says, "You've got to be—" Before he can finish, the black man springs with the agility of a cat and, spinning, kicks Roan on the side of the face.

As Roan falls to the floor the black man grabs his wrist and pins it behind him.

It takes a few seconds for Roan's head to clear, but when it does, he yells, "Get off me! What's the matter with you? Red, call him off!"

Red nods at the black man, who releases his grip on Roan and resumes his post in front of the door.

Roan gets up on all fours and then staggers to his feet. Rubbing the side of his face, he says to the black man, "You'll pay for that. Nobody gets away with sucker-punching me."

"I like the way you think, Roan," Red says. "Payback is all about settling a score, evening things out, so to speak. That's exactly why we're here, to settle a score. I'm here to find out two things: who set me up and where all my money is."

Panic is beginning to dance on Roan's chest. "Man, I don't know what you're talking about. I don't know nothing about that raid or your money. You've got to believe me."

"Hmmm. Well the truth is I don't have to believe you, 'cause I don't. Tell me something, when was the last time you talked to Buzzard or Big Country?"

Roan licks his lips nervously as he tries to figure out how to answer Red. Remembering the night he and Buzzard tied up Big Country and threw him off the bridge into the Little River, he answers, "I ain't seen or heard from Big Country in over ten years. Buzzard and me will cross paths every once in a while, but I'm not sure when the last time was we talked." Fear has filled his mouth, and like a sponge, soaks up all traces of saliva. He tries to swallow, but can't.

"Let's see if this might jog your memory," Red says. Reaching into the pocket of his windbreaker, he pulls out a small, black velvet bag whose drawstrings are pulled tight. He pitches it to Roan.

Roan catches it awkwardly.

"Go ahead and open it," Red instructs him.

Roan's hands begin to tremble. "What is it? What's in here?"

"I guess you could say it's a message. Now open it up."

Roan fiddles with the drawstrings and finally opens the mouth of the bag. He peers into the dark interior and frowns. Looking at Red, he asks again, "What is it?"

"Pour it out and you'll see."

Roan turns the bag upside down and empties the contents into his palm. When a severed finger lands in his hand, he screams and jumps back. "What the—?!" he exclaims as he stares at the finger lying on the comforter. "What kind of sick joke is this?"

"Let me assure you," Red says calmly, "this is no sick joke. Do you recognize the finger? Because you should."

His eyes wide with fright, Roan says, "Of course I don't! I don't know what's going on here. This is messed up!"

Cocking his head thoughtfully to one side, Red says, "I'm surprised at you, Roan, not recognizing your friend Buzzard's finger. What you need to be asking yourself at this point is how I ended up with Buzzard's finger."

In response to Red's query, all the blood drains from Roan's face.

Red laughs loudly. "I can see by your sudden paleness that you've connected the dots. You're right. I cut his finger off, plus the three others on that hand. He wasn't being cooperative with me and I thought some persuasion would help. But after I cut his fingers off and he still didn't give me the answers I wanted, it seemed pointless to continue the process, so I shot him in the head. You see, Roan, Buzzard didn't give me what I wanted. And now it's your turn." He pauses and taps his lighter on the table a few times. "Judgment Day has come for you, Roan, and I am the judge. Who set me up and where is my money?"

Roan falls to his knees and begins to cry. "Please, Red, don't kill me. I'll tell you what you want to know, just don't kill me."

Leaning forward, Red holds his hand behind his ear and says, "I'm all ears. Start singing."

Words start pouring out of Roan's mouth like water from a broken main. "I know it wasn't me that set you up and it must not have been Buzzard. So Big Country is who did it. I never did like him anyway. He thought he was better than the rest of us. You want me to help you find him? Because I will. You just say the word. I don't know where to start, but I'll figure it out. I've got connections—" He stops when Red holds up his hand.

Red stands up. Shaking his head slowly, he sighs. "Roan, Roan, Roan, you're not answering my questions. You're just guessing. You're scared and you'd lie to your own mother just to stay alive. You can't tell me where my money is and you can't tell me where Big Country is, so you're useless to me." He slips the small pistol out of his pocket, walks over to Roan. and fires two quick shots into his forehead at point-blank range.

With his mouth open, Roan falls over.

Turning to the black man, Red says, "Look, Tarzan, go get Skinny out of the car and you two take care of Roan just like you did Buzzard, but this time I want you to dispose of the body in and around Maryville."

"You want us to carve him up in here?"

"Doesn't matter to me, here or back at the shop. Suit yourselves. I'm getting out of here and heading home for a few days to think. I'll be in touch."

Red leaves the room, gets into his pickup truck, and exits the parking lot. In a hundred yards he sees the sign for Interstate 40. Turning on his blinker, he enters the on-ramp and merges into the rest of the westbound traffic.

CHAPTER NINE

Sitting with Debbie on the couch in his apartment, his hand between hers, March can sense how badly she wants to understand him. *But how in the world can I tell her the truth? She'll be horrified and disgusted. She'll never look at me the same way again, and she'll never want to have anything to do with me.*

As if she is reading his thoughts, Debbie says, "Listen to me, March. There is nothing you can tell me that will change my love for you—nothing. I know that whatever is blocking you is a really big deal to you, but I promise you it won't be for me." She gently massages his palm. "It's okay, you can tell me."

"Do you remember the dream I used to have after my accident?" March asks. "The one where I was standing on the edge of a cliff and April was beside me?"

"Yes, I do."

"Well that's how I feel right now, like I'm on the edge of a cliff and I'm scared of falling."

Debbie puts her hand on one of his cheeks and kisses the other. "Oh baby, don't be scared. I won't let you fall."

"I know you believe that, that you won't let me fall. But you don't know everything about me, and you don't know how learning the truth about me will change how you see me. It's like the priest that everyone in a community looks up to and loves for decades, until they learn that he's been a pedophile all those years. It changes forever how they view him."

March's example stops Debbie in her tracks as she thinks about the implications of what he has said. Slowly she says, "You . . . mean . . . you—"

"No, no," March interrupts quickly. "I'm not saying I'm a pedophile. I'm making a mess of this." He leans forward and puts his head in his hands.

Debbie watches him closely, her mind on an incessant, circular chase, trying to figure out what his big secret must be, and wondering if she shouldn't have been pressing him so hard to tell her.

Suddenly, March sits up straight and takes a deep breath. He shifts his body so that he is facing Debbie. "I'm going to do this, but if there was ever a time I wished I could see, it is now, so that I could be certain of your reaction."

Debbie pulls her legs up under her and turns to face March. "You'll just have to trust that I will be honest with you."

"I'm going to have to," March replies. "You know I told you about hitchhiking west and ending up with that crazy commune bunch in Utah. When I ran away from there I ended up in Las Vegas, which you know, too. But what you don't know is what happened while I was in Las Vegas.

"Debbie, if you've never gone without food for days, you can't imagine how desperate a person becomes. And when you are completely alone, no friends or family, you don't know who to turn to for help. So when someone suddenly offers you something to eat, no matter what they look like, no matter if something inside tells you to run away from them, your hunger will override all of that. This is one life lesson I've learned along the way: desperate people do desperate things. Stay away from desperate people, you understand me?"

Unsure if March is really asking her a question, or if he is talking to himself, Debbie says softly, "I understand."

"There I was standing in a dark alley in Las Vegas, watching what I now know were prostitutes working the streets, their johns driving up to the curb to pick one of them up to take to a motel or paying to get a blowjob while sitting in the car. I was starving and cold and tired." His memory is so visceral that he begins shaking and his voice starts breaking. "A part of me wished I could die."

Watching the pain etched on March's face and hearing the sadness in his voice, Debbie truly regrets having pressed him so hard to open up to her. "March, I'm so sorry. I shouldn't have made you feel like you have to open this chapter of your life in front of me. You can stop if you want to." She pulls back his hair and kisses the edge of his ear. She whispers, "We'll find a way to work around it."

March shakes his head. "No, if you and I are going to spend the rest of our lives together, there can't be any secrets between us. The truth is cleansing, Debbie, but it is sometimes also very painful. I've started this story, and I'm going to finish it."

He draws a ragged breath and continues, "I've also told you about Red and about me working for him as a drug courier. Well this story is when I first met him. I saw a man passing out sandwiches and hot coffee to all those women. They were laughing and seemed to be enjoying themselves.

"I stepped out of the shadows of the alley and started walking toward them. The man with the sandwiches, who turned out to be Red, offered me what sounded like the world—hot food, a hot bath, and a warm bed. I know I shouldn't have, but I got in a car with him. He took me to McDonald's and bought me whatever I wanted. Then he took me to the most amazing and beautiful hotel

I had ever seen. I took a hot shower. It was the first shower I'd had in weeks. It felt so good I didn't want to get out.

"When I finally went out of the bathroom, there was another man in the room with Red, an older man dressed in a suit and tie. Red took me aside and told me that since he had done a favor for me, he needed me to do a favor for him. He put his face an inch from mine and said that I was to do whatever the man in the suit wanted me to do. And then Red left."

Like a thermometer taken out of the sunlight and placed in a freezer, all the color slowly drains from Debbie's face. She feels a coldness in the pit of her stomach that makes her nauseous. She has heard all of March's story that she needs to hear, all that she wants to hear. Its end is predictably disgusting and degrading. She wants to clap her hand over his mouth to stop him, but knows it is a story he wants to get out, like a stomach getting rid of spoiled milk.

She clenches her fists until her nails dig into her palms as March tells the details of what happened that night. Bile bubbles up into the back of her throat and she almost throws up.

"I waited by myself in the room for probably an hour before Red came back," March says. "I looked at my options. I could run away and go back to living on the streets and risk starving to death or I could stay where I was. As a kid, those were the only options I could see. So, like I told you, desperate people do desperate things, and I decided to stay. The next four years of my life I worked as a prostitute."

March reaches for Debbie's face and searches her features with his fingers to see her reaction.

She sits quietly as he explores every inch of her face.

When he is satisfied that she is not disgusted by the sight of him, he places his large hands on both sides of her face. "Dr. Sydney helped me to learn to forgive myself for all that I've done, and I realize that I was just a kid doing what he had to do to survive. The lingering problem for me is sex. When I'm with you, and we are kissing and touching each other, I love every minute of it. The feelings of intimacy are indescribable, the joy immeasurable. But the longer we kiss, my body starts responding the way any red-blooded man's would. My cock starts getting hard. And it's at that moment that I have flashbacks of all the cocks I've seen in my life and what I had to do with them, and it makes me sick. It makes me shut down every time. That's why you feel me pushing you away sometimes."

March feels Debbie's facial muscles contracting and shifting. Creases form under his palms. He frowns and says, "You're smiling?"

"Yes, yes, yes, I'm smiling," Debbie says excitedly.

March drops his hands from her face. His forehead wrinkles. "Well you're going to have to explain that to me. Why are you smiling?"

"This is great news, March. Don't you see? We can work through this. We can! I was afraid you didn't find me desirable. Now that I know what's going on, we can talk openly about it. Instead of it being the elephant in the room that only you are aware of, we'll now approach the problem together and stop ignoring it."

March puts his arms around Debbie and pulls her face within inches of his. "God sent me an angel when he brought you into my life, you know that? You are the most optimistic person I have ever known. You make me believe in possibilities."

As he finishes speaking, their lips meet and they give each other the kiss of relief, reassurance, and rejoicing.

CHAPTER TEN

April is afraid to move. Having James's arms around her and being this close to him, her body tingles from her scalp all the way to the bottoms of her feet. Strong sexual urges keep trying to hold sway over her, and they are barely kept at bay by her feelings of compassion and hurt for him.

I'm so bad! I can't believe I can even think about having sex with James only moments after Susan has died. How selfish can a person be?! But oh, how many times have I thought and dreamed about being with him. I just don't want to move and break the spell of this moment.

She feels him lift his head from off of hers and his arms loosen their grip on her. Reluctantly, April mirrors his moves.

Looking at Susan's body, James says, "I need to call the doctor to let him know and then call the funeral home. And I need to go wake the boys and tell them." He chokes down another sob.

"Can I make the phone calls for you?" April asks.

"Would you mind?"

"No, not at all. I want to talk to Michael and Christopher, too, but I'll let you go first."

"They'll definitely want to talk to you, too, I'm certain." He turns and looks directly into April's eyes. "I'm really glad you're here and that you're a part of our lives. It's going to mean a lot to the boys." He starts walking out of the room, but pauses and turns around. "The phone numbers you'll need are underneath the phone by my chair."

But April barely hears him. She feels as if she's floating with angels on the tops of clouds. Though she's careful not to let it show, there is a smile inside her that covers her spirit in a canopy of blindingly brilliant sunlight. *This is as close to heaven as I've ever been. It's like we were meant to be.*

After finding the piece of paper with the necessary phone numbers, April is about to dial the doctor when she hears the low, muffled tones of James's voice through the wall of the boys' bedroom. She pictures them sleepy-eyed, sitting side by side in the bed as James tries to explain to them what has happened to their mother.

Just as she begins punching in the numbers, a solitary wail comes from the boys' room. It quickly turns into a duet on death as the brothers give voice to the pain and fear triggered by the announcement from their father. Their mourning song cuts through all the carnal feelings April has been harboring for James and lays open an old wound she thought had healed. Tears sting her eyes as memories of the night Ella died come flooding over her. But the memories release a tsunami of feelings connected with the event and April suddenly doubles over as if she's been punched in the stomach. She begins crying.

Whispering, she says, "Oh Christopher and Michael, I know how you feel! It's a pain like no other. But I will be here for you. I will help you through this." Tears are flowing down her cheeks and over her lips, so much so that a soft spray of tears is created by every hard consonant she utters.

Moving to Susan's bed, she kneels beside it and folds her hands on the edge of the mattress. *Dear God in heaven, forgive me for wishing Susan would die, for ever wishing that a child would lose its mother.*

Please don't punish me for being selfish. Help me to know how to help these boys. Guide my thoughts and my motives.

She is startled at the sound of sniffling from the doorway. Looking up, she sees James coming into the dim bedroom carrying both boys. Rising from beside the bed, she looks at James and raises her eyebrows.

"They wanted to come see her," James says simply. "I didn't know what else to do."

Both boys have their heads lying on their dad's shoulders but also have one eye looking sideways at their mother's bed.

April hesitates for a moment, then walks around the bed and joins the three of them. She kisses each of the boys' hands.

James kneels down and the boys unwrap their arms and legs from him and stand beside the bed.

"Is that Mommy?" Christopher asks.

"Yes it is," James answers him.

"But I thought you said she died and went to heaven. How can she be in heaven and be here, too?"

April is stunned by his question. *That is exactly the same question I asked myself the night Ella died!* She is eager to hear how James will navigate this complex topic in a way that will satisfy his son's curiosity.

James kneels down between his sons. "You boys know how you look into a mirror to brush your teeth or to comb your hair?"

Both silently nod.

"So tell me, what do you see when you look into a mirror?"

"My hair," Christopher says.

"My eyes," Michael says.

"But don't you also see your ears and chin and cheeks and neck?"

Christopher smiles, believing he understands what his father is looking for. "Yes. And my shirt and my jacket, too."

"Exactly," James says. "You see the things on the outside. That's what our eyes see—the outside of a person. It's how you recognize someone when you see them in a restaurant and you know it's them.

"But there's also another part of people that makes them special, a part that makes them like no other person on earth. It's a part you can't see, even though you know it's there."

"Huh?" Michael says.

Without noticing her own movements, April slowly kneels down as the child in her is eager to hear this secret revealed.

"What makes you two brothers special?" James asks.

"We're twins!" they say simultaneously.

"So you're the same, right?"

"Right."

"Exactly the same in every way, right?"

The boys are slower to answer this time.

"I don't like broccoli, but Christopher does," Michael says.

"And I like baseball, but Michael likes soccer," Christopher says.

"Which one of you likes to hide and scare people?" James asks.

"Me, me!" Christopher says excitedly.

"But which one of you likes to make cards for people?"

Michael silently raises his hand.

James puts his arms around his boys and says, "You boys look the same but you are very different. And what makes you different is what is inside of you. It's the part of you that makes you special, the part of you that people love. It's the part of you that was placed there by God."

The boys' eyes widen as the light of understanding that their father is sharing with them begins to make sense to them.

Nodding toward Susan's bed, James says, "What you see there is Mommy's body, the outside of her. But the inside of her, the part of her that made us smile, that made us love her, that made her the beautiful person she was, has left her and gone back to God so that they can bring joy and happiness to each other."

Fresh tears begin running down April's cheeks.

"Can I touch her?" Michael asks.

"You can if you want to," James says. "But it won't feel like Mommy, because the part of her that made her warm and alive and special is already gone."

Michael has second thoughts. Shaking his head, he says, "I changed my mind."

James looks at April and says, "Why don't you boys go lay back down and try to go back to sleep?"

Taking his cue, April says, "Come on, guys, I'll go with you and tuck you in."

Having become used to turning to April as a caregiver, the boys readily turn themselves over to her, each of them taking one of her hands. As the three of them walk out of the room, Christopher says, "Will you sing us a song?"

Smiling, April says, "Oh, I think I can do that for you."

As they pass by her bedroom, Michael says, "And play your Autoharp, too."

Making a detour into her room, April gets on all fours by the side of her bed, reaches underneath it, and pulls out the case with her Autoharp inside.

Once she gets the boys tucked in their beds, she takes out the instrument her grandmother Ella used to play, the same instrument that helped her learn to speak out loud. She strums a few chords to awaken its spirit and to feel herself connected to it. Then she begins singing,

> *Hush, little babies, don't say a word,*
> *April's gonna buy you a mockingbird.*

If that mockingbird won't sing,
April's gonna buy you a diamond ring.

If that diamond ring turns brass,
April's gonna buy you a looking glass.

If that looking glass gets broke,
April's gonna buy you a billy goat.

If that billy goat won't pull,
April's gonna buy you a cart and bull.

If that cart and bull turn over,
April's gonna buy you a dog named Rover.

If that dog named Rover won't bark,
April's gonna buy you a horse and cart.

If that horse and cart fall down,
You'll still be the sweetest little boys in town.

When April sees that the boys' eyes have fallen shut and their breathing is regular and deep, she finishes the song in a whisper,

So hush, little babies, don't you cry,
Daddy loves you and so do I.

CHAPTER ELEVEN

Hanging up the phone, March says to Debbie, "That was April. James's wife died tonight."

Sitting up on the couch, Debbie says, "Oh, how sad. How is everyone doing? And how long have we been asleep on this couch? I felt you get up to answer the phone, but until you started talking I couldn't get oriented to where I was."

March touches the mechanical clock beside the phone. "1:38 a.m.," it announces.

"You're kidding," Debbie says. "I can't believe it's that late, or maybe I should say that early, depending on how you look at it."

March locates her on the couch and sits beside her. He puts his arm around her and pulls her to his chest. "April said James is pretty upset but the boys are just trying to understand what it means when someone dies."

Laying her hand on his chest, Debbie says, "How sad for those boys. I can't imagine what must be going through their minds. It was very sad for me when my parents were killed in the car wreck, but at least I was old enough to understand what was going on. To be so young and lose a parent—" She shakes her head and pats March's chest.

With his fingernails, March lightly draws small circles on Debbie's back.

Her body melts further into his in response to the sensuous feelings running through her.

"When my mother died," March says, "it was kind of different for me than for you or for James's boys. I'd never really had my mother. She was sort of like Halley's Comet, orbiting on the outside edges of our world and occasionally coming close enough to create excitement in us. All the pain that I felt when she died was because it was the end of my hope and my dream."

March's words drift slowly into Debbie's consciousness, having to find their way through the haze of endorphins and dopamine flooding her. When he doesn't continue talking, she says, "Hope? What do you mean it was the end of hope?"

"Growing up, I always knew that Tucker was my grandmother, not my mother, even though Tucker is part of my earliest memories. The Tucker you know, Debbie, the way she is now, is not the Tucker I had when growing up. She was a harsh woman, probably in today's world her behavior would be labeled abusive. Don't get me wrong, I love Tucker, and what she did in taking us in to raise is a testament to the kind of heart she has." He pauses and shakes his head. "If you knew the way she was raised, you'd say it is nothing short of a miracle that she did as good a job as she did in raising us."

Debbie's mind has become fully engaged with March's story, with him peeling back another layer of the onion of his complicated past. "I've often wondered about Tucker's past. She never talks about it, and old people are usually always telling tales about growing up."

"And you probably won't ever hear her talking about her past," March says. "It's always been a closed door. August and April and I have talked and put together a sketchy picture of her past based on the bits and pieces each of us has learned over time." He falls silent as imagined images of Tucker as a child play in his mind.

Debbie waits for him to continue, but when he doesn't she says, "Can you tell me what you know about her past? If you don't want to, I understand. It's really none of my business. It's just that I have a great fondness for Tucker and would like to know more about her."

"My great-grandfather, Tucker's father," March begins, "was an extremely abusive man. He treated Tucker the same way cruel slave owners treated their slaves back in the 1800s. One story she has told is of being put in a dog pen in the dead of winter. The only thing that kept her from freezing to death was a hunting dog named Suzy. All she had to eat during that episode was the dog food and scraps her father would bring out once a day."

Debbie pushes herself off of March and sits up straight. "Oh—my—god, you have got to be kidding me!" she exclaims. "Tell me that is not true!"

"Nope, it's the truth. Hard to believe, isn't it?"

"And even harder to comprehend," Debbie adds. "He was a monster."

"Yes he was," March agrees. "She often missed school to work in the fields with him, and I'm talking about her having to do that when she was as young as six years old. He was abusive to Tucker's mother, too, which I'm sure is why she left him and deserted Tucker."

Tears spring up in Debbie's eyes. "You mean her own mother abandoned her and left her in the hands of that evil man?"

Hearing the disbelief and heartache in Debbie's tone, March says, "I know. I've felt the same way many times as I've thought about that."

Debbie moves closer to March and lays her head on his chest. "Hold me. A chill has run through me that I can't explain. I know these kinds of things happen, but I've never known someone personally, someone I care about, that has lived it."

March wraps his arms around her and folds her into himself.

They sit in silence for several minutes.

Finally, Debbie says, "What about the way she dresses? I've never seen her wear anything but men's work pants and shirts or a pair of overalls. And she never wears makeup or has her hair done at a beauty shop."

March squeezes her more tightly, hoping to protect her from the brunt of the next truth he will share about Tucker. "I've never heard the why of that and have never heard anyone ask her about it. But I have my own theory. On the night before I ran away from home I sat with Tucker in the front porch swing." His voice suddenly chokes off as the flood of emotions connected with that night and time in his life pour down on him like a waterfall.

Debbie feels a shudder run through March and hears the catch in his voice. She grips his clothes in fistfuls in anticipation of whatever has overpowered him.

After a moment, March clears his throat and says, "Tucker told me that her father sexually abused her from as far back as her memory went. I think when she got old enough she decided she didn't want people to look at her in a sexual way, so she decided to stop making herself attractive, which meant wearing men's clothing and no makeup."

Through her tears of empathy Debbie says, "How awful for her, and how sad, too. What ever happened to her father?"

"Don't know. All Tucker would ever say is that he disappeared when she was sixteen. I grew up hearing lots of rumors about what happened. One of them was that Tucker killed him and got rid of his body. Actually, I hope that is true, because he for sure deserved it and Tucker would have gotten at least a measure of revenge on him."

It's Debbie's turn to shudder now. "What a dark past she had. But you'd never know it because she doesn't whine about it or use it as an excuse."

March gives a short laugh. "The word *excuse* doesn't exist in Tucker's vocabulary. She is a pull-yourself-up-by-your-bootstraps kind of person. 'Quit your whining and move on' was her attitude whenever we kids would complain."

Debbie relaxes her grip on March and says, "Can I ask one more question?"

March also releases Debbie from his arms. "Sure you can."

"What about Maisy's father? Who was he and how did that happen if Tucker was so . . . Well, you know."

"Oh me," March replies, "that is the one subject that is locked behind iron doors. And if anyone tries to touch that door, Tucker's axe handle will break their hands. The subject is taboo. So I have no idea about that. Not even Maisy knew. Interesting, isn't it, that my mother never knew who her father was, and, like I've told you before, I have no idea who my father is."

"Does that bother you?"

"It used to, but not anymore. I think I'm better off not knowing because, the way my mother was, he could have been from the bottom of the sewer of society."

They fall silent again.

Just as March is about to drift off into sleep, Debbie says, "Do you think James's twins will remember their mother when they get older?"

"Probably only through pictures and stories that people tell them about her. It's sometimes hard for me to remember Maisy."

"I know what you mean. I'm the same way with my parents. I'll get photo albums out to help me remember how they looked and to refresh my memories of our life together."

March shifts his body and stretches out, with his back resting against the back of the couch. "Lay down here beside me and turn your mind off, will you? Let's get a few more hours' rest before we have to get up."

Debbie stretches out on her side, pushing herself into March. He drapes his arm over her.

She takes his hand in hers and pulls it to her chest.

Believing that Debbie has decided to go to sleep, March begins unplugging himself from his conscious world, letting his mind drift into the clouds. However, Debbie jerks him back into the present.

"I'm worried about April," she says.

"Oh my gosh," he says in mild frustration. "Why don't you shut your mind down and let yourself get some sleep. Besides, why are you so worried about April?"

"It's her attraction to James that worries me."

"Her what? What are you talking about?"

"Don't tell me you haven't noticed how she looks and sounds when she talks about him."

"You forget, I don't see like you do, so maybe I've missed something."

"I'm sorry, I still forget sometimes. I think she's in love with him."

"Debbie, James is fifteen or twenty years older than she is! You can't be serious. That's just wrong. Has she said something to you in private about it?"

"When it comes to love, March, years are inconsequential details. And thoughts of right or wrong don't always factor into the decisions of the heart. She hasn't said anything to me specifically about how she feels about him. Call it women's intuition if you want to, but I believe she loves him and wants to be with him."

"If what you're saying is true," March says, "and I'm not saying it is, do I need to talk to her? Is there something I need to do? She's been doing so great since her time at Spirit Lake, I'd hate to see her get derailed and spiral downward."

Debbie sighs. "There's probably not anything that can be done, if that's how she feels. Trying to reason with someone who's in love is like trying to reason with a two-year-old. The best we can do is stand on the shore in case her ship runs aground and breaks up on the rocks."

March gives her a playful shake. "At least I know what you really think about me."

"Huh? What do you mean?"

"I must seem like a two-year-old to you because I'm definitely in love."

Debbie pokes him with her elbow. "Oh just go to sleep, little baby. I'll tend to you in the morning."

CHAPTER TWELVE

Tucker looks at the kitchen clock for the fifth time in the last twenty minutes. *Where is that ol' fool?! I told him t' be here at eight o'clock an' I'd have some fresh coffee, hot biscuits, an' some new sorghum t' share. It's done 8:30 an' th' biscuits is cold.* Looking out the window toward the road where Smiley Carter will be coming from, she frowns. *Smiley Carter don't never miss out on free food, 'specially when it's a new can of Benton County molasses. I hope there ain't nothin' wrong.*

After sitting back down at the table, Tucker listens absently to the *Today* show playing on the TV in the living room. Five minutes later she stands up and walks toward the front door. Grabbing her jacket and keys, she goes outside. *Somethin' ain't right, I can feel it in m' bones.*

She gets inside her pickup truck, cranks it, and heads out toward Smiley's house.

She covers the three miles quickly and turns off the road into his tree-lined driveway. *His lights is on inside; that's a good sign.* As she walks toward the front of the house, she notices that the door is standing half-open. A frown furrows her forehead and creases the space between her eyes. *That don't look right.*

As Tucker gets closer, she sees a man's legs lying halfway through the doorway. "Smiley!" she yells as she breaks into a trot. When she gets to the front door, she finds his still form lying on its side across the threshold. She shoves the door all the way open, falls to her knees beside him, and screams, "Smiley Carter, if you're dead, I'll kill you!"

In a hoarse and weak whisper, Smiley says, "I believe that's the dumbest thing I ever heard you say."

Relief fills Tucker's heart, displacing the terror that was there only seconds ago. "What happened? What's wrong? Are y' all right?"

"I don't rightly know what happened or for sure how long I been lying here. I must have passed out or something. Once I come to I tried to get up, but my right leg and arm don't seem to be working right."

"Do y' feel like anything is broke? I'll try an' help y' up but not if somethin's broke. We'll call us a amb'lance if we need to. I'm thinkin' what happened is that y' had a stroke."

"Don't nothing hurt more so than it usually does," Smiley replies. "Just try sitting me up first and let's see how that goes."

Tucker walks on her knees toward his head and slides her hands under his side. Bending low over him, she grunts and begins lifting him up. She pushes him back against the door facing and pulls his legs in front of him. "Whew! No more biscuits fer you, Smiley Carter. You's as heavy as a hog that's ready t' slaughter."

"Quit trying to brag on me and bring me a glass of water," Smiley answers her.

Gripping the doorknob to help her, Tucker pulls herself up from the floor and goes into the kitchen. She returns in a moment and goes to one knee beside her friend. Holding the glass of water toward him, she says, "Here, drink this."

Smiley looks at his right arm and hand lying limp at his side. "I'm trying, but it ain't working, Tucker. Something's bad wrong. I believe I'm paralyzed." His voice breaks and his eyes redden on the word *paralyzed.*

Tucker puts her hand on the back of his head and eases the glass toward his lips. "Take a drink an' remember that neither one of us has th' letters MD after our name. We don't know nothin'. All we're doin' is guessin', an' prob'ly guessin' wrong."

When Smiley brings the glass to his mouth and tries to get a swallow of water, most of it spills out the left corner of his mouth and runs onto his shirt. "What in the—?" he sputters.

The crusty edges of Tucker's battle-weary heart flake off and fall into a black hole. She feels a fissure open. *Dear God in heaven, please don't make me walk this path again with someone I love. I don't think I have it in me no more."* She pulls her bandanna out of her hip pocket, wipes Smiley's mouth and chin, and dabs at the spilled water on his shirt. "I think I better call an amb'lance," she says.

Smiley's eyes widen. Rallying, he says, "No! Don't you dare because I ain't going to a hospital. If the Lord wants me now, let him take me. If He doesn't, then I'll live my life the way I want to without doctors and nurses telling me what I can and can't do."

Wiping tears from the corner of her eyes, Tucker says, "Y' ain't nothin' but a stubborn ol' goat! So, do you want me t' leave y' here on th' floor an' go back home?"

One side of Smiley's face smiles at her while the other side droops. "If you want to see stubborn, go look in the mirror, old woman."

"Okay, that does it. Y' ain't as bad off as you look. I'm goin' home where I don't have t' listen t' yore nonsense. How'd y' like that?"

All signs of humor evaporate from Smiley's face. "I need your help. I don't know what to do."

Tucker reaches down and grabs the front of his shirt. "Let's stand y' up an' see what happens."

Smiley grips her forearm with his left hand and tries pushing up with his left leg and foot.

Once she gets him into a standing position, Tucker leans him against the wall inside the door. "Now I'm gonna let go of y' an' see if'n y' can stay standin' on yore own."

Fear and uncertainty play across Smiley's stroke-distorted features, but he manages to remain standing by keeping his weight on his left leg.

"That looks good," Tucker says. She slips his limp right arm over the back of her neck and puts her left arm around his back. "Now let's see if y' can take a step 'r two." Cautiously she moves forward a few inches.

Smiley is able to move his right leg forward, but his foot drags across the floor.

"Good," Tucker says. "Now use me an' step with yore left foot."

He leans heavily on her and is able to take a step.

Ten minutes later they have covered a distance of only six feet. Tucker reaches for an armchair and slides it behind Smiley, then eases him into it. She wipes sweat from her forehead and looks at Smiley. "Well here's where we are," she begins. "There ain't no way y' can stay here by yoreself. You are gonna have t' move in with me, an' I'll take care of y'."

Looking exhausted and defeated, Smiley says, "I'll do whatever you say. This is one bridge I ain't never crossed. You'll have to lead the way."

Surprised that he didn't put up a protest at her suggestion, Tucker says, "Okay then, I'll need t' throw some of yore clothes an' things t'gether t' take with us."

"There's a suitcase under my bed," Smiley tells her. "The top three drawers of my dresser will have all the clothes in them that you'll need to bring."

Tucker walks into his bedroom, reaches under the bed, and pulls out the suitcase. After she sets it on the bed and opens it, she turns to his dresser and stares at it. *I ain't never handled 'r touched a man's things, unless it was August's or March's. What have I talked m'self into? If Smiley's livin' with me, I'll be havin' t' wash his clothes.* A thought suddenly hits her and arrests her breathing. *Who's gonna help him change clothes?!* Then another thought slams into that one and panic seizes her. *Who's gonna help him wash himself?!*

CHAPTER THIRTEEN

Be still, Christopher!" April admonishes. "I'm trying to finish fixing your hair so we can leave."

Christopher looks into the bathroom mirror to see April's efforts to comb his hair and keep it in place. He sticks his finger inside his buttoned-up shirt collar and twists his head back and forth. "It's too tight!" he complains.

Unfortunately, just as he decided to twist his head April was pulling a comb through his hair. His movement causes her to turn his hair into a bird's nest of twisted hair.

Stomping her foot, April yells, "Christopher! Now look what you've done. Is that how you want to look at the funeral?"

His bottom lips sticks out and tears well up in his eyes. "I want my mommy to do it."

Immediately, April drops to her knees and hugs him. "I know you do. I'm sorry for sounding so cross with you. I just want you to look nice for the service. It would really make your mommy proud to see you looking handsome, don't you think?" She lets go of him and looks him in the face. She pulls some toilet paper off the roll, puts it to his nose, and says, "Blow."

Christopher complies by giving a hard blow through his nose.

His brother, Michael, appears in the doorway of the bathroom and says, "Daddy told me to see if you all are ready." Pointing at Christopher, he says, "What's he crying about?"

"None of your business!" Christopher snaps at him.

"Tell your father that we'll be there in just a minute," April says. "We're almost ready."

Michael turns and runs through the house, through the front door, out to the car where James is waiting.

April quickly combs Christopher's hair into place then picks up her hairspray and sprays it. "That'll hold it," she says. "You scoot on out to the car. I'll be right behind you."

As Christopher runs out of the bathroom to join his brother, April looks at herself in the mirror. *I hate the way I look in black. It makes me look so pale and anemic. I wonder what James thought about the dress. He didn't say a word about it. Stop it! This is about James and the boys,* she chastises herself, *not about you. Keep focused on your job of managing the twins.* She walks out of the bathroom, flipping off the light as she passes through the doorway.

When she gets to the car, she looks in the backseat to be sure the boys are securely buckled in, then she gets inside.

"The boys look really handsome, April," James says. "You did a nice job getting them dressed and ready." He shifts the car into reverse and backs out of the driveway.

April watches him. *He looks exhausted. Those bags under his eyes and his gray complexion make him look ten years older.*

James turns and catches her looking at him. He holds her eyes for a moment, then blinks and turns his head to the front while shifting the car into drive.

April also turns and watches the road. "When we get to the funeral home," she says, "you take the boys and sit down front. I'll just sit with the audience."

"You will not," James says. "Don't be silly. You're a part of this family now. You sit with me and the boys. We'll put them in between us."

Slipping on her sunglasses, April smiles.

Walking into the funeral home, April is unprepared for the flood of memories that hits her. The sweet and musky smell of flowers brings back memories of her grandmother Ella's funeral. When they enter the chapel, she imagines it is Ella in the open casket at the end of an aisle flanked by chairs. Standing between Christopher and Michael, she takes both their hands and follows behind James as he makes the slow walk to the front of the chapel. The four of them sit in the front row.

As April sits and listens to different friends and family give eulogies to the memory of Susan, she becomes more and more uncomfortable. *The woman sounds like she was a saint. How can I ever compete with her? I've never done anything with my life. Heck, I'm not even finished with college. What do I have to offer a man like James? He'll forever be comparing me to Susan, and I'll lose that contest every time. Maybe I'm fooling myself with any thoughts of drawing his attention.*

After James pulls to a stop behind the hearse in the cemetery for the graveside ceremony he, April, and the boys exit the car and make their way to the small tent pitched over the grave site. The funeral director escorts them to the front row of a dozen or so chairs that are filled by Susan's and James's relatives. Thirty or forty more people stand close by as witnesses to the grief their friends are enduring, hoping that just by being present they can help shoulder some of the heaviness of the loss.

April gazes into the yawning, rectangular hole underneath the suspended casket, barely hearing the pastor's recitation of scripture.

Ella, I miss you so much. You left me way too soon, before your job with me was finished, I think. How different my life might be if I could have continued growing up with you as my mother. I made so many mistakes and lost my way. In doing that, I dishonored you, and I want you to forgive me for that. It wasn't your fault, and I certainly don't blame you, though for a time I may have.

Sometimes I still have these waves of sadness come over me when I remember losing you. I hope you'll watch over me as I try to help Christopher and Michael survive their mother's death. I want to save them from the dark place I fell into, and you can help me do that. Be my angel and point me in the right direction. Help me let go of this girlish fantasy of me and James being together. He could never have feelings for me, I can see that now. I should be honored and grateful that he trusts me enough to help him with his boys. They need to be my main focus.

Later that evening, after all the friends and family have left the house, James and April are cleaning up the kitchen and putting food away in the refrigerator and freezer. Exhausted, they focus only on the tasks, without engaging in conversation.

When they are close to being finished, April says, "Why don't I go give the boys a bath and put them to bed? You go ahead and take your shower and go to bed, too. I'll take care of the rest of this later."

Too tired to protest her offer, James says, "That sounds nice, thank you. I believe I will." He walks past her like a sleepwalker.

She reaches up to touch his arm as he passes, but stops herself.

In the bathroom, April starts running the bathwater and then goes into the boys' bedroom. They are half-asleep on the floor, watching TV. "Hey, guys," she says, "let's get our pajamas together and let me give you a quick bath. You'll sleep better if you're clean."

Exhaustion keeps the door closed on their normal urges to complain about taking a bath. They get up and walk to the bathroom, knowing their fate is sealed.

April follows them in and helps them take off their clothes.

They crawl into the warm bathwater and sit motionless.

April reaches for the bar of soap on the edge of the tub and wets it with one of her hands while gently splashing water on the boys with her other hand. Then she soaps them up, having to lift their arms for them as if they were marionettes. With their energy-depleted voices silenced, the only sound is the water dripping and splashing into the tub.

After rinsing them off, she helps them out of the tub and towels them dry. "Okay, you all put your pajamas on while I go turn back your beds."

As April walks out of the bathroom, the boys sit on the floor and start putting their feet into their pajama bottoms.

By the time April has finished turning back the boys' beds, they appear in the doorway of the bedroom. They walk toward the welcoming pillows and folds of sheets and blankets and crawl into the cotton womb. Their eyes are already closed when April pulls the covers up and kisses them goodnight.

Closing the bedroom door behind her, April lets out a long sigh. *What a day. I don't remember the last time I was this exhausted.* She looks at the closed door to James's bedroom. No muted sounds emanate from the other side. *Sounds like he's already passed out, too. Good!*

She returns to the bathroom and turns the shower on. She strips off her clothes and steps into the warm liquid tranquilizer, lifting her face as she eases into the spray. As the tension begins leaving her, it triggers an audible groan. She slowly turns in the waterfall and chills run up and down her as the water hits her back. Tilting her head back, she soaks her hair and closes her eyes.

Fifteen minutes later, she shuts off the water and opens the shower curtain to reveal a steam-filled room. She towel dries her hair and dries herself off. She wraps the towel around her torso and cracks open the bathroom door to look out to be sure no one has gotten up. Secure in the knowledge that she is the only one in the house who is awake, she pads across the hallway into her bedroom. When she closes the door behind her, she lets the towel fall away and pitches it across the back of a chair. Sitting down at her vanity, she begins coming out her hair.

Suddenly, there is a small knock on her door. She freezes, listening to be sure she didn't imagine it. Again, there is a small knock. Envisioning the twins standing on the other side of the door wanting something from her, April grabs her short satin robe off a hook on the wall and puts it on as she strides to the door.

Feeling aggravated at having her bedtime routine interrupted, she opens the door abruptly and says, "What in the world do you—?"

At the same time, James is saying, "I'm sorry for disturbing you, but—"

April stares at him. His tangled, damp hair tells her he hasn't been out of the shower very long. He is wearing his black monogrammed housecoat and he's barefoot. His eyes drop from her face and run down the length of her, then quickly return to her face. A tingle runs up her spine.

"I'm sorry," he says softly. "I know you have to be exhausted, but I couldn't fall asleep without telling you how much I love you for what you did today. It meant the world to the boys and it meant a lot to me, too. It would have been much harder without you."

April feels like the mallet of a bass drum is beating inside her chest. She opens her mouth to speak, but James holds his hand up.

"Don't say anything. I just wanted to say that to you. Go to bed and rest." Bending down, he kisses her on the cheek, then turns and walks down the hallway.

CHAPTER FOURTEEN

A stroke?!" August exclaims into the phone receiver. He listens in silence to the person on the other end. His eyes widen. "He's staying with you? The two of you in your house? Why isn't he in a hospital?" A frown creases his brow as he listens. "I suppose that sounds like him, but I don't like it. It's a lot for you to take on, Tucker. Are you sure you can handle everything?" He jerks the receiver away from his ear and Tucker can be heard yelling. When her voice is silent, he puts the receiver back to his ear. "I'm sorry, you're right. You can handle it, I'm sure. Can I talk to him?"

After a few moments he says, "Hey, Dad, Tucker just told me what happened. Don't you think it would be better if you let a doctor see you or if you went somewhere to get some rehabilitation?" As August listens to Smiley Carter's weakened voice, tears well up in his eyes. He squeezes them shut and the tears spill out onto his cheeks. Nodding, he says, "I know you don't like doctors, but we need to find out why you had a stroke and you need some medication to prevent another one. There may be a clot they need to clean out of one of your arteries." Once again he listens quietly to Smiley. "Yes, sir, I'll not hound you about it. I know you're a grown man and have lived a long time without people telling you what to do. I don't have to like your decision, but I will respect it. Let me talk to Tucker again."

When he hears Tucker's voice August says, "Do I need to leave right now and come home to see about him?" He listens closely to Tucker's reply. "Okay then, I'll wait until the weekend. If anything changes, call me day or night, okay?" After a brief pause, he says, "Okay. Bye now. I love you."

As Tucker hangs up the phone, she looks at Smiley lying under the covers on April's bed. "He'll be home this weekend. I told him there weren't no need fer him t' come home right away. Seems t' me you is gittin' a bit stronger as th' hours go by, ain't y'? Y' ain't quite as weak as y' was when I brought y' here this mornin'."

"If you says so," Smiley replies. "I still feel like I'm as weak as a baby. My arm is still not responding."

"Well look here," Tucker says, "these kinds of things take time. Y' know they do. You're gonna have t' be patient."

A pained expression crosses Smiley's face.

"What's th' matter?"

"I hate t' tell you this, but I gotta go pee."

"Don't y' think I knew you'd have t' go eventually?" She reaches down and pulls the covers back. "Swing yer legs over th' side of th' bed so's I can help y' up."

Using his left hand, Smiley pulls his right leg to follow his left leg over the side of the bed. He sits up.

Tucker stares at the zipper on his pants. Imagining what's behind that zipper, Tucker almost gags. *If he can't get himself out an' pee on his own, I don't know if I can do it fer him 'r not.* "Look here, why don't we just take yore pants off an' leave 'em off. Y' don't need 'em fer now anyway, not as long as you stay in April's bed."

"That's a good idea," Smiley agrees. He unbuckles his belt with his left hand and unfastens and unzips his pants.

Tucker grasps the cuff of his pants and tugs his trousers off. She reaches out her hand, grasps his offered left hand, and pulls him to a standing position.

They negotiate the eight feet between them and the bathroom. Once inside, Tucker stops him in front of the toilet. She reaches down and lifts the seat. "I'm hopin' y' can take care of things by yoreself from here."

"I don't know if I can stand up by myself without you helping me," Smiley says uncertainly. "If you'll just hold me up, I can manage with my left hand, I think."

Oh my lord almighty! I don't even want to be in the same room when he pulls that thing out! She closes her eyes. "Okay, I'll hold y' up like this an' you do yore business." Keeping her eyes closed, she feels Smiley moving and then hears the sound of him peeing. She works to keep her mind focused on images of her working in her garden in the spring.

Eventually Smiley says, "I'm done."

Tucker helps him back to the bed. "Let's prop you up in here," she says. "I'm gonna fix us somethin' t' eat." Focusing her efforts on getting Smiley settled in the bed and the pillow stuffed behind his back, she doesn't notice his face. But when she's about to stand up, she looks at him and sees his cheeks are shining with tears. "What th' matter? Are y' hurtin' somewhere?"

Smiley shakes his head. "When you was growing up, did you ever imagine that one day when you were old, you'd be taking care of a black man? No need to answer that question because I never dreamed I'd have a white woman taking care of me. Tucker, you've become a really good woman, a kind woman. It's been an amazing transformation to watch over the last ten years or so. I know having me here ain't easy for you. I don't know how, but someday I'll make it up to you." As he finishes speaking, he gently lays the palm of his left hand on the side of her face.

Tucker flinches at his touch but doesn't pull away. "We've seen some times, ain't we? This here is just another fence t' climb over. I'll see y' through this an' I'll expect y' t' make it up t' me ten times over, that's fer sure. Now let me go fix us some food." Smiley removes his hand from her face and she gets up off the bed.

Walking into the kitchen, Tucker argues with herself. *Don't trust him 'cause all men is after th' same thing. It's Smiley Carter, for Pete's sake! Get a grip on yoreself. He's th' one man that ain't never done anything outta th' way toward you. But he's th' same man that had sex with Maisy an' fathered August. A man like that ain't t' be trusted. If things was turned around, an' he'd found me on th' floor after havin' a stroke, what would he do?* Tucker stares blankly into her refrigerator as she lets this last scenario play out in her mind. She reaches for the jar of salad dressing. *Well that settles that. There ain't no doubt that Smiley Carter would take me in an' do fer me exactly what I'm doin' fer him.* After removing a stick of baloney, she lets the refrigerator door close itself. *An' if'n he needs me t' give him a sponge bath, then that's just what I'll do. An' curse th' mem'ry of my father.*

CHAPTER FIFTEEN

The night after March and Debbie slept on the couch together March reaches inside his kitchen cabinet and takes out two plates and two glasses. The smells of spaghetti sauce and French bread fill his small kitchenette. He places the plates and glasses on opposite sides of the small dining table, turns to the stove, and stirs the spaghetti sauce. Using the tip of his finger, he tastes it. *Needs more salt.* After he locates the saltshaker on the back of the stove, he sprinkles some into the sauce and stirs it again. Holding his hand over the top of a pot on the back eye, he feels the steam rising from the water boiling inside. He opens the package of spaghetti noodles and drops them into the water with a twisting motion so the noodles will be less likely to stick together in clumps.

He presses a button on his wristwatch. "6:55 p.m.," a tinny voice announces. Taking the dish towel from his shoulder, he wipes the sweat off the sides of his face. *She should be here any minute. I hope I don't lose my nerve. I've played it out a dozen ways all day long, which is why I hardly got anything accomplished at work, and there's no reason not to take a chance.*

The ringing of his doorbell suddenly interrupts his thoughts. March takes a step to leave the kitchen when he hears the spaghetti boiling over. The water hisses like an angry crowd at a bad vaude-ville act as it hits the hot eye underneath the pot. He turns back to the stove to turn down the eye and slide the pot halfway off. The doorbell rings again. "Come on in!" he yells in the direction of the front door. The only response to his cry is the doorbell ringing once again. "What the—?!"

Certain that the boiling spaghetti has quieted down, he hurries into the living room and toward the front door. "I'm coming!" he says in exasperation.

He turns the doorknob that is locked on the inside and swings open the door.

"I'm sorry, I forgot my key," Debbie says. "Whoa, you look like you've been working out in a gym. Your face is red and sweating. What's up?"

When she steps inside, March closes the door and says, "Everything started happening at once in the kitchen and then the doorbell kept ringing and I couldn't leave the stove and . . ."

Debbie puts her hand on his chest and says, "Hey, it's okay. I'm not upset. Let me come help you." Taking his hand, she walks toward the kitchen. "What's up with you tonight? I told you when you called me earlier that I could pick up some takeout and bring it with me."

"I just wanted to do it myself," March replies. "You're always the one doing the cooking, or we do takeout or go to a restaurant. Everything should be ready. We just need to put it together." As he finishes speaking, they walk into the kitchen and the buzzer on the oven goes off. "That should be the bread," he says.

"Well, everything smells delicious," Debbie says. "Can I take the bread out of the oven?"

"Thanks," March replies. "I'll drain the spaghetti while you do that."

Debbie opens the oven door and, grabbing a potholder, extracts the hot, golden loaf of French bread. She lays it on the cutting board resting on the counter, takes the serrated knife, and slices it. "How was your day today?" she asks.

"Not too bad," March responds. "It just seemed like I couldn't finish anything I started, for some reason."

"I know what you mean. I hate days like that. It's like I don't get one thing finished before someone gives me something else to start. At the end of those kinds of days I feel like all I've done is spin my wheels."

March turns from the sink and carries the colander of drained spaghetti over to the stove and dumps it into the pot of sauce. "Yeah, I know. I felt like a dog chasing his tail all day; lots of energy expended but going nowhere." He mixes the spaghetti and sauce with the large spoon, then carries the pot to the table and places it on the trivet between their plates.

Debbie joins him, carrying the sliced bread still resting on the cutting board. She raises a piece of bread to his mouth. "Here, take a bite. It's best when it's hot, if you know what I mean." She nudges him with her elbow.

March laughs and she pushes the bread into his mouth.

She kisses him on the cheek and laughs, too.

When he finally chews and swallows enough of the bread that he can speak, March says, "Are you trying to choke me to death?" Feigning an expression of innocence, he adds, "And I have no idea what you mean when you say, 'It's best when it's hot.'"

"Oh brother! Sure you don't, you poor innocent little child."

Suddenly, March embraces her. Tilting his head down, he says, "Kiss me, Debbie."

Rising on her tiptoes, Debbie covers his mouth with hers. She gently bites his lip and then pulls away. "So is it spaghetti you want, or is it the dessert?"

"Whew! Has anyone ever told you what an unbelievable kisser you are? You take my breath away."

"You know," Debbie says huskily as she tugs on his shirt, "we don't have to eat the spaghetti."

March grasps her hand and shakes his head. "No, let's eat first. There are some things I want to talk to you about."

There's an audible catch in Debbie's throat. She backs away from him. "Is there something wrong? Is it bad? Don't make this a buildup with what I think is a romantic dinner when it's really a 'let's just be friends' dinner."

"Debbie, take a breath and relax. Nothing is wrong. I just want to talk to you about some of the things we discussed last night, that's all. Can we do that?"

"I'm sorry I'm such a fraidy cat. I get spooked too easily, don't I? Sure, let's sit down and enjoy this March-prepared feast."

They sit down across from each other and Debbie serves their plates.

"Oh man," March exclaims as he scoots his chair back from the table, "I forgot to pour the tea."

"No, no," Debbie says, "let me do that. You keep your seat." She takes the glasses to the refrigerator and puts some ice in them. She locates the pitcher of tea and fills the glasses.

When she places the glass in March's outstretched hand, he says, "Thank you," and takes a long drink.

After they eat a few bites in silence, March says, "There are some things I need to say to you, Debbie. First of all, I love you. I think those may be the three most important words in the English language. I remember the first time you said them to me my soul filled with a warmth and light I had never experienced before. I love you in a way that I've never loved anyone. I care about what you think, what you feel, what you are doing, what excites you, what saddens you. I want to know you in a way I've never known anyone else. I'm not sure how this will sound to you but it's like I want to open you up and crawl inside you and live there so that I can learn every detail there is to know about you. That's how fascinated I am by you."

"Oh March," Debbie says in a whisper.

"The second thing I want to tell you," March continues, "is that I cannot imagine my life without you. I don't want to imagine my life without you because if you leave me, then the light in my soul will go out and an ice castle will take its place. You see, I used to think that my heart was a stone castle, a castle I built over the years to protect myself from getting wounded. But when you came into my life, the heat and fire of your spirit revealed the castle to be made of ice and it slowly began to melt. I don't want to go back to living in that cold, dark place. Living there used to be okay, because I didn't know there was another option. You've shown me . . . You've shown me that love can break down walls and heal souls. What a powerful gift you've given me."

He rests his arms on the table and extends his hands toward Debbie.

She grasps one of his hands with hers. When he taps the table with the back of his other hand she places her prosthetic hand in his. "March Tucker," she says, "my heart is going to burst. It can't hold all these words you are pouring into it."

"There's only been one issue that was holding me back from you, Debbie, and it's what we talked about last night. My issues with sex are dark and twisted. Dr. Sydney told me once that I would have to face those demons one day or I would be destined to live alone. When I finally lanced that boil last night and you did not pull away from me in disgust and horror, and when you said we can work through anything together, even that issue, I had no more reasons standing in my way."

Through her tears, Debbie asks, "Standing in your way of what?"

"Standing in my way of this." March lets go of her hands and gets up out of his chair. He walks around to her chair and gets down on one knee at her side. "Give me your hand." Once he feels her warm hand securely in his, he says, "Debbie Cooper, will you marry me?"

The dam that Debbie had been pushing back against, as the swirling river of emotions created by March's tender and heartfelt words kept rising, suddenly bursts in a shower of tears and a cry from deep within her. Throwing her arms around him, she buries her face in his neck and says his name over and over.

March puts his arms around her and pulls her onto his knee, then, putting his arms under her, he lifts her as he stands up and begins walking down the hallway. He pushes open his bedroom door, walks in, and carefully lowers her onto the bed. He lies down beside her, facing her.

Debbie begins slowly unbuttoning his shirt. When she gets to his belt, she pulls his shirttail out of his pants and unbuttons the last two buttons. She slips her hand under his T-shirt and explores his chest and stomach.

March reaches his hand underneath the back of her shirt. He feels the moisture of sweat on the small of her back, then slides his hand up to where her bra strap crosses her back. Pinching and twisting the catch, he releases it.

"Oh, March," he hears her say.

She pushes him on his back and moves on top, straddling him on her knees. She takes his hand and lifts it toward her chest.

The phone beside March's bed rings loudly.

They both jump as if someone had fired a gun at them. Then a nervous laugh escapes from each of them.

The phone rings again.

"Let's ignore it," Debbie says. She leans down and kisses him.

The insistent phone repeats its demand to be answered.

"I'll try to, if you can," March replies.

The answering machine kicks on. "March!" comes a frantic voice. "This is August. Pick up the phone! Something's happened to my dad! March! Answer the phone!"

CHAPTER SIXTEEN

In a flash, March pushes Debbie aside as he slides out from under her. Sitting on the edge of the bed, he picks up the receiver. "August, it's March. What happened?" He listens for a moment, then says, "August, slow down, you're not making any sense. Now slow down and tell me exactly what happened."

Frowning, March listens intently as August talks.

Debbie moves behind him and lays her cheek on his back.

After several moments, March says, "Sure I want to go with you. When are you wanting to leave?" He pauses. "What about April?" Another pause. "Let me call her and tell her what's happened and see what she wants to do. It may be more complicated for her to get away. I'll call you right back, okay?"

March hangs up the phone.

Debbie shifts positions and sits beside him. "What in the world is going on?"

"It's Smiley Carter. It sounds like he's had a stroke."

"Oh no!" Debbie gasps. "How bad is he?"

"August said Tucker found him inside his house lying on the floor. No one knows how long he'd been lying there. He's alert and talking but the whole right side of his body seems to have some paralysis or weakness."

"That he's alert and talking is a good sign," Debbie says. "What hospital is he in?"

"Well, that's one of the problems," March replies. "He's not in a hospital because he refused to let Tucker take him there or call for an ambulance, either. He's actually at Tucker's house. She's put him in April's bedroom and she's taking care of him."

"You have got to be kidding me! Tucker is taking care of a black man who is paralyzed and needs help with, what? Dressing himself? Feeding himself? Bathing? Going to the bathroom?"

Shaking his head, March says, "I know, I know. It's crazy, but apparently that's how the two of them decided to manage things. August wants to go home to see him for himself and determine if maybe Smiley needs special care and then see if he can convince him to get it."

"We're going too, then," Debbie says as she gets off the bed. "When are we leaving?"

"I've got to call April to see if she can even get away to go with us."

"I think I'll run home and pack me a few things. Is that okay with you?"

"Sure."

Debbie bends down and kisses him on the lips.

March says, "I'm sorry we got interrupted."

"Don't worry. I'll remember where we left off." She turns to leave when March grabs for her.

"Wait a minute," he says. "You didn't answer my question."

"What question?"

"*The* question. You know . . ."

"Oh, *that* question. Silly boy, if you don't know the answer to that, then how about this for an answer." She pushes him on his back, lies on top of him, and puts her lips on his. She opens her mouth and pushes her tongue through his lips. Their tongues dance in excitement. Quickly, she pulls away from him and stands up, leaving him lying on his back open-mouthed. "Does that answer your question?"

Smacking his lips together, March says, "I think I understand, but maybe you better do that one more time just to be sure."

Debbie playfully kicks him in the shin. "Call your sister. I've got to run." As she walks out of the bedroom and down the hallway, she calls out, "Be back soon."

A broad smile spreads across March's face. *Thank you, God, for bringing that angel into my life and leading me out of the darkness.* Sitting up, he reaches for the phone and dials the number for April's private line in James's house. On the fifth ring, April answers. "Hey, baby sister, I almost thought you weren't going to answer." He listens to her reply. "Yeah, I'll bet your reading stories to the boys at bedtime means even more to them now. You are doing a wonderful thing for James and his family. But listen, something has happened back home." He pauses. "No, Tucker is fine. It's Smiley Carter. It sounds like he's had a stroke. August called me after Tucker called him. We're going to head home tonight, so that we can be there by morning. Can you go with us?"

After a long pause, March says, "I figured it might not be easy for you to get away on such short notice. Do you want me to wait on the phone while you talk to James about it?" After her reply, he says, "Okay then, I'll be waiting on your call. August is waiting on me to call him back and let him know something, so the sooner you call me, the better."

Two hours later August pulls his car into James's driveway. The front door opens immediately and April steps outside carrying a small suitcase. She walks quickly to the car as August gets out to open the trunk. August takes her bag from her, puts it beside the others, and closes the trunk. They both get in the front seat.

From the backseat, March says, "Glad you got to go with us, April."

"James was really sweet about it," April says. "He said how could he refuse me after all I've done for him the past few days." As August backs out of the driveway, she says, "So give me more details about Smiley. What hospital is he in?"

Looking in the rearview mirror at March, August says, "You didn't tell her?"

"Tell me what?" April says.

"I just gave her the basics," March answers. "I knew there'd be time to fill her in on the drive home."

When neither August nor March continues with an explanation, Debbie speaks up. "It seems Smiley has refused to be taken to a hospital or to a doctor."

"You just wait till I talk to him," April says. "He's never refused me for anything I've asked him. He's just being stubborn with Tucker. So if he's not in the hospital, where is he? Don't tell me he's staying alone in his house!"

"Actually," March says, "he's staying with Tucker."

"In your bedroom," August adds.

There are a couple of beats of silence as these last two bits of information filter into April. She says, "You mean to tell me that Smiley Carter is living with Tucker? A man is staying in Tucker's house? I mean, a man—?"

"A semicrippled man," March interjects.

"Who has to have help dressing himself," August adds.

"And who has to be bathed by someone," Debbie says.

All four of them shake their heads and fall silent, trying to sort through all the implications of the situation they just described.

April is the first to break the silence, "Look, we've all talked about Tucker and her issues with men in general. I just can't imagine her taking care of a man, even if it is Smiley."

"I know what you mean," August chimes in. "There's no doubt the two of them are close friends and they care about each other, but when I picture Tucker giving him a bath—" August gives his body a shake. "It gives me the willies."

"What you two are forgetting," March says, "is that people can face their issues and they can change. Maybe Tucker is still growing and becoming. I know I am." He puts his arm around Debbie's shoulders and she snuggles up to him.

April notices the movement and turns around. "Well it's nice to see whatever you two were arguing about a few days ago, you got things worked out."

"Yes we did," Debbie says.

"Actually," March says, "we've got some pretty important news we need to tell you about."

August tries to see his brother in the darkness of the backseat. "What's up, brother?"

"I asked Debbie to marry me and she said yes."

April screams and climbs over the back of her seat, spilling into March's lap. "I knew it! I knew it was going to happen eventually! Oh my, that is the greatest news! I'm so happy for both of you." She hugs and kisses them.

"You are the man!" August calls out excitedly. "That is fantastic. What an amazing story the two of you have."

"What do you mean?" Debbie asks.

"Well, if you'd never been in the accident with your parents and lost your arm, you'd have never gone to Patricia Neal. And if you'd never gone there for therapy, you'd have never gone there to work. If March hadn't run away from home and gotten injured, he would never have gone to Patricia Neal, and you all would have never met. So, it's like the worst things that happened to both of you ended up being significant adjustments to the course of your lives and eventually brought the two of you together. That just can't be happenstance."

"I know what you mean," April says. "I feel the same way about me and James and his boys. It's like God brought me into James's life at Spirit Lake so that He could help me find direction in my life. What neither of us knew is that that new direction was intended to help prepare me for this tragic time in the life of him and his boys."

March listens closely to his brother and sister, then says, "It sometimes seems like the only way of making sense of your life is by looking backward and seeing how all the twists and turns make sense, because while you're in the middle of living it, it looks and feels chaotic and out of control."

"So," Debbie speaks up, "you're saying that God killed my parents and took my arm so that I could meet March? What kind of God is that?"

"Let me comment on that one," August says. "I remember having a conversation with Smiley about this very thing. I believe what he would say to you, Debbie, is that God didn't kill your parents or take your arm. He would say that Satan is responsible. He told me that Satan is the King of Chaos and Jesus is the Prince of Peace. Satan tries to turn us from God by creating chaos and destruction, but Jesus can step into the midst of that storm and say, 'Peace. Be still.' God is constantly holding open doors of opportunity to escape. But it's up to us to see them and follow His lead."

August's insightful comments gives them all something to chew on and digest. In silence, they continue their journey toward Dresden.

CHAPTER SEVENTEEN

The sun is approaching the horizon and its rays are kissing the brown leaves in the tops of the tall oak trees as August turns onto the road leading to Tucker's house.

Switching off the car radio, August says, "Hey, you guys, it's time to wake up. We're home."

In the backseat, Debbie and March unfold themselves from each other's arms.

"Sorry about that, August," March says, "I meant to stay awake and keep you from getting sleepy. I guess you managed okay in spite of me, though."

"Not a problem," August replies. "For some reason I'm one of those few people who doesn't get sleepy when they're driving."

April gives a screech that sounds like a windup siren as she comes awake. Stretching her arms as she arches her back, she says, "I think I passed out soon after we left Knoxville and missed all the rest stops. My bladder feels like it. Don't hit any bumps or I won't be responsible for the results."

"Mine feels the same way," Debbie agrees.

"What time is it?" March asks.

"Around 6:30," August answers. He pulls into the driveway in front of Tucker's home.

The clicking of seatbelts being unfastened indicates the eagerness each of them has in debarking from the four-wheeled ship that has transported them the length of the state and is now being moored safely in front of their grandmother's house.

August is the first one to get out. "We'll get the bags out of the trunk later," he says as he closes his door. Not waiting on the others, he walks quickly to the front door and steps inside, where he meets a startled Tucker.

"What th'—?! August, what in tarnation are y' doin' here? Besides, y' like t' have give me a heart attack."

"I came to see about my dad. How's he doing?"

"You mean that lazy, demandin' ol' man lyin' in bed back there in April's room? He's doin' well enough fer now, but he won't be after I shoot him."

Frowning, August says, "What's the matter? I got the impression from you on the phone that he was in bad shape."

"He was when I found him lyin' on th' floor of his house an' when I brought him over here. But since he had a night's sleep, he's had some kind of miraculous recov'ry."

The front door reopens and April, March, and Debbie walk inside.

"Land of Goshen!" Tucker exclaims. "Y' didn't tell me th' rest of th' bunch was with y'. Come on in, ever'body."

"So, how is Smiley doing?" April asks.

"Apparently," August says, "he's much better today than yesterday because it sounds like these two are right back to their bickering selves."

"What do you mean?" March asks.

From the far end of the house, Smiley calls out, "Who's here? Is somebody here? What's going on in there? What about that cup of coffee?"

Pointing in the direction of his voice, Tucker says through gritted teeth, "That's what I'm talkin' 'bout. Who'd of ever thought he was one of them 'give 'em an inch an' they'll take a mile' kind of people? Ever since he opened his eyes at five o'clock this mornin' he's been actin' like he's a king an' I'm his slave. Well this slave girl knows how t' use a gun an' a axe handle. I'm fixin' t' use both of 'em on him if he don't shut up."

August puts his hand over his mouth to conceal his smile and April turns her face away as she laughs silently.

Without making an effort to hide his amusement at this familiar dance of irritation between his grandmother and her friend, March holds out his hand and says, "Here, give me the gun. I'll go shoot him for you. No sense in you having to go to the trouble. Sounds like you've been put out enough this morning."

August and April are unable to contain themselves any longer. Their brother's hyperbole-filled comment unleashes peals of riotous laughter from them.

March doubles over he laughs so hard.

"Go ahead!" Tucker says, trying to feign being indignant. "Make fun of me. But y' better get ready t' call th' sheriff 'cause—"

She is interrupted by another cry from the end of the house. "Is that all you kids I hear? August, is that you?!"

August heads toward the bedroom and the others follow. "Yes, it's us, Daddy. We heard you were in bad shape and decided we needed to see you for—" He stops talking when he makes the turn into April's bedroom and sees Smiley sitting up in bed.

The first thing he notices is that his father's normal smile droops on one side. The other thing that strikes him is that his father looks older and more tired than when he saw him just a few days ago.

"Well come in here all of you," Smiley says warmly. "Give an old man a hug."

Each of them willingly obeys his request.

April kisses both of his cheeks. "You had us scared."

After March hugs him, Debbie steps up and gives him a hug, too.

"You better hurry up and make this girl legal, March, or she's gonna get away from you," Smiley says. "I'm telling you, she's a keeper."

Before March can respond, Tucker walks into the crowded room. "I s'pose this is exactly what y' was wantin', people makin' a fuss over y' an' seein' t' yore ever' whim. Don't ya'll encourage him, 'cause you ain't th' one havin' t' take care of him."

"I want you all to take a look at Tucker," Smiley says. "This here woman is an angel of God for certain. If she hadn't come and rescued me, there's no doubt I'd probably have died right there lying on my own floor. She's swooped in and taken care of me like I was a little baby. Yes sir, I owe my life to Tucker."

Tucker's face turns crimson. "He's just tellin' tales so's I'll keep him here an' take care of him, when th' truth is I ain't sure he's needin' anybody t' take care of him. Take a look at him. Does he look like anything's wrong with him?"

August looks with concern at Smiley's face and is about to comment, when Tucker gives him a sharp look that hooks his attention. She makes a scowl and shakes her head at him.

Turning to look at Smiley, she says, "See there? There ain't nothin' wrong with y'. Any day now I'm gonna turn y' out, just like puttin' a calf in th' pasture. So y' better watch it."

"Ain't she something?" Smiley says. "Listen how she tries to cover up that heart of love and concern that beats within her. You are one of a kind, Tucker."

"We'll see about that," Tucker replies. "Now ya'll come into th' kitchen. I was just about t' start cookin' breakfast when y' barged in."

Following her instructions, the four of them retreat from the bedroom and head into the kitchen.

"Ya'll sit down at th' table an' I'll start cookin' us up somethin'," Tucker says.

"So how is he really?" August says.

"One thing's fer certain, I don't want nobody actin' like he ain't doin' no good. He don't need t' know that. He needs t' believe he's doin' good an' he's gonna git better soon. So don't be carryin' on with him, ya'll hear me?"

A collective and simultaneous "Yes, ma'am" comes from the congregation assembled at the table.

Debbie slips her hand into March's hand, then leans over and whispers in his ear. Getting up, she walks back down the hallway but turns into the bathroom.

"Oh good grief!" April exclaims. "That's right! I forgot about how bad I had to pee." She gets up from the table and, walking quickly down the hallway, calls out, "Hurry up, girl! I'm next!"

The hissing sound and the aroma of bacon frying in the black cast-iron skillet fills the air in the kitchen.

"Nobody fixes a breakfast any better than you, Tucker," March says. "I've eaten my share of breakfasts in lots of places and I've had lots of mornings I didn't get any breakfast, but one of my favorite childhood memories is breakfasts at our little kitchen table in the old house. No matter how little we might have had to eat, you made sure we got a good, hot breakfast."

"That is the truth," August says. "I remember one of our special treats for breakfast was her homemade apple fritters. Mmmm, were they ever delicious."

"What was delicious?" April asks as she and Debbie return to the table.

"Tucker's homemade apple fritters for breakfast," August says. "Do you remember them?"

"Remember them? She taught me how to make them," April answers.

"Yeah, but are yours as good as hers?" March taunts.

"Oh now you've done it!" April says as she jumps up from her chair. "Tucker, do you have any canned or frozen apples?"

Though her eyes are focused on the bacon as she turns it, Tucker's ears and heart are soaking up the beauty of the memories and the banter of her grandchildren. Smiling, she says, "There's three or four pint jars of apples in the pantry."

"I've got to watch you do this," Debbie says as she gets out of her chair. "I've never seen anyone actually make apple fritters."

"Be sure you take notes when you do," March says, "because I could get used to having them every morning."

"Yes," Debbie replies, "and you could also get used to becoming as big as the side of a barn, too."

Laughing, August says, "Oh that girl has a sharp wit and matching tongue. You are not going to stand a chance with her after you're married."

Tucker drops the meat fork onto the floor and turns around quickly. "After you're what?!"

"Way to drop the egg, August," April chastises him.

"It's okay," March says. "I was just waiting for the right pause in the conversation to make the announcement. It's true, Tucker, Debbie has agreed to marry me."

"Whooo-eee!" Tucker cries. "Come here, Debbie!"

Debbie walks into the open embrace of Tucker's arms.

"I thought th' boy was gonna mess 'round an' let you git away. This is wonderful news!"

Smiley's voice cuts in from down the hallway. "What's going on in there? Somebody come get me and bring me in there. I'm missing out on everything!"

They all laugh.

As August stands up to go get his father, Debbie says, "Let me go help you. I'm not a physical therapist or anything like that, but I've had lots of experience with people who've had strokes."

"That'd be great," August says.

A few minutes later, Smiley Carter and August walk slowly down the hallway side by side. Debbie is following closely behind, talking low with subtle suggestions to both of them.

April sees them and starts singing, "There he comes just a-walking down the street, singing doo-wah-diddy-diddy-dum-diddy-doo. Smiley Carter's just a-walking down the street, singing doo-wah-diddy-diddy-dum-diddy-doo."

Tucker and March join with April in singing the last phrase.

August helps Smiley into a chair at the table. "Look at you!" August says. "You made it in here just fine. I hardly had to help you at all."

"Well," Smiley says, "you can't expect a man to lie in bed when there's a party going on in the next room. So I want to know what I missed out on that made Tucker squeal like a schoolgirl."

"Let me say it," April says. Before anyone can object, she announces, "March and Debbie are getting married!"

Smiley slaps March on the back. "Decided to take ol' Smiley's advice, didn't you? That is wonderful. I'm happy for both of you. When's the date?"

"We haven't gotten that far in our negotiations," March replies with a smile.

Debbie comes up behind him and rests her arms on his shoulders. "Negotiations?" She grabs a handful of his beard. "I'll show you some negotiations!"

As March howls, everyone laughs.

CHAPTER EIGHTEEN

Y ou want this last biscuit, March?" Tucker asks. "I'd hate t' throw it out."

Sticking out his hand, March says, "Don't you dare throw out one of your biscuits! If the manna that the children of Israel ate in the wilderness tasted anything like your biscuits, then I'm not surprised some of them gathered up more than they were supposed to and got in trouble for it."

"Ya'll hear that? March says m' biscuits are like manna from heaven."

"Who taught you to make biscuits like that?" August asks.

"I'm sure m' mama did, but I don't really remember it. I can remember rollin' out biscuits when I was seven years old, an' it wasn't just fer fun that I did it. It was m' job."

"I'll tell you what's good," Smiley speaks up. "These apple fritters April made were as fine as I ever ate."

Beaming, April says, "Thank you, Smiley. I made them for James and his boys one morning and you'd have thought they were eating a Krispy Kreme doughnut. I never heard that many groans and moans of pleasure. I was afraid they were going to lick their plates."

"You sure those weren't groans and moans from them having bellyaches?" March teases her.

"March Tucker! I'll come over there and slap you!" April says.

"Still got that quick temper, don't you, sis?" March says. "I'm just kidding."

"Look here, ever'body," Tucker suddenly says, "we need t' go somewhere an' celebrate March and Debbie's engagement. Let's go somewhere special an' it'll be my treat."

"You don't have to do that," Debbie says.

"I know I don't, but I want to. So where do ya'll wanta go?"

"We could go eat lunch at the Hearth in Martin," August suggests.

"No," Tucker says. "We can go there anytime. I want it t' be more special than that."

"Okay," August says slowly as he rubs his chin. Snapping his fingers, he says, "I know the perfect place. Let's go to Reelfoot and eat at Boyette's. I went there one time for my high school basketball sports banquet. First of all Reelfoot is a beautiful place and secondly Boyette's food is outstanding. What about that idea?"

"What's Reelfoot?" Debbie asks.

"It's a large lake the other side of Union City that was formed by an earthquake in the 1800s," March says. "Isn't that right?"

"Right," August agrees. "It's surrounded by huge cypress trees and they even grow out in the middle of the water. The cypress knees are the most interesting feature about them."

"Trees with knees? Now wait a minute," Debbie says, "are you all spinning another one of your all's yarns, trying to suck me in? I've learned to doubt all three of you when you start talking about your lives around here."

"I'm serious," August answers her. "They are part of the root system that comes up out of the ground, sometimes three feet high. You've never seen anything like them."

"Reelfoot might be a pretty place," Smiley says, "but it has a reputation for being dangerous, especially after dark. People have been known to disappear without a trace. You all ever hear of the Night Riders?"

"What are they?" April asks. "I've never heard of them."

"It's a secret society," Smiley says, "sort of like the KKK. Nobody knows for sure how long they've been around, but my daddy said they were around when he was young. They pretty much rule that area of Lake County. Those people over there are different from most folks, sort of like clans. I've heard stories of them killing a man and butchering his body like a hog's, then scattering his body parts all over the lake so the law can't never find him."

Debbie gasps in horror.

"Oh my gosh," April says in a whisper.

"You ever been over there?" Augusts asks his father.

"No siree, and you won't catch me over there, leastwise not after dark. I don't think there's any black folks live around that lake. One black man moved in there a long time ago and they found him hanging from a tree. He had a hundred fish hooks stuck in him with fishing line attached that was tied off in the tree limbs—a message from the Night Riders. I'm telling you kids, it's a bad place. But now that don't mean we can't go over there in the daytime, just so we get on the road back home before the sun starts going down. I'm like August, I've heard it is a beautiful lake."

March has been listening intently to Smiley's stories and the reactions of his siblings and Debbie. Turning his head in the direction he supposes Tucker is sitting, he says, "You're mighty silent on this topic, Tucker. Have you ever been over there, or have you heard any of these tales Smiley's talking about?"

Everyone at the table turns their attention to Tucker, whose eyes appear glazed over. All the color has left her face.

"Uh-oh," August says in a low tone. "I haven't seen that expression on her face since I was a kid. She's somewhere else right now."

"What's the matter?" March asks.

"She looks like she's turned to stone," Debbie whispers to him. "She's as white as a sheet and she looks like she's staring at something a thousand miles away."

"I know what to do," April says. She goes to the sink and moistens a washcloth. Kneeling beside Tucker, she gently rubs her face with the cloth. Using the same tone of voice she uses with James's twins, she says, "Tucker, it's April. I'm right here with you. We're all here. You can come back now. It's safe here."

Suddenly Tucker gasps and she blinks rapidly. She looks around the table as if everyone is a stranger, until her eyes alight on April. "M' April? Is that you?"

"Yes, Tucker, it's me. Are you back now?"

Tucker looks up and sees everyone staring at her. "What's th' matter with all you folks? What're y' starin' at?"

"I'm staring at the most beautiful grandmother in the world," March says. "Oops, I forgot, I'm blind, aren't I?"

Everyone laughs at his self-deprecation, thankful to him for relieving the tension of the moment.

"Have you ever been to Reelfoot Lake, Tucker?" March repeats.

Tucker picks up her plate, walks toward the sink, and says, "Maybe I have an' maybe I haven't."

"Somebody needs to make a decision," August says. "Are we going to Boyette's to celebrate the upcoming nuptials of my baby brother and his beautiful fiancée, or not?"

"Ain't no reason why we can't go," Tucker says. "But we girls are gonna clean up this kitchen first, while you two boys give that old man at the end of the table a bath."

There is a squeal of delight and laughter from the girls at the loud groans and protests from all three of the men.

March speaks up, "Let me just say that this is one event that's going to make me very happy that I'm blind."

An hour later everyone is assembled in Tucker's living room.

"How do we want to divide ourselves up to drive over there?" August asks. "We can't all fit in one vehicle."

"Ya'll kids go on an' ride t'gether in yore car," Tucker says. "Me an' Smiley will go in my truck."

August looks at April, who takes his cue and says, "I'll drive for you, if you want me to, Tucker. It's a pretty long drive over there."

"No. There ain't no need fer that. I'll be fine. I'll just follow ya'll."

Clapping his hands together, August says, "All righty then, I believe we're ready to go!"

CHAPTER NINETEEN

Once they get loaded in the vehicles and head out on the highway, Debbie says, "What happened back there with Tucker when she turned into a statue?"

"It's called a flashback," March answers her. "It happens when someone has suffered some sort of trauma in their past and, without warning, something in the present, like a word or phrase or even a sound or smell, triggers all the memories and feelings of the trauma. Then the person goes through a time warp and is transported back to that very moment. It's what happened to me the other night in my apartment, if you remember that."

"It happens often to people who suffer from post-traumatic stress disorder," April adds.

Debbie puts her arm through March's arm and squeezes it. "You all are such an amazing family. All of you have survived your difficult pasts and become such incredible people, never complaining about the past or using it for an excuse like lots of people do."

The three siblings absorb Debbie's sincere words of praise in silence, as scenes from their past flit across a movie screen in their memories.

March breaks the silence. "I suppose one of the most important things Tucker taught us was to never make excuses. She told us we were responsible for how we acted and felt, not someone else who we might be pointing to as the reason for our behavior. We watched her live that kind of life, so it was hard not to follow her example. Though I will have to admit there was a time when I did feel sorry for myself. It's probably one of the things that contributed to me running away from home."

"I'll chime in on that note," August says. "I for sure felt sorry for myself. I wasn't black and I wasn't white. That made it hard for me to find a place to fit in in school. But between Tucker and Smiley, they basically told me to get over it and live the kind of life I wanted to live, regardless of my circumstances."

"Okay, both of you don't hold a candle to me when it comes to feeling sorry for yourself," April says. "I was the queen of feeling sorry for myself. I dwelled on it, wrapped it around me, sucked on it like a pacifier, and made it who I was. I thank God that he delivered me from that awful pit. It was my family and Spirit Lake that rescued me, or there's no telling where my life would be right now."

Putting his arm around Debbie, March says, "And now we're going to add another amazing person to our family who is cut from the same cloth. Not one time have I ever heard this woman complain about losing her arm or use her handicap as an excuse."

April reaches across the back of the seat and squeezes Debbie's knee. "We love you just like you're family. You're the sister I never had. Trust me, living with brothers is no picnic."

"What?!" August exclaims. "March, I believe our sister has impugned our character. I'm crushed by her sly accusation."

They all laugh.

"Honestly," Debbie says, "I've never met a family like yours. I'm completely captivated by each one of you, and it's really going to be an honor to become a part of your family." Her voice chokes off and she buries her face into March's arm as tears begin to flow.

March puts his hand on the back of her head.

April wipes her own tears off her cheeks. She opens the glove compartment and says, "Don't you have any Kleenex or napkins in here?"

"Sorry, ladies," August says, "I'm not used to having to deal with all these emotions bubbling over in my car."

"If you'd get you a girlfriend, you would," April chastises him.

"I've told you, I don't have time for a relationship right now. I'm too focused on getting through school."

"Yeah, whatever you say."

After a few minutes of riding in silence, Debbie says, "I want to ask another question."

"You all will learn," March interjects, "that there is no end to this woman's questions."

Ignoring him, Debbie continues, "How do you think Smiley Carter is? How difficult was it to manage him in the tub?"

"Funny you should ask that," August says, "because I noticed that he leaned all over me and March when we were getting him into the bathroom, but when it came time to get in the tub, he stepped right in with hardly any hesitation or help from us. He almost acted surprised at how easily it happened. But then he quickly became helpless again."

"It seemed to me," March adds, "that he did the same thing when it came time to get him out and dry him off and dress him."

"Yes," August agrees, "you're exactly right. Sometimes he acted helpless and sometimes he acted like he didn't need any help at all."

"That's interesting," Debbie says.

When she doesn't continue, March says, "What does that mean? What are you thinking?"

"Well," Debbie begins, "think about Tucker's attitude about Smiley and his stroke. On the one hand she says she's tired of him acting helpless, and then on the other hand she acts like he can't do anything without help. And I thought I noticed the same things as you two mentioned as far as Smiley's behaviors are concerned."

"What are you trying to say?" April asks. "I'm not sure I'm following you. Just spit it out."

"This is just my opinion, but I think Smiley had a stroke, however, as some people do, he recovered most all of his functional ability within twelve hours. But he doesn't want anyone to know he's doing better. And Tucker pretends she's fed up with him, but she really wants him to need her help."

"Why would they do that?" March asks.

"Bottom line? I think it's because they would like to live with each other. They are both older and alone, winter is about to set in, and they don't want to go through it by themselves. However, they need an excuse to move in with each other. This stroke incident is just the excuse they both need."

The siblings sit in stunned silence, weighing the evidence for Debbie's theory.

After several minutes, April says, "Oh my gosh, I believe you could be right."

"As far-fetched as it sounded when you first said it," August says, "I think all the evidence points in that direction."

"Oh my lord," March says, "lawyer August Tucker gives his summation."

Turning to March, Debbie says, "But what do you think? Am I right? Because sometimes you see things that we people with sight don't see."

"I'll admit that things never felt just right when I heard Tucker complaining so much about Smiley. It was like she was trying to cover up something she didn't want us to see. So I guess you may be right."

"So how would you three feel about them living together?" Debbie asks.

"Actually," August says, "as I've had time to think about it, it really is the best thing for both of them, and I'm fine with it. They're getting older and none of us live here so we can keep an eye on them. This way they can help each other."

"I certainly don't mind," March says. "I'm truly color-blind. When people in town start hearing about it, they'll probably talk. But we all know that won't bother Tucker or Smiley."

"At first," April says, "it kind of creeped me out that Smiley was sleeping in my bed and living in my bedroom. But you know what? I'm close to being on my own anyway and don't really have need of a place to live when I'm out of school. Why don't we just let them live out their charade as long as they want to? It's really kind of sweet what they are doing."

"And what you all are doing is sweet, too," Debbie says. "You all are just awesome."

March holds up his hand. "Now don't you start crying again. My sleeve hasn't dried out from when you drenched it earlier."

CHAPTER TWENTY

A
s the two-vehicle caravan slows down while passing through the community of Samburg, Debbie asks, "Are we almost there?"

"Just a few more miles," August answers. Snapping his fingers, he says, "I just had an idea. What do you all think about stopping at the state park before we go eat at Boyette's?"

"That sounds like fun!" April says. "I think they have a boardwalk that goes around part of the edge of the lake. It'll be really pretty."

"Walking and stretching my legs sounds good to me," March says. "I've got my personal artist with me who can paint a beautiful picture with words so that I can see what you all see."

Debbie smiles. "It's a really interesting and challenging thing to do. We take in so much when we look at something, that we don't even realize all the details at a conscious level. March has taught me to look for and see those details."

"Oh my gosh!" August exclaims. "What are we thinking about? Smiley can't walk around and do the boardwalk, and Tucker won't want to."

April's countenance falls. "Awww, I hate that. It was going to be so much fun."

This twist in their plans has the same effect on their enthusiasm as a lead sinker tied onto a fishing line. The group falls silent, trying to think of a workable alternative.

They drive over the spillway as they enter Tiptonville and are suddenly able to glimpse the sparkling blue water of the lake.

"Oh, wow," Debbie says, "it is beautiful."

A hundred yards later, August turns his right blinker on and pulls into the parking lot of the state park's interpretive center. "I've got an idea." He slows to a stop, gets out of the car, and walks to Tucker's pickup behind them.

"What's going on?" March asks.

April has turned around, watching August. "He's back there talking to Tucker and Smiley. I don't know what he has in mind. But he's already heading back and he's smiling, so it must have worked."

Opening the door of his car, August says, "Everybody out! We're going to see the sights."

As they begin pulling on their coats, Tucker drives past them, then makes a U-turn and returns to the highway.

"So what did you get worked out?" April asks.

Zipping up his jacket, August says, "I told them what we wanted to do and asked if they would like to drive around and see some of the sights from her truck while we did our thing. They didn't even think about it before they both said it was fine with them. As a matter of fact, Tucker seemed like she had no interest in even getting out of her truck. I noticed her door was locked and she only rolled her window down about six inches for us to talk."

The four of them exit August's car. March stretches his arms and arches his back. "Ah, that's better." He waits until Debbie touches his arm with her elbow, then he reaches and puts his fingertips on the back of her arm. As she starts walking, he matches her pace while keeping on her side and half a step behind. "Don't ya'll think it's a little odd that Tucker wouldn't roll her window all the way down to talk to August?"

April speaks over her shoulder as she and August lead the way, "March, we're talking about Tucker. Don't you think the words *odd* and *Tucker* sort of go together?"

Shrugging, March says, "You're right. I just thought it was peculiar."

Suddenly there is a loud screeching sound to their left. They all jump.

"What the heck is that?" Debbie says.

"Oh, look," August says, "it's a huge enclosure of some kind."

They follow the sidewalk in that direction. When they get close, a bald eagle sails from one end of the net-covered enclosure to the other and lands on a perch fifteen feet away from them.

April screams and Debbie pushes herself into March.

In awed tones, August says, "Unbelievable. It is huge! I never knew they were so large."

"I need some help here," March says.

Regaining her composure, Debbie says, "I'm sorry. There is a net-covered enclosure that must be almost thirty feet high, a hundred feet long, and forty feet wide. It has a bald eagle in it that none of us saw until it swooped toward us. At the last moment it flared its wings and stopped on a perch right beside us."

"This sign says these eagles have been injured and are being rehabilitated," April says.

"I've heard that Reelfoot has become a significant player in the comeback of bald eagles," August says. "They come here by the hundreds during the winter."

As if agreeing with August's statement, the caged eagle gives a cry, pushes off its perch, flaps it wings, and flies to a perch in the top of the enclosure. At the same time a chorus of cries comes from the direction of the lake. Five or six eagles fly out of the tops of the cypress trees and start climbing higher and higher into the sky.

Initially overwhelmed in stunned silence, Debbie recovers her voice and says, "Oh March, it is magnificent. This captive eagle flew to the top of the enclosure as if he was going to escape, but he landed on a perch. Then this group of eagles in the tops of the cypress trees over by the edge of the lake seemed to be answering his cries. They flew into the air and climbed higher and higher in a series of circles. Right now they look as small as crows, they are so high. The sky is the color of a blue jay's neck feathers and there's not a cloud in it."

"Look!" August cries out.

Gripping March's arm, Debbie says, "They're falling out of the sky. The eagles are sailing down like military jets. I can't even describe how fast they are traveling."

April screams in excitement.

"They are catching fish!" Debbie says excitedly. "I can see through the trunks of the trees that the eagles turn at the last instant before hitting the water. They lower their legs and with a splash they reach down and pluck a fish out of the lake. Then they fly into the trees to eat their catch. It's all in one motion, like an artistic, choreographed ballet."

"Come on!" August calls out. "Let's go out on the boardwalk and get closer."

March hears the sound of his brother's and sister's pounding feet on the planks of the boardwalk as they race to gain a visual advantage. "You go with them," he says to Debbie. "I'll just wait here."

"Why would I do that?" Debbie asks.

"I just don't want you to miss whatever it is they are hurrying to go see. It's not that important for me to walk out there . . . You know what I mean."

Turning to face him, she says, "I think I know exactly what you mean, but did you ever stop to think that maybe it is important to me for you to go with me?" She walks directly into him, bumping him backwards a step. "I want to see it with you." She pushes him with her chest and he retreats another half step. "If we're going to share the rest of our lives with each other, we're going to share everything." Slipping her arms around him, she gently presses her body into his and then jerks him into her, squeezing him tightly. "You and me, big guy, that's the way it will be. I want you to share with me what you see with your eyes and ears."

"But I can't—"

Placing her finger on his lips, Debbie says, "No buts. You do have eyes, maybe not like mine, but you see things, March. You've never looked at me, but you've seen me. When you run your fingertips across my face to read my expression, I feel like you are seeing not just my face, but my soul."

March slowly raises one of his large hands and lays it on the side of Debbie's face.

She leans into it and closes her eyes.

He lays his other hand on the other side of her face. With his thumbs he traces her closed eyelids from the bridge of her nose to the outside of her face, then does the same to her eyebrows. Tilting her face up toward him, he bends down and touches his lips to hers. In a whisper, he says, "I love you, Debbie Cooper."

She whispers back, "I love you, March Tucker."

When she whispers, her warm breath touches his face and he has a memory of a blanket he slept with when he was a child. He begins to weep.

"Oh March," Debbie says. She kisses each of his tears when they reach his lips.

From the cypress trees, August yells, "Hey, you two! Go get a motel room!" His hearty laugh bounces across the boardwalk and jumps in between them.

Debbie releases her grip on March just as he lets go of her face. They both laugh.

"You're just jealous!" March yells back.

"Come on, you two!" April calls out.

Debbie puts her elbow into March's hand. "Let's go." She heads toward the boardwalk with March by her side. When they reach the beginning of the boardwalk, Debbie says, "This boardwalk is about four feet wide and has some turns at odd angles. I'll be walking on the right side of the boardwalk so that you will be walking in the center of it."

"Lead the way," March says.

As they begin passing between the giant cypress sentinels, Debbie says, "These trees have such an unusual shape. The base of the trunks start spreading out until they are four or five times the size of the trunks themselves. Scattered all around the base, whether the tree is completely on land or whether it is sitting in the lake, are those things August called knees. Some of them are three feet tall."

"How big around are they?" March asks.

"Well they are varying sizes. Some of them I could reach around with my hand, but others would take both of my hands to reach all the way around."

"Are they pointed like a spike on the end?"

"No, they have a smooth, blunted end."

"How tall are the trees themselves?"

"Oh my gosh, I don't know, March, maybe forty feet. And the tops, though they don't have any foliage on the limbs, spread out like an umbrella, sort of like the trunks spread out at the bottom. Seeing them all along the edge of the lake makes me think of guards on the top of a castle wall, protecting the inhabitants."

Passing between the silent warriors, they suddenly break through their phalanx and are struck by the unfettered cold December wind blowing across the open water.

Thirty feet away, April calls to them, "Out here! This is the observation point for seeing the eagles."

While walking toward April and August, Debbie says, "The lake is truly magnificent, March. It has a very irregular shoreline, with lots of coves and peninsulas, at points disappearing from view only to reappear further around the edge. And there are tops of cypress trees rising out of the water at random all the way out to the middle of the lake."

"The air smells so clean and crisp," March says. "Reminds me of western Colorado."

When they reach the observation station, Debbie places March's hand on the rail surrounding it. "This deck is about fifteen feet wide."

"Gotcha," March replies.

"Have you ever seen anything so beautiful?!" April gushes. "The colors, even though it's winter, are so sharp and vibrant."

"It is," August agrees. "If I'd known it was like this, I would have been making trips over here before now. It's spectacular."

Pointing up, Debbie says, "Is that an eagle way up there?"

March lifts his head. "Where? I don't see it."

"Just ignore him," Debbie says. "His smart mouth has no filter sometimes."

"A Tucker trait, for sure," August says.

April shields her eyes with her hands while peering into the sky. "Gosh, that bird is so high! I can't tell what it is."

"It's making large, slow circles," Debbie says. "I think that's where the expression *a bird's-eye view* must have come from. There is no telling how far away it can see."

"Maybe that's the way it is with God," March says. "He sits higher than anyone or anything and can truly see everything."

April walks over to her brother and gives him a hug. "I like it when you talk about God, March. Growing up we never went to church and Tucker rarely mentioned His name except in a prayer or as a way to threaten us." Folding her arms across her chest, she gives her best impersonation of Tucker. "God's a-watchin' you kids. Y' better behave 'r he'll send y' t' th' bad place."

All four of them erupt into a chorus of laughter.

Looking at his watch, August says, "We better be heading over to Boyette's. Tucker and Smiley will be waiting on us."

Debbie asks, "I wonder if they saw anything interesting while driving around?"

CHAPTER TWENTY-ONE

As they pull into the parking lot of Boyette's restaurant, April says, "There's Tucker and Smiley waiting on us. I wonder how long they've been waiting?"

"I don't know," August replies, "but if it's one minute longer than Tucker thinks she should have had to wait on us, we'll all hear about it."

Laughing, March says, "You can be sure about that! I wouldn't be surprised if the sun and moon didn't check with Tucker before they rise and set to be sure they match up with her expectations. She never needed an alarm clock to wake up by or a clock to tell her when it was bedtime."

Braking to a stop, August says, "Do you remember the time she poured a bucket of water on us because we wouldn't get up and get ready for school? Remember her rule?"

Without prompting each other, the three siblings all say in unison, "I'll only call y' one time t' git up." They break into laughter at their imitation of Tucker.

"Did she really pour a bucket of water on you?" Debbie asks.

"A bucket of cold well water!" March exclaims, shivering at the memory. And then we had to haul our worn-out mattress down the stairs and outside to dry in the sun. But you know what? I never had to be called twice again. People might question Tucker's techniques, but when you learned a lesson under her, you never forgot it."

"Come on," August says, "let's go get some grub."

When the four of them open their doors to get out, Tucker and Smiley also open the doors on her truck parked beside them.

"Let me help you, Dad," August says as he trots over to the passenger side of Tucker's truck. "Have ya'll been waiting long?"

"Long?!" Tucker huffs. "We been sittin' here long enough t' put in a crop. What took ya'll s' long?"

April walks up to Tucker and grabs her arm. "Oh Tucker, it was the most amazing thing. We'll tell you all about it inside the restaurant." She leads Tucker in the direction of the front door.

As the six of them enter Boyette's they are greeted by a cacophony of sound—loud talking, boisterous laughter, the tinkling of silverware striking plates, and scurrying steps on the worn wooden flooring as the numerous waitresses shuttle back and forth between the tables and the kitchen. In a scene reminiscent of an old Western movie, a hush gradually falls on the patrons in the restaurant and everyone turns their attention to the motley crew that has just entered.

"What just happened?" March whispers to Debbie.

"I'm not sure," Debbie whispers back. "Everyone is staring at us."

Sitting on a wooden stool behind the cash register, a woman with deep wrinkles in her face, undoubtedly enhanced by cigarette smoke and too much exposure to the sun, says, "Do you all need some help?" Her voice has the texture of a wood rasp.

April steps forward. With a chill in her voice, she says, "For starters, we'd appreciate you showing us to a table for six, if that wouldn't be too much trouble."

The old woman waves her hand, and a teenage waitress approaches. "Find them a table, Tiffany."

125

"Yes, ma'am," Tiffany replies. She grabs a handful of menus and says, "Ya'll follow me."

They walk past several tables of diners until Tiffany stops at a pair of empty tables. As she moves chairs and pushes two tables together to accommodate the party of six, the sounds in the restaurant slowly return.

At the far end of the dining room a middle-aged waitress with black hair and gray roots carries a plate of food and sets it on the table in front of a man.

Nodding in the direction of Tucker and her family, the man says, "What are ya'll doing letting people like that in here? When I was growing up around here, you'd have never seen that happen."

She follows his line of sight and says, "I've got nothing to do with that. I just work here. But you know how the law is nowadays. You have to be careful or somebody will sue you."

Picking up his fork and lifting a bite of white beans, the man mutters, "We used to be the law around here."

Meanwhile, Tucker looks up from her menu and says, "I wonder if their catfish is any good?"

"It is delicious!" August says. "That's what they are really known for."

The waitress approaches their table and says, "Have you all decided what you want to eat?"

Tucker says, "We wanta table full of fried catfish, hush puppies, cole slaw, white beans, an' fried taters."

Looking around the table, the waitress asks, "So all of you want the all-you-can-eat catfish dinner?"

April starts taking everyone's menu from them and stacking them to give to the waitress. "Yes, that's what we want."

"Do you want fillets, steaks, or fiddlers?"

"Fillets," Tucker answers.

When the waitress heads to the kitchen to turn in her order, April says, "You know, I believe this is the first time all of us have been together in a public setting like this. You'll have to admit we are a rather diverse-looking bunch—a crippled man, a blind man, and a woman wearing men's clothes. I'll bet some of these people almost swallowed their hush puppies whole."

August says, "I'm thinking the thing they were looking at was the color of our skin. I've always heard Lake County was a little backward about those kinds of things."

Smiley Carter speaks up. "That's what I was telling you all about before we drove over here. Those are not just rumors. People over here are different. They've probably never seen black and white folk mingling together like us, leastwise not around here."

Suddenly, March pushes back from the table. "Well they need to get over it." Standing up, he shouts, "Hey! Everybody listen up!"

Silence moves across the dining room like a wave in the ocean, starting at the tables closest to them and expanding until it reaches all four corners.

March points in the direction of August. "That's my brother and that's his father with him." Pointing toward April, he says, "That is my sister. All of us have different fathers." Next he points toward Tucker. "And that's our grandmother who raised us." Then he rests his hand on Debbie's shoulder. "And this is my fiancée. If any of you don't like it or have anything you want to say about it, then let's step outside and discuss it face-to-face."

The dining room is as silent and still as a little league ball field in winter. Many are staring at March with their mouths open. Others have their tea glasses halfway to their mouths. And some appear frozen, gripping the handles of forks sticking out of their closed mouths.

After several seconds of silence, March says, "Good! Everyone enjoy your meal!" He sits back down and scoots forward.

Everyone at his table stares at him.

"I'm sorry if that embarrassed any of you," he says. "I just don't like people being prejudiced toward people that I love. Even though nobody said anything to us, it was like I could hear their thoughts. And they were all mean, hateful thoughts. It made me mad, and I wanted to shut them up."

Laying her hand on top of March's, Debbie says, "Well you certainly achieved that."

At the end of the table, Tucker says, "I ain't never been prouder of y', March. You've grown up t' be a real man."

"I remember when he wasn't nothing but a pesky little ant," Smiley says. "I wish I could have had a picture of the expressions of all these folks in here. For certain, there wasn't going to be anyone who wanted to tangle with March."

Before anyone has a chance to say anything else, three waitresses appear at their table, their hands and arms full of platters of steaming food.

"Oh man," August exclaims, "you guys better get ready for some mighty fine eating."

At the opposite end of the dining room, the middle-aged waitress approaches a table with a pot of coffee. "You need anything else? Maybe some more coffee?"

The man at the table looks up at her and smiles broadly. "How could I want anything else? This has turned out to be the luckiest day of my life."

The waitress sets the coffee pot on the table, reaches into her apron, and produces his ticket.

When she hands it to him, he meets her hand with a folded hundred-dollar bill. "Keep the change, dearie. It's been well worth the price of admission."

Stunned, she walks away as she stuffs the bill into her bra.

Looking across the dining hall at the table where March is sitting, the man grins and rubs a red, jagged scar that runs from the corner of his left ear down to the front of his tattooed neck.

Red watches March and his family leave the restaurant. When he is certain they won't notice him, he walks to the front, where he can see them getting into their vehicles. Once they back out and pull onto the highway, he hurries outside to get in his pickup truck and follow them. Just as he opens his door to get inside, he notices his rear tire is completely flat. Swearing loudly, he slams the door and peers down the road at the license plate of the car March is riding in. *If Big Country is living in Knox County, what in the world is he doing way over here in West Tennessee?*

CHAPTER TWENTY-TWO

Yawning, March says, "I don't know about the rest of you, but I'm getting sleepy. This has been a whirlwind of a day, capped off with that delicious meal at Boyette's."

Debbie puts her arm through his and hugs him. "This man is definitely an early-to-bed-early-to-rise kind of person. I can't get him to stay up late for anything."

With sarcasm in his tone, August says, "Anything? Are you sure?"

Debbie blushes.

"Oh shut up, August!" April says.

"My big brother is just jealous," March says. "Just because I've got the most beautiful woman in the world and he's so busy with school he doesn't have time for women, or at least that's what he says." He concludes with a laugh.

Joining in laughter with March, Tucker says, "Sounds t' me like th' hormones is runnin' pretty high in here."

"To me," Smiley says, "it sounds like a bunch of pretty normal young people. I've got my suspicions that August has got some action on the side he's not letting any of us know about."

"Ask me no questions and I'll tell you no lies," August replies.

"What's goin' on with you, April? You gotta feller up there at school that's chasin' y'?" Tucker asks.

Smiling, April says, "There might be someone. Time will tell."

"You just be sure you're focused on your studies. Don't get distracted by some hairy boy."

"Hey, wait a minute," March protests. "I believe I'd fit that description."

Everyone laughs.

Smiley stretches and yawns loudly. "I'm like March. I believe I'm ready for bed, too. April, you use your bed tonight and I'll bed down here in the living room with August and March."

"No way," April says. "That's your bedroom now, for as long as you need it. Debbie and I can share the bed in the spare bedroom, can't we, Debbie?"

"Absolutely," Debbie replies.

"You always were my favorite," Smiley says warmly.

"That sound you hear, little brother," August says, "is the sound of you and me being kicked to the side of the road. I'm his son, but yet April is his favorite. That's just wrong!"

Throwing her arms around Smiley's neck, April kisses him on the cheek. "You all leave Smiley alone. He just happens to have very discriminating tastes in people." Turning to Debbie, she says, "Come on. We'll get some extra covers for August and March to use."

"I reckon ya'll got it all figured out," Tucker says. "This ol' woman's headed t' bed, too. Ya'll sleep tight."

A chorus of "good night, Tucker" accompanies her as she heads toward her bedroom.

Later, as April and Debbie lie side by side in the dark, April says, "I'm really happy for you and March. I think you make a strong couple. It's like you balance each other out. I just can't imagine how it would be to date someone who is blind."

"Honestly," Debbie replies, "I never imagined myself being with someone who is blind, but as I often tell March, he's not really blind. Oh, I know what you mean, but he can see so many things that I don't see. Everyone is intimidated by his size, but I think he's the most gentle man I've ever known. Yet he's also strong, not just physically, but strong-minded and strong-willed. I can't believe how much I love him."

"I know what you mean," April says. "Can I tell you something if you promise to keep it a secret?"

Debbie rolls on her side to face April. "Sure you can."

"I'm in love, too."

"How wonderful! Who is it? Someone you met at school? Why haven't we met him yet?"

"No, it's not someone from school. And you all have met him." April hesitates, then says, "It's James."

Debbie is thankful for the darkness so that April can't see her expression of disappointment. "James? Really? You love a man whose wife has just died? And isn't he quite a bit older than you?"

Turning away from Debbie, April says, "I was afraid you would think that way. That's what everyone is going to say." She sits up and pulls her knees to her chest. "If you and March can love each other in spite of your handicaps, why can't James and I love each other in spite of our ages? What's the difference?"

"I didn't mean to sound judgmental. It's just that this has been an emotionally intense journey that James has been through and you've accompanied him along the way. It's really easy to get feelings confused—compassion, empathy, respect, admiration, love, appreciation—all of those are really powerful. Do you know if James has the same feelings for you?"

"He's told me he loves me and that he doesn't know how he could have made it without me. And . . ." She pauses. "And he's kissed me."

"James kissed you?!"

"Yes. He came to my bedroom in his bathrobe to tell me goodnight. And he gave me a kiss. It was almost like a dream. It makes me feel warm, you know where, just remembering it. It's like God placed us in each other's life at just the time we needed someone the most. He was there for me at Spirit Lake, and I was there for him while his wife was dying." Lying back down, she says, "I think it's beautiful, even if no one else does."

Meanwhile, March works at making himself comfortable on the couch. He punches his pillow to work it into a shape that fits.

From the recliner, August says, "What in the world are you doing over there? It sounds like you're hitting a punching bag."

"I'm just trying to get this pillow worked into shape." Grunting, he turns on his side while trying to keep the blanket from sliding off and onto the floor. "This couch needs to be about ten inches longer."

"I told you I would take the couch and you could have the recliner."

"It's even shorter than this couch. I'll get comfortable in a minute."

After a few minutes of silence, August says, "March, I'm really, really happy for you and Debbie. I'm glad you found someone you want to share the rest of your life with. I really like Debbie and enjoy being around her."

"Thank you, brother. I'm glad you like her. She has been like an angel from God for me. I was lost in so many ways when we first met. I had absolutely no direction in my life. Heck, I didn't even know who I was for a while. And I thought that I had built a stone wall around my heart. I was going to live alone for the rest of my life. I was tired of being hurt by people and for sure didn't think anyone could ever love me. But Debbie showed me that my stone wall was actually built out of ice. The warmth of her heart melted my wall and awakened hope in me. Hope—that is such an important thing. And when you've given up ever having it again, and then you find it—" Emotions rise from his chest and choke off his voice. He wipes tears from his eyes.

"I'll tell you what it looks like to me," August says. "It's like Debbie, or maybe the hope she gave you, has become an anchor for you. In spite of your blindness, you seem so confident and sure of yourself, or maybe secure in yourself. I just know it's a beautiful thing to see. You're an awesome man, March. And I love you." He uses his shoulder to rub the unexpected tears from his cheeks.

In a hoarse voice, March says, "And I love you, August."

They lie in silence for several minutes when March says, "You still awake?"

"Huh? Yeah, sure."

"Can I ask you something?"

"Sure you can. What's up?"

"I want you to be honest with me. Just tell me the truth because it really won't change anything, but I just want to know."

"Know what? What are you talking about?"

"Do you think Debbie's pretty?"

"What?! Are you kidding me? March, she is one hot-looking lady."

Smiling, March says, "Well, I know what I think she looks like and she feels beautiful to my hands and heart. Does she have a nice figure?"

August kicks the leg rest of the recliner to the floor and sits up. "March! Don't tell me you can't tell if she has a nice figure. I mean,

I just assume you guys have slept with each other and even a blind man can tell what a woman's body feels like and if it has curves."

"We haven't had sex. I know, we're probably the only people our age who are dating who haven't. I've got some issues related to things that happened to me in Las Vegas, but we've finally started talking about them and we're going to work things out. I don't know why, but I'm curious about how she looks to sighted people."

"Well, let me put it to you this way," August says, "Debbie is so hot-looking that I've been thinking about putting a move on her, and if I do, you will lose out because no woman can resist the charm of August Tucker."

Moving like a cat in the dark, March slips off the couch and silently approaches August. At the last instant he pounces on him in the recliner. "Then I'll just kill off the competition," he laughs.

The crash of the tumbling recliner and August's cries for help mixed with laughter echo through the house.

CHAPTER TWENTY-THREE

The next day Red awakens in his motel room. Looking at the clock on the bedside table, he sees 11:27 a.m. Slowly sitting up on the edge of the bed, he runs his hand through his hair. He walks unsteadily to a desk, picks up the half-empty bottle of Jack Daniels, and pours some into a glass. He gulps it down in one swallow and lets the burn work its way to his stomach.

After relieving himself in the bathroom, he returns to the desk and picks up the phone receiver and dials a number. "Hey, Tarzan, it's me. Have you all seen or heard anything?" After a pause, he says, "Well I have. I saw Big Country yesterday as big as life. He wasn't thirty feet away from me."

He pauses again as Tarzan expresses his amazement.

"I know. I felt like I was that blind hog who found an acorn. But there's a new piece of information in this situation. Big Country is blind." He listens. "No, it doesn't change a thing. It just raises more questions. Like, what happened to him that made him blind? And the biggest question is, if he's living in Knox County, what was he doing over here at the opposite end of the state?" After another pause, he says, "I don't know the answer to any of those questions. I couldn't follow him because I had a flat tire. But here's what I want you to do. Start looking at the angle that maybe he was in an accident of some kind. There has to be a record of that, an accident record, hospital record or something. You'll have to check back for the last two years. Anybody who treated Big Country will remember him. A man that size is hard to forget. Call me if you learn anything. I'm going to do some snooping around here."

He hangs up the phone, heads into the bathroom, and starts the shower.

Thirty minutes later, Red steps out of his motel room into the bright sun. Squinting, he pulls his sunglasses out of his jacket pocket and slips them on. "First stop is Boyette's," he says out loud.

He gets in his truck, drives the three miles between the motel and restaurant, and pulls into the parking lot. Inside he finds the same woman sitting behind the cash register. Neither her clothes nor her expression look any different from yesterday. Smiling at her, Red says, "Mornin'."

Staring at his scar, the woman replies, "You can seat yourself. We don't get really busy until later this afternoon."

"Thank you. I'll do just that in a minute. But first, I'm needing some information."

The woman's right eye twitches and she finally takes her eyes off Red's scar and looks him in the eye. In a flat tone she says, "I don't know anything about anything except what goes on inside this restaurant. And we don't sell information here. We sell food."

Red holds up his hands. "Whoa, I'm not looking for trouble. It's just that I was in here yesterday and saw an old friend I haven't seen in years. By the time I figured out who he was, he was leaving the restaurant. I tried to catch him but he was already driving away when I got outside. Besides that I had a flat tire and couldn't have chased him anyway. I was hoping maybe you knew him or some of the people he was with and could tell me where they live."

"Mister, do you have any idea how many people we fed yesterday? And you expect me to remember one man?"

"I know, it sounds impossible. But my friend is the kind of guy who's hard to miss and even harder to forget. He's well over six feet tall, weighs probably two seventy-five, and has a full beard."

Looking disinterested and unfazed by Red's description, the woman says, "I've seen several duck hunters who look just like that."

Color begins to move up Red's neck. The corners of his smile twitch. "Look, lady, you're not trying. Even if he might not look out of the ordinary from some of your other diners, the group of people he came in with for certain did. There was an old nigger with a limp, an old woman dressed in men's clothes, a young half-nigger man, and two good-looking girls. Plus, my friend is blind. Don't tell me you didn't notice them or that you don't remember them."

Just then two State Troopers enter the restaurant. Red's back is to them and when the woman looks past him and speaks to them, Red grabs her arm and says, "I'm talking to you, lady! Don't try to ignore me. Now tell me what I want to know."

From behind him Red hears a man say, "Is there a problem here, Ruthie?"

Red whirls around. Whatever was about to come out of his mouth, he swallows it upon seeing the troopers. Smiling, he says, "No sir. I was just joking around with Ruthie."

One of the troopers says, "I don't believe I was speaking to you, sir." He looks over Red's shoulder. "Ruthie? What do you say?"

"There's no trouble, Andy. This fellow was on his way out the door, weren't you?"

Red turns and looks at Ruthie, then back at the troopers. After a slight hesitation, he says, "She's right. I'm just leaving. I apologize if I upset anyone."

Red exits the restaurant and the two troopers follow him. When he opens the door on his truck, one of them says, "Could I see your license and proof of insurance, please, sir?"

Surprised to discover the troopers on his heels, Red says, "Is there a problem, officer?"

"Not if you have your license and proof of insurance and everything checks out."

Red reaches into his hip pocket and pulls out his billfold. He takes out his driver's license and hands it to one of the troopers. "My registration is in the glove compartment. Can I get inside and get it?"

"Yes, sir, please do."

While Red is retrieving his registration, he notices one of the troopers walking to the back of his truck and writing something in a notebook. Red gets out of his truck and hands the registration to the trooper, who walks away and gets inside his cruiser. Red watches him talk into his radio.

"You're a long way from home, aren't you?"

Red is startled by the other trooper, who has circled his truck and come up behind him. "Well, sort of. I grew up around here but haven't lived here since I was eighteen. I just come back every once in a while to see familiar sites and to see if anything has changed."

"You live in Knoxville?" the trooper asks.

"Yes, sir."

"What kind of work do you do?"

"I don't like being tied down to any one thing. So I sort of dabble in lots of things. I do some real estate and I do some contract work for people who need problems solved."

The unsmiling trooper stares at him. The sound of his partner closing the door of their cruiser draws his attention from Red.

The second trooper walks up and hands Red his license and proof of insurance. "You've got an interesting history. I don't know what you're doing around here or what you were trying to do with Ruthie, but I encourage you to head on back to East Tennessee. At this moment I don't have anything to hold you on, but the more time you stay around here, the more time I have to think of something. And trust me, I'll think of something. Do we have an understanding?"

Red's face turns crimson and his eyes narrow. "I'll tell you two what I understand. You've been out of the academy, what, a year or two? And you think you're the baddest thing on the road. Let me tell you something. I've had troopers like you for breakfast. I've not done anything wrong and you can't run me out of town like this is the Old West."

As he finishes talking, a sheriff's patrol car pulls in beside his truck. The driver steps out and sees the confrontation. "Hey there, Red," he says. "How long you been in town?"

The troopers look at the officer. "Hey there, Sheriff Dale," one of them says. Motioning toward Red, he says, "You know this man?"

Sheriff Dale stands with the troopers on one side of him and Red on the other. "Who, Red here? Sure I do. He grew up here. We used to play some ball together in high school. Is there a problem?"

"We walked in Boyette's and observed him grabbing Ruthie. It looked like trouble brewing so we stepped outside with him to check out his papers."

Looking at Red, Sheriff Dale says, "What's that about, Red?"

"Just a misunderstanding, that's all. Even Ruthie told them it wasn't anything."

Turning back to the troopers, the sheriff says, "I'm sure you radioed in and had him checked out. Is he clean?"

"There's nothing outstanding on him. I guess if you're willing to vouch for him, Sheriff, we'll go on and get the lunch we came here for in the first place."

"Sure, sure, I've got this. You two go on ahead with your lunch."

Red and Sheriff Dale watch the two troopers as they head back inside Boyette's. Turning to the sheriff, Red says, "Thanks, man. I owe you for that one. If you hadn't shown up when you did, I would have taught those two greenhorns a lesson."

"And if you had," Sheriff Dale replies, "you'd have gone back to jail once again. When are you going to learn that you can't do everything you feel like doing? We have laws exactly because of people like you. But you think you are the law."

Reds eyes widen. "What about when you and I were part of the Night Riders? We were the law around here. All you've done is make yourself legitimate by being elected sheriff of the county, but there's really no difference."

The sheriff puts one foot on the bumper of Red's truck. "Look here, Red, times have changed. The Riders don't exist anymore, and yes, I am the sheriff, but I do everything by the book. No more of this making up our own laws and punishment. Things had to change or this county was going to die. No one wanted to come here because of the reputation of lawlessness. Factories were leaving and businesses were boarding up. Now things are looking better. Tourists come here all the time from all over the country." He pauses and pokes Red in the chest with his index finger. "And I don't need you coming in here and messing things up. So tell me, why are you here, and how long are you planning on staying?"

"You sound like you don't want me here. What kind of welcome is that for an old hometown boy?"

"Just answer my questions, Red."

The two men stare unblinking at each other.

Finally, Red says, "I just wanted to come back and see some familiar sights and maybe see some old friends. But clearly some of my old friends aren't friends anymore."

"Then maybe you need to head on back to wherever you came from."

"Is that some kind of order?"

"Take it any way you want to."

Turning away from the sheriff and walking to the driver's side of his truck, Red says, "Fine then! I'll go get my stuff and go back to East Tennessee where people are a lot more friendly."

Just before Red steps inside his truck, the sheriff says, "By the way, whatever happened to your brother? I lost track of him after he went to prison. He's not living around here, is he?"

"The last I heard," Red replies, "he was living around Dresden. They tell me he found religion while he was in prison and now he's some sort of preacher." Laughing, he gets inside his truck. "My brother—a preacher! Now that's a good one."

CHAPTER TWENTY-FOUR

Driving east on Highway 22, Red pulls into a convenience store on the edge of Dresden. He stops in front of the gas pumps and gets out. As he begins filling his truck, a mud-spattered red pickup drives up on the other side of the pumps and stops. The driver steps out and starts filling up.

"Hey, kid," Red says, "you from around here?"

The teenage boy looks out from under his camouflage cap at Red. Keeping one eye on the changing numbers on the pump, he answers, "Yes, sir."

"I'm wondering if you might know where a man named Hal Forrest might live. Last I heard he lived somewhere around Dresden."

"The name doesn't ring a bell with me, but you might ask my granddaddy." He motions toward the cab of the truck.

Red returns the handle to the gas pump and walks over to the passenger side of the red pickup. Smiling, he looks through the window.

The window lowers and reveals a white-haired man with a ruddy complexion and gray stubble. He, too, is wearing a camouflage cap. His right eye squints as he says, "Howdy."

"I hope you can help me," Red says.

"Will if I can. What do you need?"

"I'm trying to find an old friend of mine. His name is Hal Forrest. The last contact I had with him he was living around Dresden."

The old man rubs his calloused hand across the bottom of his chin, producing a sound like sandpaper rubbed against a pine board. "Hal Forrest? Hmmm, that name doesn't ring a bell. What does he look like?"

"He's around fifty years old and a little over six feet tall. Unless he's changed, he always wears cowboy boots with silver tips on the toes. The last time I saw him he had a ponytail. He always drove a Harley, too. I've never known him to own a car."

From the other side of the truck, the teenager speaks up. "That sounds like Preacher, doesn't it, Granddaddy?"

The old man's eyes widen. "Why sure! You're right. Preacher is all I've ever heard anyone call him. Don't know if Hal Forrest is his name or not, but that description sure fits him."

Chuckling, Red says, "Preacher? I did get word once that he'd become a preacher, but I didn't believe it. When I knew him he was a long way from being a preacher. I don't guess either of you know where he lives, do you?"

"I believe he lives out on the Davis farm," the old man says. Turning to his grandson, who has joined him in the cab, he asks, "Isn't that right, Tommy?"

"I think so," his grandson agrees. "I know I've seen a motorcycle parked outside a single-wide trailer out there."

"How do I get there?" Red asks.

Pointing, the old man says, "Take that road there into town. Then follow Highway 54 toward Paris. About five miles out of town you'll see Beulah Baptist Church on your right. Take the next road to your right. The Davis farm is about three miles on your left."

Looking at his grandson, he says, "Where's that trailer at that you were talking about?"

"You take that little gravel road past where the hay barn was that burned down last summer. It's the same road I use when me and Zack go duck hunting in the bottoms. You can't miss that trailer. It's the only thing out there."

Turning back to Red, the old man says, "There you go, mister. That ought to get you there."

Red puts his foot on the running board of the red pickup and says, "The only problem I'll have is trying to figure out where a barn used to be."

The man laughs and says, "I guess you're right about that. Okay, there's a huge oak tree that stood close to that barn. The fire killed it, but it's still standing there. You can't miss it. It's the biggest oak tree you ever seen."

Satisfied that he's gotten as clear directions as he can from these two, Red pats the roof of the truck and says, "You two have really been helpful. I really appreciate it. I can't wait to see Hal's, I mean, Preacher's, face when I show up unannounced."

"I really don't know Preacher, but I ain't never heard anybody say anything bad about him, and in a small town like Dresden, that's pretty unusual."

Red returns to his truck and follows the road that takes him into the downtown. He stops at a four-way stop. As he pulls forward he takes in the large county courthouse that is the centerpiece of the town square on his left, but also notices the police department on his right. Being careful to drive slowly, he comes to a complete stop at another four-way stop. Taking Highway 54 he leaves the downtown and heads east toward Paris.

Eventually he sees a church up ahead. Slowing, he reads the name "Beulah Baptist Church" on the sign in front. He turns on his blinker and turns off the highway onto a tar- and gravel-surfaced secondary road. He looks at his odometer and, after traveling two and a half miles, he slows. Soon he spies a mammoth tree and turns onto a one-lane gravel road. A field of green winter wheat lies on the right side of the road, while the left side is thick woodland. As he searches for the single-wide trailer, Red sees a flock of ducks flying at treetop level in a V formation.

Suddenly a clearing in the woods appears. Sitting in the back of the opening is a small trailer with a motorcycle parked in front. Smiling, Red pulls into a lane that takes him to the trailer. As soon as he gets out of his truck he hears two gunshots in rapid succession. He drops to the ground, rolls toward the rear of the truck, and scans the edge of the woods, uncertain where the shots came from. Silence as loud as the earlier booming gunshots now fills the air.

Staying low to the ground, Red eases back to the cab of his truck and, keeping his head down, crawls inside and removes a nine millimeter pistol from the glove compartment. He ratchets a shell into the chamber and pushes off the safety. Able to get a clearer view of both sides of the truck, he again scans the edge of the woods. A cluster of possumhaw bushes on the passenger side moves. Red grips the pistol and slides out of the truck. Peeping around the front bumper, he sees a tall man wearing a small game hunting vest emerge from the woods carrying a shotgun in the crook of his arm.

The man stops when he sees Red's truck and he takes on Red's role of scanning the area for signs of danger. After a minute, he takes slow, deliberate strides toward the trailer.

"Well I'll be," Red says under his breath. Holding the hammer of his pistol with his thumb, he squeezes the trigger and eases the hammer down, then pushes the safety on. Standing, he says, "Well if it isn't my long lost brother! Man, I thought someone was shooting at me!"

Preacher stops and stares.

Red walks toward him. "Surprised, aren't you? I'll bet I'm the last person in the world you expected to see today."

"What are you doing here? And how did you find me?"

Red extends his hand to his brother, but Preacher ignores the gesture. "Gee, Hal," Red says, "is that anyway to greet family?"

"We share the same mother, but we haven't been family in a long time."

"This is about you having to go to prison, isn't it? Look, I didn't make you take the fall for that murder. You did that on your own. Surely you can't hold that against me."

"The only reason I took the full blame was because I didn't think Mama could stand the humiliation of both her boys going to prison for murder. I thought I could count on you to take care of her while I was doing time. That was just another foolish mistake I made. It was years before I learned the truth, that you left soon after I went to prison without letting her or anyone know where you were. She died of a broken heart, you know. One son stuck in prison, and the other son abandoned her."

Red looks away. "Yeah, that's one thing I feel bad about having done. She was a good woman and deserved better."

"We both made more than our fair share of mistakes when we were young," Preacher says. He waves his hand. "I'm sorry I even brought it up. That's all in the past and it's better off left there. I thought I had let all of that go and had forgiven you. But seeing you face-to-face like this, all that hatred came boiling back up again. I guess I've got more work to do in that department. Why don't you come inside?"

"I thought you'd never ask," Red replies.

Once inside, Red glances around at the spare furnishings and says, "Apparently you're not used to having company over."

"I live a pretty simple life," Preacher replies. "But that's the way I prefer it. You want something to drink?"

"That sounds good."

"I've got tea, coffee, and water."

Red looks at him.

"No, there's no alcohol in here."

"Then I'll take coffee. So what I heard is true, isn't it? That you've become a preacher."

As he scoops coffee into the coffee maker, Preacher says, "I share with other people what I understand about God and his word, the Bible. If that makes me a preacher, then I suppose I am."

Taking a seat in one of the two cane-bottom chairs in the kitchenette, Red says, "Do you know how hard that is for me to believe? My brother, the hard-driving, hard-drinking Night Rider who nobody messed with is now a preacher?" He shakes his head.

Preacher sits in the other chair as the smell of coffee fills the air. "The first few years I was in prison I stayed angry all the time. But an old man who'd been in prison for decades told me that I was wasting my time. He said, 'Boy, you need to be a man and accept your punishment. Figure out what you're supposed to learn from being here. Decide what kind of life you want to live and start living it while you're in here. And above all, get to know God because only He can get you through this.' I took his advice and began a journey that took me to the Cross. That's where I found the thing that had been missing from my life, and that was peace." He pauses and says, "You ought to think about making the same journey."

Red holds up his hands. "Hold it right there. Don't start preaching to me about all that love and forgiveness and being kind to your fellow man. What I've learned in life is that if you want anything, you've got to take it. If somebody's in the way, that's too bad for them."

Looking at the scar on the side of Red's face, Preacher says, "Looks to me like you might have gotten in someone else's way."

"Don't you worry," Red snaps, "he got what was coming to him."

Preacher gets up from the table and fills two coffee cups. "Why did you look me up after all these years?"

Red hooks two fingers into the handle of one of the mugs and takes a sip of the steaming, black coffee. "I'm not really sure. I've had an unusual couple of days. I saw a man I haven't seen in years and I thought, 'I haven't seen my brother in years. I wonder if I can be lucky enough to find him.' I stopped in Dresden and asked around about you and danged if I didn't get directions right to your trailer."

Snapping his fingers, Preacher says, "Say, how'd you like me to fry these squirrels I killed a while ago? We can eat a late lunch together."

"Fried squirrel . . . Do you know how long it's been since I ate fried squirrel?"

"Maybe too long."

Two hours later, Red and Preacher exit the trailer. Red gets in his truck. Sticking out his hand, he says, "It was good to see you, brother. Maybe we'll see each other again sometime."

Preacher shakes his hand. "I don't know what kind of angle you're working, Red, but it's not going to take you where you want to go. The only way you'll ever find true satisfaction is when you quit living for yourself and start living for Christ."

Laughing, Red starts his pickup. "Tell you what, you put in a good word for me to the man upstairs and maybe he'll help me see the error of my ways. Take care." He follows the gravel road back to the blacktop and drives slowly toward the highway.

An older model pickup truck approaches him from the opposite direction. As they pass each other Red looks at the large man driving the other truck. Two seconds later he slams on his brakes. *That wasn't a man! That was that woman in man's clothes who was with Big Country at Boyette's!*

CHAPTER TWENTY-FIVE

After hearing the familiar three sharp knocks followed by one solitary knock on his front door, March waits for the sound of Debbie entering his apartment.

"Hi, March. It's me."

Rising from his chair, he opens his arms to welcome her. Her perfume sweeps over him just before she steps into his embrace. "Mmm, you smell good."

Giving him a quick kiss, Debbie says, "But of course I do. And you look handsome."

"Thank you. Do you have a nice restaurant picked out for us tonight?"

"Yes sir, just as you asked. It's a little Italian restaurant named Mama Lucia's. Someone at work told me about it. They said it's a simple mom-and-pop kind of place, but the food is fabulous. What I don't know is why you're wanting something small and intimate for tonight."

He runs his hand over her hair, then traces the bottom of her jaw with his thumb. Putting his thumb on her cool lips, he says, "No questions allowed. Not yet, anyway."

March feels Debbie's face broaden into a grin. "Okay, Mister Mysterious. I'll play along with your game."

Forty minutes later, Debbie parks her car and shuts off the engine. "The restaurant's just a block away. We can walk it."

When they open their doors, the sound of Gene Autry singing "Rudolph the Red-Nosed Reindeer" fills the air.

"How sweet!" Debbie exclaims. "One of the stores has Christmas music playing."

March picks up the refrain of the song and sings with the recording.

Debbie hugs his arm as they walk toward the restaurant and joins in singing with him.

As the song finishes, March asks, "Is everyone staring at us?"

Laughing, Debbie says, "As a matter of fact, they are."

"Good. That just means they recognize great singing when they hear it."

Debbie pulls back on his arm. "We're at an intersection. There's a curb about three feet in front of you."

March follows her lead and comes to a stop beside her. When she starts moving, he transitions easily across the curb, through the intersection, and up the curb on the other side.

A little bit farther, Debbie says, "Here we are."

Walking inside Mama Lucia's, they are greeted with the strains of "White Christmas" sung by Dean Martin. The muted voices of diners can be heard as well.

"I like this place already," March says, smiling.

"Table for two?" a man with an Italian accent asks.

"Reservation for Tucker," Debbie replies.

"Yes, I have a very special table for you. Follow me, please."

Once they are seated, the man asks, "Can I get you something to drink?"

"Bring us two glasses of wine, please," March says.

"Excellent. I'll have them brought right out."

Pausing until their escort to the table has left, Debbie says, "Wine? I don't think I've ever known you to drink any kind of alcohol."

March pulls at the corner of his sweater and clears his throat. "This is a special night, so I thought it deserved a touch of elegance and class."

"Special how?"

"First, I want to see the inside of this restaurant. Describe it to me."

"Okay, let me see . . . I guess the first thing you'd notice is that the lighting is dim, not in a dark, cheap way, but in a way that makes for intimate conversation. There are about a dozen tables. In the middle of every table is a lit candle in a wine bottle. It's obvious they've been used for years because the wax drippings have made the bottles look as big around as a cantaloupe. One wall has a soft spotlight on it with black-and-white photographs of singers like Dean Martin, Frank Sinatra, Tony Bennett, and Nat King Cole."

"It sounds perfect," March says. He slides his open hand across the table and smiles when he feels her warm hand in his. "Ever since we announced to my family last week about our engagement, I've been thinking that we needed to celebrate it ourselves. I mean, you had barely agreed to marry me before we had to make that mad dash to Dresden to see about Smiley Carter."

March is interrupted. "Here is your wine, the best of the house. How about a plate of our famous spaghetti and meatballs or lasagna?"

Recognizing the voice, March asks, "So are you the greeter and waiter, too?"

The man laughs, a laugh that has the texture of the Italian dough in the kitchen—soft, giving, and warm. "Young man, I am that, plus I wash dishes, cook sometimes, and sweep the floors when we close. This is my restaurant."

Debbie says, "But the name of the restaurant is Mama Lucia's."

"Yes, I know. Mama Lucia was my mother, God rest her soul. I was her only child and was raised in this restaurant. She left it to me. Excuse me, but I have to hurry back to the kitchen to make sure my daughter doesn't burn it down."

"Bring us whichever you think we would like," March says, "the spaghetti or the lasagna."

"Very good, sir."

March listens to the man's footsteps fade. "This place means something to him. It's more than just a restaurant. It's his life. I'll bet a lot of his customers are ones he's had for years. He knows them on a first-name basis. They are like family to him. And he loves his daughter deeply. He doesn't for a moment think she's going to burn down his kitchen. He wants to go in there because he takes so much pride in seeing how accomplished she is at what she does."

"I love how you do that," Debbie says.

"Do what?"

"How you see all of that simply by listening."

"That's how I fell in love with you. Your voice makes me think of a gently flowing creek as it passes over and between rounded stones. Only a gentle, loving spirit produces a sound like that, and it's just one of the reasons I enjoy hearing you talk."

He hears her sniff back her tears.

"March," Debbie says, "I don't know what to say."

"This time you don't have to say anything. You know, the other night when we agreed to marry each other, it was in the middle of a very intense moment. Now that you've had a chance to think more clearly, I want you to be absolutely honest with me and tell me if marrying me is really what you want to do."

There is a moment of silence, and March feels an old fear raise its head. He holds his breath.

In a voice husky with emotion, Debbie says, "Listen to me carefully because I want you to hear and understand perfectly what I am about to say."

Fear grabs a mallet and beats so hard against March's chest that he is certain the front of his shirt must be moving in rhythm.

"Before the car accident," Debbie begins, "I dated a lot and always enjoyed the company of guys. I had the dream of getting married one day and raising a family. But after I lost my arm, the guys I had dated stopped calling. Oh sure, at first they gave a pity date. However, I could see in their eyes that they looked at me differently. So, I gave up on my dream of marriage and a family. And even though at first I was sad, I accepted it and eventually became content with being single. Then, out of the blue, a burly bear of a man showed up in my life with walls as thick as the Great Wall of China."

Hearing the smile in Debbie's voice as she says this, March feels a soft breeze in his chest. He breathes. Fear lays down its mallet and returns to the mausoleum of crippling emotions.

Grinning, he says, "I was a piece of work, wasn't I?"

"No," Debbie replies, "you were a train wreck and I didn't like you. Still though, I was intrigued by you. I was certain there was something behind that wall that was worth getting to know."

Still grinning, March says, "Intrigued—I like the sound of that."

"Oh shut up. I'm being serious here."

"Sorry. So, was what you found behind the wall what you expected?"

"Honestly, I'm not sure what I expected," Debbie replies. "What I discovered was that you had every reason to be the kind of person you projected to the world. Once I understood that, I was willing to be patient until you decided to open a gate and let me through the wall."

Suddenly a man standing beside their table clears his throat. "I apologize for intruding, but I have your spaghetti and meatballs. You are still interested in eating, aren't you?"

The spell of intensity that shrouded the young lovers' table suddenly lifts in the glare of this unexpected interruption.

March clears his throat and sits back in his chair. Tapping the table, he says, "Right here, please."

The aroma of tomato sauce and Parmesan cheese rises from the plates of steaming spaghetti.

"Smells delicious," Debbie says.

"And a loaf of our famous, homemade Italian bread," the server says. "Made exactly the way my great-grandmother made it."

"I don't see a knife to slice it with," Debbie says.

"Oh, we don't recommend slicing. You pull it apart." In a lower voice, he adds, "I know that sounds weird, but that's the way our family has always done it. Trust me, it tastes just as good."

Debbie stifles a laugh. "Then we'll follow your family tradition. Thank you."

"Can I get you anything else?"

"No," March says.

Once the server is out of earshot, Debbie says, "You didn't have to be so short with him."

"Well, his timing sucks. We were having such a great talk and then he shoved himself in the middle—"

"I know, I know," Debbie says. "Come on, let's keep this night as perfect as it has been so far." She tears off a piece of bread and lifts it to his mouth. "Take a bite."

The warmth and smell of fresh bread kisses the inside of March's nostrils. He smiles and opens his mouth. The soft bread melts in his mouth as he crunches the crusty exterior. "Oh my gosh," he says. "That is unbelievable. You try a bite."

A groan of pleasure escapes from Debbie as she chews a bite of the savory bread. "Oh my, I think I just had an oral orgasm."

March barely stops himself from spewing his mouthful of wine across the table. But he can't stop his combination coughing-choking-and-laughter. When he finally catches his breath, he says, "That's the funniest thing I've ever heard you say. What did you call it again? An oral what?"

"Oh hush! You just want to hear me say the word out loud again. I'm sure I've never used that expression before, but I've also never had warm bread that tasted that good."

"I can't wait until you try the spaghetti and describe how that affects you," March says. "Just please warn me before you do, so that I don't have my mouth full."

For the next few moments, they eat in silence, experiencing the magic that authentic Italian cooking can produce.

Finally, Debbie says, "I need to finish answering your question, don't you think?"

And just that quickly intimacy descends on their table as if they pulled down window shades around them.

March begins, "I remember how scared I was when you took that first step inside my walled kingdom. I felt almost helpless to defend myself because nothing I did intimidated you."

"March, I am drawn to you like the tides are to the moon. You have a power over me that I don't understand and can't explain. I want to marry you and be with you for the rest of my life. I want us to raise a family together and grow old together."

From the tables close to them comes the sound of hands softly clapping. Then come voices saying, "Congratulations," "Wonderful," "How precious," "Beautiful," "Thank you."

"What's going on?" March asks.

"Oh my, March," Debbie says, "it appears we've been putting on a show without knowing it. Everyone around us is smiling and applauding."

"Well I'm ready to go to my apartment and finish this conversation in private, if you are."

"I thought you'd never ask."

CHAPTER TWENTY-SIX

As soon as March and Debbie walk through the door of his apartment, they hungrily embrace. March kisses her as if he is drowning and her mouth will supply him with the breath he needs to stay alive.

Surprised by his eagerness, Debbie quickly responds and opens her mouth. Her tongue finds his. Something like the feeling of electricity rushes through her. She feels her body heating up.

March pushes her up against the front door and presses his body against hers. He puts his hands on her hips and lifts her off the floor. She quickly wraps her legs around him and squeezes. Pulling her mouth away from his, she says, "I want you, March."

His breath feels hot against her face. "And I want you."

"Are you sure you're ready for this?"

March responds by carrying her to his darkened bedroom.

Debbie slips her hands under his sweater. Her fingers use the lubricant of the small beads of sweat on his back to skate crisscrossing patterns.

He growls in her ear, "That feels good."

She raises the tips of her fingers until her fingernails lightly drag across his slick skin. They slice downward past his kidneys and trace the border of the waistline of his pants.

March squeezes her hips in reply. He pulls her shirttail out of her pants, slips one of his large hands underneath, and begins massaging the small of her back.

"Mmmm, you could do that all night, and I wouldn't get tired of it," she says.

After a moment, he gently grips her thighs, pulls her legs from around him and lowers her to the floor until she is standing.

She begins unbuckling his belt as he removes his sweater and T-shirt.

With a light touch he deftly begins unbuttoning her shirt.

She stands unmoving as March's actions bring him closer to the one area she is most self-conscious about. For once she is thankful that he is blind. When he starts to slip her shirt over her shoulders, she says, "Why don't you let me do it. I'll have to take off my prosthesis."

March kisses her on her forehead, then her eyelids, then each cheek, and then on her lips. "I want to do it. If we're going to share our lives, then that means everything."

Debbie bites her lip. "If you say so."

He slips her shirt off of her and brushes the back of his hand across her bra-covered breasts, sending a shiver through her. Then he locates the harness that holds her prosthesis in place, loosens it, and removes the artificial arm. Tenderly he removes the protective sock from the end of her arm. His fingertips trace and retrace every centimeter of it.

"So now that you've seen it," Debbie whispers, "do you have any questions, or are you having second thoughts?"

March lifts the end of her arm to his mouth and kisses it, holding his lips against it for a long time before lowering her arm. "I think it's sexy."

Debbie suddenly realizes she is crying. "You are the most unusual man I have ever known. Only God could have sent a man like you into my life. Thirty seconds ago I didn't believe it possible that I could love you any more. But you've shown me that was wrong, because now I love you even more. You've done for me what I never believed was possible."

"What's that?" March asks.

"You've made me feel whole again."

He pushes his body up against her and she backs up until she feels the bed on the back of her legs. His hands reach behind her and unfasten her bra. As he tosses it aside, Debbie feels the comfort of the weight of her unfettered and eager breasts.

March's large hands cover each of her breasts and massage them. Debbie reflexively squeezes her legs together at the surge of pleasure.

"They're so soft and warm," March says. "As soft as a baby's skin. And they're larger than I expected. I'd always wondered what they would be like."

He gently squeezes her nipples and a small cry escapes from her.

"I'm sorry! I didn't mean to hurt you," March says.

"That wasn't a cry of pain, you silly man," Debbie replies.

She unfastens his pants and unzips them, feeling his own bulge of excitement lying just behind the zipper.

When his pants fall to the floor, March steps out of them. He pushes her down onto the bed, and she scoots on her back as he removes her pants and panties. After removing his underwear, he crawls onto the bed on his hands and knees, keeping her underneath him.

Hovering over her, March says, "You are the most beautiful woman I have ever seen."

Debbie reaches and pulls him down on top of her as she spreads her legs. "Come to me, lover. Find the depths of me. For you are my one true love."

CHAPTER TWENTY-SEVEN

April eases shut the door to the twins' bedroom. *My god, I didn't think they would ever go to sleep!*

She hears James in the kitchen. Entering the room, she smiles and says, "What are you up to?"

James turns away from the open refrigerator. Holding up a dish, he says, "I had to have another piece of that apple pie you made. It was delicious! You want to join me?"

"Sure. I'll get the plates." After feeling like James has ignored her for a week, April works to keep her excitement in check. She walks over to the cabinet and removes two plates. As she does so, she glances down at her chest. Being careful to keep her back toward James, she quickly unbuttons two more buttons at the top of her shirt.

James says, "Didn't you tell me that Tucker taught you to make pies?"

Standing on the opposite side of the small island in the kitchen, April says, "Yessiree, that pie is a Tucker special. The only difference is that I didn't have any of her canned apples to use."

James slices two equal pieces of pie and then serves them onto the plates. "I know just a little about cooking, so I'm curious to know the secret for having such a flaky crust."

April laughs. Wagging her index finger in the air, she says, "Don't you know that chefs never reveal their secrets? Besides, Tucker would somehow find out if I ever told you, and then I'd have heck to pay."

"Well that's the last thing I'd want to happen to you. And I wouldn't want to have to face Tucker myself, either. So you go ahead and keep that secret to yourself. I'm going to warm my piece in the microwave. You want me to warm yours?"

"Yes, please."

When James turns to open the microwave, April takes two forks out of the drawer in front of her and joins him.

He turns his head to look at her. She notices that he glances down at her open shirt. Just then, the timer on the microwave goes off, and he opens the door. Handing the plate to her, he says, "Be careful, it may be hot."

Keeping her eyes on his, April takes the plate and says, "I'll be careful."

James stares at her for a moment, then blinks and turns his attention to sliding his plate into the microwave.

April feels her heart beating in her throat. *Calm down. It's obvious he's looked at me. All I need to do is follow his lead.* "Tucker always says a glass of cold milk is the best thing for washing down apple pie. Do you want some?"

Without looking at her, James answers, "That does sound good. Yeah, pour me a glass, too."

April sets her pie down in front of one of the two barstools at the end of the island. She sets out two glasses and then goes to retrieve the milk from the refrigerator. Just as she finishes filling the second glass, James sets his plate in front of the other barstool.

Before he sits down, April pretends to accidentally drop the top to the milk jug. "Just call me fumble fingers," she says.

"I'll get it," James says as he stoops to the floor.

At the same time, April bends at the waist and reaches to pick up the top, her head only inches from James's.

Their hands grab the top at the same time and James looks up, laughing. "Looks like we both—" When his eyes reach the open top of her gaping shirt, whatever he was about to say gets lost. His laughter gets choked off as well.

April keeps perfectly still, letting him look. "Looks like we both what?" she says softly.

James's head snaps up and he stands.

As April stands, she notices the tops of his cheeks are pink. She feels heat building inside her, and she fights the urge to rip her shirt off and take James to the floor.

He sits on the barstool and takes a bite of the pie. After gulping down half of his glass of milk, he exclaims, "Boy, Tucker was right! Apple pie and milk are a perfect combination."

April climbs onto her barstool and takes a bite. "Mmm," she moans, "Even if I did make it, that really tastes good. Kind of gives you a good feeling all over, doesn't it?"

James pauses and looks at her. "You didn't put some kind of magic spell on this pie did you? You know, like when Sleeping Beauty ate the poison apple. Because I'm feeling a little strange."

Nudging him with her knee, April says, "So, you think I'm trying to kill you?" She laughs. "What do you mean, you feel a little strange?"

James lays his fork on his plate and turns on his stool to face her.

April mirrors his move, but to keep their knees from bumping she slips one of hers between his. She focuses on his mouth, waiting for even the slightest movement toward her.

"April, I haven't officially been a widow for even a month."

April feels as if someone has thrown a glass of cold water in her face. She looks down at her lap. "I know that, James. I understand."

"But at the same time," he continues, "it's been a long time since I've been with a woman. Susan was so sick for so long that we didn't have a physical relationship."

As if someone has thrown a gallon of gas and a lit match on her, April's sexual urges and feelings flare back up inside her. Without intending to, she squeezes his leg between hers.

James lays his hand on top of her thigh. "You are an amazingly attractive young woman."

"Daddy, we're thirsty." The sound of Michael's voice startles them so badly that April falls backward off her stool, and James barely catches himself from falling.

James rushes to his boys, who are standing in the doorway of the kitchen. "I thought you guys were asleep," he says.

"We want a drink of water," Christopher says while rubbing his eyes.

April gets off the floor, rubbing the back of her head.

"Is April okay, Daddy?" Michael asks.

James whirls around. "Oh my gosh! April, are you all right?" He quickly walks over to her.

Though she is gritting her teeth, she manages to force a smile. "I just hit the back of my head on the cabinet, but I'm fine." The mixture of pain and aggravation has worked like a fire extinguisher on any carnal urges she was having. *Kids! Why can't they stay where they're supposed to?!*

"You need to put some ice on that," James says. "There's an ice pack in the freezer. Why don't you get it and go on to bed. I'll take care of the boys."

April grabs the ice pack out of the freezer and walks out of the kitchen without saying a word. Once inside her bedroom, she flings the ice pack across the room. *Everything was moving along perfectly until the twins showed up! James was within a breath of kissing me. Who knows when there will be another opportunity like that?!*

April strips off her clothes and slips on her robe. She picks up the discarded ice pack from the floor, lies back on her bed, and gingerly slides the ice pack underneath the back of her head. She winces in pain. After several minutes she closes her eyes.

Immediately visions of her and James together fill her head. The more she concentrates on the images, the more her frustration subsides. It is replaced by the familiar warm feeling she always gets when she thinks of her and James.

She sits up on the edge of her bed. *Why should I let a little interruption interfere with what was about to happen between me and James? I know he's still thinking about it, just like I am.*

April cracks her bedroom door open so she can see the twins' room. Their door is shut and only a dim light from their night-light is showing at the bottom of the door. She opens her door wider and sees James's door is shut as well, but light is spilling across the hallway floor from under it. Walking across the hallway, she puts her ear to his door. *Perfect! He's taking a shower.*

Silently she opens the bedroom door and makes her way to the bathroom. The door is only partially closed and steam is rolling out of the opening. She eases inside the steam-filled room. For a moment she watches James's silhouette inside the large, glass-walled shower. Then she unties her robe and lets it fall to the floor. Opening the shower door, she steps inside.

At the sound of the door, James turns and sees her. Water sprays off of his back, framing him in silver droplets. He opens his arms and April steps into them, pressing her cool body against the warmth of his. She lifts her face and he kisses her deeply.

Suddenly the blaring sound of April's alarm clock beside her bed shocks her with the force of an electric cattle prod. She bolts upright. The sudden movement, coupled with the daylight flooding her bedroom, sends searing pain through her head. Covering her eyes, she cries out and falls back onto her pillow.

She rolls onto her side and pulls the covers over her head. *Is my dreamworld going to be the only place I will ever be with James?*

CHAPTER TWENTY-EIGHT

Sitting down on the edge of the bed in his motel room, Red grabs the receiver on the phone and dials a number. "Tarzan, this is Red. Have you found any leads to Big Country yet?"

Tarzan replies, "I did track down a lead to the hospital that I think he was treated at. It wasn't in Knoxville. It was in Maryville. But hospitals won't dish out information as easily as they used to. I did find a nurse who finally admitted to treating him. Unfortunately she didn't feel like cooperating, even with my means of persuasion. So I've hit a dead end over here. What about you?"

"I don't know what I've got," Red growls. "I've been watching a house for a week that I thought would give me a clue, but I haven't seen anything that's given me a concrete lead. All I've seen is a strange-looking old woman who never leaves her property and hardly ever even leaves her house. I'm tired of being patient, tired of this crummy motel, and tired of hanging around this one-horse town. So I'm going to try something different tomorrow."

"You want me to come to West Tennessee and help you?" Tarzan asks.

"No, you keep snooping around. If I need help, I'll call." Red hangs up the phone.

The next day Red drives out to Tucker's house and pulls into the driveway. He slips on a pair of sunglasses and pulls a ball cap low on his brow. He reaches over on the passenger seat and picks up a clipboard. He pats his pants pocket and feels his small pistol.

He strides up to the front door and knocks. After a moment, the door opens halfway and Red sees the woman he's been watching for a week. Touching the bill of his cap, he says, "Morning, ma'am. I'm here on behalf of your electric company. The last time your meter was read, it showed almost three times the amount of electricity was used than the amount you normally use. So I've come to check out your appliances and heating and cooling systems to make sure everything is all right. That is, if you don't mind."

Tucker stares at him, keeping her hand on the door. "I don't b'lieve I know you, do I?" Nodding at his truck she adds, "An' how come y' ain't drivin' an official truck?"

"No, ma'am, you don't know me. They hire independent contractors to do this kind of work, and we drive our own private vehicles. I hate to be a bother to you, but there might be something seriously wrong. Last week someone in another county had their house burn down simply because there was some bad wiring. And it was a fairly new house. If you're busy, I'll try to be as quick as I can with the inspection."

Backing up and opening the door wider, Tucker says, "I'll let y' come in an' look 'round, but I'm keepin' my eye on you."

Walking through the door, Red says, "I don't blame you, ma'am. You can't be too careful nowadays." In a flash, he throws his clipboard and loose papers in Tucker's face, slams the front door with one hand while pulling out his pistol with his other hand.

Startled, Tucker stumbles backward several feet until she falls into her recliner. "What the—?!" Looking up at Red, she sees the pistol pointed toward her.

"Listen to me," Red says. "I have no intention of hurting you, but I will if I have to. Over a week ago I saw you at Boyette's restaurant over in Tiptonville, didn't I? You were there with several other people, weren't you?"

Tucker folds her arms across her chest. "Whether I was 'r whether I wasn't ain't none of yore business."

Using the barrel of his pistol, Red pushes up the bill of his cap, then removes his sunglasses. "Look lady, all I want is information. You don't have anything to be afraid of, if you tell me what I want to know."

"Mister, I ain't got nothin' t' be afeared of one way or th' other. Matter of fact, I don't 'member th' last time I was afeared."

Red stares at her in silence. Shaking his head slowly, he says, "Okay, let's try this another way. You were at Boyette's with an old nigger man, a pretty blonde-headed girl, a young man that looked half-white and half-nigger, another young woman, and a big, big man with a beard. I want to know what the connection is between all of you."

Cocking her head to one side, Tucker says, "Looks like y' tangled with th' wrong person sometime in th' past an' got yoreself cut up pretty bad. Seems t' me y'd wanta be more careful who y' tried t' mess with." She unfolds her arms and rests them on the armrests, letting her hands hang over the side. The fingertips of her right hand touch the axe handle she keeps propped beside her chair. "I don't think y' wanta mess with an ol' buzzard like me. It could prove hazardous t' yore health."

Red's eyes open wide in disbelief. "Lady, you have lost your mind."

"Y' ain't th' first person what's said that through th' years."

Taking a step toward her, Red says, "This pistol may appear harmless, but let me assure you it will kill you as dead as a .357 magnum will. This is not a game I'm playing with you."

"Didn't figure y' was, an' I ain't neither."

Red takes another step toward Tucker. His face is turning crimson. "I'm looking for that big, bearded man who was—"

Suddenly Tucker swings her axe handle and strikes Red in the mouth. He cries out in pain and falls backward into the entertainment center. It collapses under him, sending the TV crashing to the floor, where the front of it explodes with a loud pop. His mouth spews blood and expletives in equal proportions as he works to regain his footing.

Tucker rises from her chair and starts toward him when Smiley Carter calls from his bedroom, "Tucker! Is everything all right in there?"

Tucker freezes.

Red's head snaps in the direction of the hallway.

Halting steps are heard coming toward them. "What's all the commotion in there?" Smiley asks as he steps into the living room.

Red looks at Smiley then at Tucker. "You're shacking up with this nigger?" He turns back to Smiley, raises his pistol, and fires a shot.

Smiley's head snaps backward and he collapses onto the floor. A pool of blood starts forming under his head.

Dropping her axe handle, Tucker cries, "Smiley!" She makes a move toward him.

Red swings the pistol toward her. "Stop right there, you crazy woman."

Tucker stops.

Wiping the blood from his mouth, Red says, "You can't do anything for him, unless you want to join him in the sweet by-and-by. Now back up and sit back down in your chair."

Tears run down Tucker's round cheeks as she looks at Smiley's form on the floor. She turns toward Red and squints her eyes. "I ain't gonna let y' kill me, 'cause I'm gonna live long enough t' take y' t' hell with me."

Red laughs. "You are a piece of work, woman! Crazy or not, I admire your spirit. Too bad it's not going to do you any good." As Tucker sits down, he pulls a chair in front of her and sits in it. "The big, bearded man who was with you at Boyette's, how do you know him?"

"Why do y' wanta know?"

"It's none of your business!" Red screams.

"Then I ain't tellin' y'. An' you ain't gonna kill me, neither."

"I'm not? And why not?"

"'Cause you think I know somethin' you wanta know. An' y' think I'll tell y'."

Red runs his hand through his hair. He gets out of his chair and walks over to a wall with several picture frames hanging on it. "This must be that good-looking blonde I saw with you. Now, I know she's not your daughter, so who is she? Your granddaughter, maybe?"

When Tucker gives no reply he steps over to the demolished entertainment center. Pushing around the pieces on the floor, he spies a broken picture frame. Bending over, he pulls the picture out of it and stands up. "Well, well, what do we have here? Hail, hail, the gang's all here. Is this some kind of family photo or something?"

Tucker responds by folding her arms over her chest and sits in stony silence.

Holding the photo beside his face and turning it so Tucker can see it, Red points and says, "This big fellow is a man I know as Big Country. He used to be a business associate of mine, but he betrayed me. Now I want to get my money back that he stole. That's only the fair thing, don't you agree? So tell me where I can find him, and I'll be on my way."

Tucker stares, unblinking.

"I don't know what his connection to you and Dresden is. As a matter of fact, I don't know why anyone would want any connection to this run-down town. The only thing I ever knew that was any good out of Dresden was this woman I met years ago. I was working as a carnival worker at the time. She was one hot piece of merchandise. She called herself Amazing. And she was." He whistles low. "Only problem was she came up pregnant and said I was the daddy. Lucky for me the carnival was leaving town and I skipped out before she could hang any kind of legal collar around my neck."

Pitching the photo to the floor, he looks at Tucker. "What in the world are you crying about now? That old nigger? If you are, then you're not only crazy, you're sick!"

Sobbing, Tucker bends over and puts her face in her hands.

CHAPTER TWENTY-NINE

March awakens in his bed, unsure of what time it is. Lying on his left side, he is immediately aware of Debbie's warm body spooned against the front of him. His right hand is on her breast. He feels the rhythmic rise and fall of her chest and abdomen as she breathes. The slow and even beat of her heart reinforces the sense of peace he awoke with. He takes his hand off her breast and lays it on the side of her thigh. Like a skier traversing mountain slopes, he slowly slides his hand up her thigh to her hips, then down the slope to her waist, and up again to her shoulder.

Debbie stirs and rolls over to face him. Kissing his chest, she says, "Good morning, lover."

"What time is it?" March asks.

"That's the first thing you're going to say to me after last night? 'What time is it?' You're a real romantic, aren't you?"

"Sorry, it's just that I find it confusing when I'm not oriented to time."

"My turn to apologize. I didn't think about that. This is the first time I've awakened with you in bed. There are still things I need to learn about you and what it's like to be blind." Debbie kisses him again. "It's 8:43 in the morning."

Putting his hand on the side of her face, March kisses her. "My turn to say, 'Good morning, lover.' Last night was the most incredible experience of my life. You were tender and eager at the same time. I felt set free by you."

She pulls her fingers through his chest hair. "Set free from what?"

"From all my past and the darkness that surrounded it. It was like the sun burning away a fog. It just seemed to disappear. Then I got lost in just us and us being together in the moment." He feels Debbie's hand work its way down his chest and past his abdomen. She grasps his rising erection. He gasps.

"Look what I found," Debbie giggles. "Is this a good morning wake-up call, too?"

Smiling, March says, "It can be, if you want it to be."

Debbie pushes him onto his back and then straddles him. "Prepare yourself to be fully awakened."

After their lovemaking, Debbie gets out of the bed. "Why don't you go get your shower while I fix us some breakfast?"

"That wasn't breakfast?" March asks. Suddenly a pillow hits him in the face. "Hey, you're hitting a defenseless man here."

"My daddy used to say that love will fill your heart, but it won't fill your belly. Get on in the shower, but you better hurry or I'll have it all eaten. I'm starving!"

When March finishes his shower and gets dressed, he walks into the kitchen. The sound of music on the radio and the aroma of food fills the air. "Even if you hadn't spent the night with me last night, I could still tell you are here by the smell of your cooking."

"You know, that could either be a compliment or a criticism," Debbie replies.

Walking to her voice, March smiles. "It is most definitely a compliment. You must be making us sausage omelets, with some bell pepper, cheese, and just a little cinnamon. You're the only person I've ever known to put that touch of cinnamon in an omelet." He finds her facing the stove and puts his arms around her.

"That cinnamon was my mother's special secret," Debbie says. "She said her mother used to do it, too. Now go sit down, or you're going to get burned."

As he sits down, March hears a plate slide across the table toward him. He bends over and sniffs loudly. "I'll try and wait until you sit down with your plate before I start eating, but I'm not making any promises."

Debbie's plate bangs loudly on the table as she sits down. "What you don't know is that I've already eaten two omelets while you were in the shower."

March makes a grab toward her plate, "Then give me that one, too!"

She slaps his hand. "Mind your manners! What would Tucker say if she saw you do that?"

Giving his best attempt at imitating Tucker's train-whistle voice, March says, "Keep yore hands t' yoreself, y' little troublemaker. Y' act like y' ain't got no raisin'."

They both laugh.

Once they've eaten a few bites in silence, Debbie says, "Have you thought about when you want to get married? I mean a specific date."

"I don't want to wait a long time," March replies.

"Good. Neither do I."

"Is Christmas too soon?"

"I thought about Christmas, too. But then I remembered an old saying I heard one time—Whatever you are doing on New Year's Day, you will be doing all year long. Why don't we get married on New Year's Day?"

"I really like that idea. It's all about new beginnings, plus it will make it easy for me to remember our anniversary every year." March laughs.

"Just like a man, making the practical decision," Debbie says. "Then we agree? January first?"

"January first it is."

"I want to ask you about something else, but I don't want to hurt your feelings."

Fear, anxiety's constant companion, pulls the hairs on the back of March's neck. Swallowing his half-chewed mouthful of food, he says, "Don't let that stop you. Always ask me whatever is on your mind. If it hurts my feelings, then I'll deal with it."

"Okay then," Debbie says. "Have you ever thought about shaving your beard off? I've never seen you without a beard."

"You don't like my beard?"

"That's not it. If I didn't like it, I wouldn't have been attracted to you. I guess I'm just curious to see what you look like without it."

March takes a sip of coffee. "First of all, you haven't hurt my feelings. I'm actually relieved that that's all you were wanting to ask. As far as my beard is concerned, I'll have to trust you as to what really looks better—with or without the beard. It's not that big a deal to me, now. I guess it used to be in another life but not anymore."

Debbie gives a squeal of delight. "I can't wait! This will be fun. Let me go get some scissors out of your bathroom." She scoots back her chair and pads quickly into the bathroom.

Laughing, March says, "You can go get the scissors, but you're not touching this beard until I finish eating breakfast. Who would have thought that cutting off my beard would be such an exciting thing?" He makes quick work of the rest of his breakfast.

Walking back into the kitchen, Debbie snaps the scissors repeatedly and gives a maniacal laugh. "Are you sure you want to trust me?"

"Dang," March says, "I just had a chill run down my back. It sounded like Freddy Krueger just entered the room."

"I'm going to push the table out of the way because this is going to make a mess everywhere."

The plates and silverware dance and rattle as the legs of the table vibrate.

"Are you ready?" Debbie asks.

"I am your lamb, ready for the shears," March replies.

As she begins cutting, Debbie says, "How long have you had your beard?"

"I started growing it when I was about eighteen, I think. When I ended up in the emergency room of the hospital, they had to remove it because of all my injuries and the stitches they had to put in. But I immediately started letting it grow back."

"Why did you grow one in the first place?"

"I don't think I knew why at the time. But looking back at it now, I think it was a way to hide. It made me look mean, which worked to my advantage in the line of work I was in."

Debbie keeps the scissors constantly busy as they talk. "What I want to do is trim it as close as I can with the scissors and then get a razor and shave your face. I can already tell you that you have a strong, square jawline. The difference in how you look is going to be very dramatic."

Several minutes later Debbie makes one final pass over March's cheek with the razor. "That's it," she says. "Let me stand back and look at you. March, you look ten years younger! You have a dimple in your left cheek when you smile. I never knew that."

"I'd forgotten about that," March says.

"You have a beautiful, handsome face. Your features are striking. I love it. Please don't cover it back up with your beard."

"I told you, you'd be the one to decide about it. My face, just like the rest of my body, belongs to you now."

Debbie puts her hands on both sides of his face. "It's so smooth." Then she kisses him. "Okay, now I've got a serious mess to clean up. You've got hair all over you. Take your clothes off here and go rinse in the shower again. I'll clean this up."

Listening to the sound of Debbie sweeping the floor, March begins unbuttoning his shirt.

"Oh, I almost forgot," Debbie says. "While you were in the shower I heard on the news about a murdered woman found in a trash Dumpster in Knoxville. She was a nurse who worked at the Blount Memorial Hospital in Maryville. Isn't that where you were before you came to Patricia Neal Rehab?"

March stops unbuttoning his shirt and turns to Debbie. "Yes it was. Did they mention the nurse's name?"

"Yes, it was Naomi something. I didn't catch the last name."

CHAPTER THIRTY

Picking up the twins' shoes from the living room floor, April hears keys jingling outside the front door. She pauses at the metallic sound of a key being inserted in the lock. Smiling, she waits for James to open the door and come in. When he appears in the doorway, April notices dark circles and bags under his eyes. She says, "You were up and gone this morning before I even woke up. Being on Christmas break has made me a little lazy. It seems like these extra long hours you've started working on Thursdays are hard on you, aren't they?"

"I'll have to admit they are," James replies. "When this new schedule was proposed, it sounded like a good idea. But the long hours and the commute are really wearing me out. Plus we had more than the usual portion of drama among the girls today."

Taking his valise from him, April says, "Come on in the kitchen and tell me about it. I left a supper plate for you that I'll warm up. The boys are already asleep."

"You'll get no argument from me," James says as he follows her into the kitchen. "I don't think I've noticed you wearing that perfume before."

Pleased that he noticed, April says, "I took the boys to the mall today and ended up trying out some new fragrances. Do you like it?"

Taking a seat at the kitchen table, James says, "Yes, it's nice. Somehow it suits you. Susan told me once that the same perfume can smell different on different women. It's all about how their individual body chemistry interacts with the combination of scents in the perfume."

Slightly annoyed at the mention of his memories of Susan, April chooses to say nothing in response. She takes the plate of food out of the refrigerator and places it in the microwave. "So what was the drama at Spirit Lake today?"

"As usual, it was the insertion of a new resident into the group that started it. I swear, about the time we get a group of girls working with each other, a new girl arrives and disrupts the homeostasis. Today three of the girls actually got into such a big fight that I didn't think we were ever going to separate them. There were bloody noses, busted lips, and probably a couple of black eyes will eventually show themselves." He slides up his sleeve, points, and says, "One of them even bit me!"

April's forehead creases with concern. She lifts his arm to get a closer look. "My gosh, James! A dentist could use this imprint to make a mold from. I can see every one of her teeth. Did you clean it with antiseptic?"

"Yes, we washed it really good and then ran some alcohol over it."

"That's ridiculous for a teenage girl to act like that! It's something a four- or five-year-old would do. You better make sure that girl has had her rabies vaccination."

James smiles. "It just comes with the territory. You remember what kinds of girls are sent there. They all arrive with a lot more baggage than just their suitcases."

April retrieves the plate of food from the microwave and sets it in front of James, who quickly digs in.

"Every time I eat your cooking I think about sending a thank-you note to Tucker. Not many people your age are as accomplished in the kitchen as you are."

Feeling like a puppy who's just had her belly rubbed, April blushes slightly and says, "Thank you, but maybe you're just easy to please when it comes to food."

"No, that's not it. I've never told this to anyone, but Susan, as wonderful a wife as she was, wasn't all that great a cook. She tried hard, but that just wasn't a skill she possessed. She said when she was growing up her mother wouldn't allow anyone in the kitchen. So she never learned how to cook."

Irritated at another reference to Susan, April says, "I'm going to get some ointment to put on that bite. It doesn't need to get infected." She walks out of the kitchen in spite of James's protests.

When she returns, he is finishing up the last few bites of supper. Once he finishes, she takes his arm and slides up his sleeve. She squeezes a generous portion of ointment onto her fingertip and gently rubs it onto the bite marks. "Is it sore yet?"

"It's a little tender, but not too bad."

"Am I hurting you?"

"No, you're fine."

She hears some of the stress of the day gone from his voice and feels his arm relaxing in her hand. Glancing at his face, she sees that his eyes are closed. Slowly she gets out of her chair and stands behind him. Holding her breath, she lays her hands on his shoulders and begins massaging the muscles between his shoulders and neck.

She feels him inhale deeply and exhale slowly. Taking this as an encouraging sign to continue, she pushes harder with her thumbs, working loose the knots in his muscles. His body vibrates with a groan of pleasure.

April begins to feel flushed with excitement. She puts her hands on his neck and massages the back and sides of it.

James slowly turns his neck from side to side as she releases the tension in the muscles. When he raises his hands and grips her wrists, she leans forward to kiss him on the cheek. Just before her lips touch him, he pulls her hands off his neck and says, "April, we need to talk."

With newly released hormones coursing through her, April eagerly moves in front of him and sits down. She looks directly at his full lips, imagining them being covered by hers.

"Last night," James says, "we got interrupted by the boys."

Scooting forward to the edge of her chair, April says, "I know. I thought about it all day today."

"Yes," James says, "I thought about it a lot, too. I thought about what might have happened if the boys hadn't interrupted us."

April's heart is beating so hard, she fears it is going to burst. Unable to find her voice, she simply stares at James.

James returns her stare. Then, swallowing, he looks away. "This is not going to be easy to say, April, but I don't think you need to work here anymore."

As if she's just been in a car crash, April hears the sound of screeching tires, crashing metal, and breaking glass. Her heart, which just a moment ago was thundering in her chest, now lies still. Her mouth goes dry. She blinks rapidly.

"Let me explain," James continues. "I've been living in denial— denial that you are attracted to me and denial that I am attracted to you. Which simply means that I knew it but didn't want to admit it. I knew if I admitted it, there would be consequences."

At this hopeful sound, April finds her voice. "But what's the problem? We both want each other."

James looks directly at her. "The problem is we want each other for the wrong reasons. April, I'm old enough to be your father. And

I believe that that's what you are looking for. Your whole life you've suffered from what I call father hunger. That's not unique to you. It's very common in girls who've never had a warm, loving relationship with their father. Even though you're not aware of it, I represent someone who can fill that need. What I know is that making me your lover will end up devastating you."

April finds herself unable to hold back her tears. They run down her cheeks. Her voice breaking, she says, "And why do you want me?"

"My reasons are coarse and vulgar. I want you to help satisfy my sexual urges. I'm a man and you are an attractive, available woman. While there's nothing wrong with those urges, I care about you too much to treat you like that, to use you in that way. I refuse to be that selfish."

April's lips begin to tremble. "But I thought we were going to be together, that God brought us together and we would share our lives."

Shaking his head, James says, "I know. And I'll take a lot of the blame for that. I should have talked with you immediately when I sensed that things were going the wrong way. I hate myself for not doing it."

Grabbing his hands, April says, "I love you, James. I don't want to leave you, and I don't want to leave the boys. What are you going to tell them?"

"I hate it the most for their sakes," James replies. "They love you so much. And what you've done for them in being a special friend during this most difficult passage of their lives is something I can never repay you for. I'll just tell them that you got another job and couldn't do it and take care of them, too. They will be very sad, but they'll adjust."

Suddenly April's tears stop. Standing up, she says, "So that's it? Just like that? You ask me into your life and the lives of your children, and now you're going to throw me out?!"

"April, don't be so loud," James says. "You're going to wake up the boys. I'm so sorry that—"

"I don't need you to feel sorry for me!" April snaps. "As a matter of fact I don't need you to feel anything for me. I despise you! I hate you! All men are alike. They only think of themselves."

James reaches toward her.

April slaps his hands away. "Don't touch me!" She spins around and starts walking out of the kitchen.

"What are you going to do?" James asks.

April turns around and says, "I'm going to call a taxi to take me to August's. Then I'm going to pack my things and get out of your life. You'll never hear from me again!"

CHAPTER THIRTY-ONE

Preacher turns into Tucker's driveway, switches off the engine of his Harley, and coasts to a stop. He takes off his leather gloves, turns down the collar of his leather jacket, and walks up to her front door. He is about to knock when he notices the door is standing ajar. "Hello, Tucker!" he calls out. "It's Preacher. Are you in there?"

Taking a step back, he turns and walks around to the back of her house. *There's her truck, so she's close by somewhere.* He looks toward her barn for any signs of movement. Seeing none, he walks back to his motorcycle and unfastens one of his saddlebags. He lifts out a black hardcover case and sets it on the seat. With a small key he takes out of his pocket, he unlocks the case and takes out a nine millimeter pistol and its clip. In a very smooth, practiced motion, he slips the clip into the handle of the pistol and pulls back the slide. A bullet springs into the chamber.

Moving more cautiously this time, Preacher approaches Tucker's front door. Holding the pistol low in his right hand, he pushes against the door with his left hand. As it swings open, he says, "Tucker! Smiley Carter! Is anyone home?!" The hairs on the back of his neck stand up in response to the eerie silence in the house. "If anyone is in there, I'm coming in, and I'm armed. Speak up, if you hear me." This time he doesn't wait for a response and steps inside, holding his pistol in front of him with both hands.

His eyes immediately take in the splintered remains of the entertainment center and the shattered pieces of the television set. In his peripheral vision he sees something out of place on the floor. Turning, he spies Smiley Carter's body. "Smiley!" he cries. In two steps he is on his knees beside the body. He starts to move him until he sees the pool of dark blood beneath Smiley's head. The bright shine that fresh blood has is already gone as the top of the pool is starting to dry.

Preacher puts two fingers on Smiley's neck, searching for a pulse in his carotid artery. Breathless, he waits for a faint push against the pressure he is exerting on the artery. "Yes!" he exclaims. "Smiley, this is Preacher. I'm going to call an ambulance. Hang on. Don't you dare die on me."

Scanning the room, he spies the telephone and dials 911. When his call is answered, he says, "This is Preacher. Who am I talking to?" He listens to the reply. "Great! Listen, Caleb, I need an ambulance and the sheriff out at Tucker's place. And they can't get here fast enough. I've got a man down with a head wound. He's unconscious with a faint heartbeat. Hurry up!"

Preacher slams the phone down, brings his pistol back up, and proceeds down the hallway. He stops at the closed door of the bathroom. Squatting beside the door, he taps the door with the barrel of his pistol and says, "Come out with your hands up." Hearing nothing, he reaches up and opens the door. He steps inside and notices the shower curtain is closed. Sweat beads up above his upper lip and at his hairline. In one motion he steps toward the curtain, grabs it, and jerks off the curtain rod.

No one is there.

When he turns to leave the bathroom, he sees movement and quickly raises his gun to fire until he sees his reflection in the mirror about to shoot back at him. He curses softly. *Sorry, Lord, that one just slipped out. I promise I'll do better.*

He exits the bathroom and walks past the open door of an empty bedroom. He looks under the bed and in the closet. After finding nothing, he moves toward Smiley's bedroom at the end of the hall. Once he's made sure no one is in there, he heads back through the living room and into the kitchen. Drawers have been pulled out and lie on their sides with their contents scattered all over the floor. A roll of duct tape lies by itself on the kitchen table.

In the distance he hears the sounds of sirens. *It's about time!*

On the other side of the kitchen, the door to Tucker's bedroom is shut. Preacher clicks off the safety on his pistol. Moving silently, he steps to the door and rests his ear against it. He hears a metallic click on the other side and jumps away from the door. "There's no place for you to go," he says. "The sheriff is on his way. Lay your gun down and come out with your hands up."

When there is no response, Preacher steps back a few feet, bends down low, and runs straight toward the door. He hits the door with his shoulder, and it jerks out of the frame. When he hits the floor, he rolls and jumps up with his pistol ready. He sees no one. As pieces of wood from the doorjamb continue floating down to the floor, he hears the metallic click again and notices the wand on the bedroom blinds is tapping against the metal slats due to its position above a floor register.

Slowly, Preacher stands up and wipes the sweat off his face. He shoves the pistol into his waistband. Hearing the ambulance and sheriff's car arriving outside, he rushes to the front door.

The two EMTs approach the house. "Right in here," Preacher says. When they step inside, he points to Smiley and says, "I didn't move him. The pulse is very faint. He has a head wound."

Leaving them to do their job, Preacher meets Sheriff Ron Harris at the bottom of the porch steps.

"What's happened?" the sheriff asks.

"I was just dropping in for a visit," Preacher replies. "I found Smiley Carter unconscious in the floor with a pool of blood under his head, and Tucker is nowhere to be found. There was some sort of commotion because the entertainment center is in a shambles and the TV is shattered."

Frowning, Harris says, "Did you check the barn?"

"I didn't walk over there, but I didn't see anything from a distance. Her truck is here, and she wouldn't have walked any great distance to go somewhere else."

"So where do you think she is?"

"I don't have a clue."

Pointing to the pistol in Preacher's waistband, Harris says, "What's that for?"

"Something felt wrong here. The door wasn't closed when I got here. I called out and no one answered. After I checked to see that Tucker's truck was here, I decided there might be someone else inside the house. For all I knew Tucker and Smiley were dead. So I went to my motorcycle and got my pistol."

Nodding his head, the sheriff says in a low voice, "Does this have anything to do with the undercover job you're working on with the TBI?"

"I don't see how it could."

"Okay then, let's step inside."

One of the EMTs is coming out the door as they are going in.

"How is he?" Preacher asks.

"He's alive, but barely. It looks like a gunshot wound to the head."

As the two men step inside, Harris asks Preacher, "Did you touch anything?"

"Only a couple of doorknobs and the phone."

"I'm going to look around."

As Harris walks away, Preacher says to the remaining EMT, "Is he going to make it?"

"He's unresponsive, but we do have a heartbeat. We're taking him to the hospital at Martin to get him stabilized, then they'll probably send him to the Med in Memphis."

As if on cue, the other EMT reenters the house with the gurney and positions it parallel to Smiley.

"Can I help?" Preacher asks.

"Thanks. We've got it," one of them answers.

Preacher watches as they lift Smiley onto the gurney and strap him in place. Sheriff Harris walks back into the living room as they are rolling Smiley out to the waiting ambulance.

"It doesn't look like robbery," Harris says.

"I agree," Preacher says.

"I noticed the light flashing on the answering machine. Let's see who has called her."

"I'm surprised she has an answering machine," Preacher says. "Her grandkids probably made her get one."

The sheriff takes an ink pen from his shirt pocket and pushes the play button on the answering machine with it.

"You have one message," the machine announces. There is a moment of silence and then a voice says, "This message is for Big Country. If you ever want to see your grandmother alive again, you'll return what you stole. Just put it back where you stole it from and everything will be square. Do not involve the police in this, or you'll never see your grandmother again." The machine clicks off.

The two men look at each other.

"Who in the world is Big Country?" Harris asks.

Shaking his head, Preacher says, "I have no idea. I've never heard anyone called that."

"Do you recognize the voice?"

"No. It sounded like a black man, don't you think?"

"Agreed. I wonder if this guy has made a mistake. Maybe he hit the wrong house and Tucker has nothing to do with whatever he thinks she does."

"The kids need to come home so we can talk to them," Preacher says.

"Yeah, but who's going to call them to tell them Tucker's been kidnapped and Smiley Carter may be dead?"

CHAPTER THIRTY-TWO

March rolls on his side and flips and punches the pillow beneath his head.

"What's the matter?" Debbie asks sleepily.

"I can't go to sleep."

Sitting up, Debbie lays her hand on his arm. "Why not?"

"Something's wrong. I can feel it."

He hears her click on the lamp on her side of the bed. "What do you mean something's wrong?" she asks.

March throws back the covers and gets out of bed. "I don't know how to explain it, but something is wrong somewhere. Call it a sixth sense if you want to, or ESP. Whatever it is, it's bad, really bad." He rubs his hand on his recently clean-shaven cheek then across his mouth. "I don't want to keep you awake. I'm going to go sit in the living room."

March makes his way into the living room and sits in his recliner. He pushes the button on his clock, and it responds by telling him it is 1:14 a.m.

From the edge of the living room, Debbie asks, "Do you want me to call Tucker or August or April to make sure nothing has happened?"

Surprised to hear her voice, March says, "What are you doing up?"

"You don't seriously expect me to go back to sleep knowing that something has happened, or perhaps someone is in trouble, do you?"

"No, I guess not. I should have just gotten up and not said anything. But don't call anyone, because I might be wrong. Then I would just be upsetting someone else." He motions to her, "Just come sit in my lap and we'll wait and see if I'm right."

Debbie eases into his lap and spreads the comforter from their bed over them. "I've never seen you like this. I'm scared."

"It's been a long time since I've felt this way. I'm scared myself."

Debbie gently strokes his face and kisses his cheek.

Suddenly, the phone at March's elbow rings.

Both he and Debbie jump. Debbie gives a cry.

After the second ring, March picks up the receiver. "Hello," he says. He listens to the caller. Without warning, he stands up, dumping Debbie onto the floor. "Is she all right?!" he cries. After another pause, he turns to Debbie and says, "Debbie, do you know how to get to the UT Medical Center?"

"Yes."

Into the receiver, March says, "Yes, she knows where it is. We'll meet you there." After hanging up the phone, March reaches down toward Debbie. "I'm sorry, Debbie. Are you okay?"

Taking his hand and pulling herself up, Debbie says, "Sure, I'm okay. But what was that phone call about?"

"It was August. A policeman came to his apartment a few minutes ago to tell him that April is in the hospital."

"What's wrong with her?"

"We don't know. The officer wouldn't tell him."

Debbie grabs his hand and begins walking toward the bedroom. "Then hurry, let's get dressed. It won't take us long to get there at this time of night."

March keeps his fingers on Debbie's arm as they hurry through the doors of the hospital's emergency room entrance. He hears snippets of conversation and a couple people groaning as they pass through the waiting area. The hospital's intercom pages the names of doctors.

Debbie suddenly stops. She says, "We're the family of April Tucker, who was brought in this evening. Where is she?"

After a moment, a woman says, "Down that hallway. Second door on the left."

Debbie immediately starts moving and March has to take a couple of quick steps to keep up with her.

March picks up the sound of August's voice farther down the hall, and he calls out to him, "August!"

"Here comes my brother and his fiancée," August says.

Debbie slows her pace and comes to a stop.

"What's going on?" March asks. "Where's April, and how is she?"

"March," August says, "this here is Officer Henderson. He's a policeman."

"Hello, Mr. Tucker," the deep voice of a black man says.

The adrenaline March has been holding back begins leaking through the dam he has put up. His voice rises as he asks, "What's a policeman doing here? What's going on?!"

Debbie slips her arm through March's arm and says, "Let's give them a chance to tell us what has happened."

"At approximately 11:30 tonight," the officer begins, "April was found outside the emergency room entrance. Apparently she'd been dumped there. She had been beaten and was unconscious."

Without warning, March grabs for the policeman. Grasping a handful of his jacket, March jerks him toward him and says, "Who hurt my sister?! Where is he?!"

Both Debbie and August cry out, "March!" Debbie pulls on his arm as August tries to unlock his fingers from their grip on the officer's jacket.

"March, let go!" Debbie says.

As suddenly as he had grabbed the policeman, March releases his grip and takes a step back. Like trying to shake loose the images of a nightmare, March shakes his head. In a calmer voice, he says, "I'm sorry. I shouldn't have done that. I'm very sorry."

"It's okay," the even voice of policeman says. "No harm meant. No harm done."

"Please," Debbie says, "go on with your story."

"As I said, your sister had been beaten and dumped outside the ER. Her blood alcohol content indicates she'd been drinking heavily."

"Wait a minute," August says. "As far as I know April hardly ever drinks. The most I've ever seen her drink is a couple of beers."

"I agree," Debbie says.

"Hmmm." The officer mulls this information over. "That may be true," he says, "but she was very drunk tonight. The other thing you need to know is that she was raped."

Debbie gasps, "Oh my god!"

The dam that has held back March's adrenaline bursts open. He clenches his fists until he feels his fingernails biting into his palms. In a growl, he says, "Whoever did this is a dead man. I will find him and I'll kill him."

"Everybody take it easy now," Officer Henderson intones. "Let's not be making threats."

"Mister," March says, "that is not a threat. That's a promise."

"Have you arrested a suspect?" August asks.

"No, sir. There are no clear suspects. April hasn't yet been able to tell us what happened. She keeps drifting in and out of consciousness. The only name we've heard her say is James. Do you all have any idea who that could be?"

"You have got to be kidding me," August says with alarm. "Not James!"

"You know this man?" the officer asks.

"She's his nanny," Debbie says. "But he couldn't have done this."

"Why do you say that?" the officer asks.

"Well, I mean, he's not that kind of person. He's a therapist and—"

"Anybody can do anything, given the right set of circumstances," March interjects.

A door close by opens and Officer Henderson says, "Here's the doctor. I'll let you all talk with him while I go check on a couple other things."

"I'm Doctor Oliver," a woman says with a young-sounding voice.

"How is she?" Debbie asks.

"She's pretty banged-up. She has a fractured eye socket and a broken nose. She may lose a couple of teeth, as well. She received several blows to her body, but X-rays show nothing is broken there. Lots of minor scrapes and bruises. But all in all I believe she'll be okay physically."

"What do you mean, she'll be okay physically?" March asks.

Doctor Oliver clears her throat. "This will be difficult for you to hear. April was raped vaginally and anally. And semen was found in her mouth, too."

Debbie bursts into tears and pushes her face into March's arm.

Like a roaring bear, March cries out, "Arrr!"

Running footsteps approach them. "Is everything okay here?" Officer Henderson asks.

"Yes, Officer," Doctor Oliver says. "I was just finishing up. Once April becomes more coherent I think she'll be better able to tell us exactly what happened."

"Can we see her?" August asks.

"Sure, that'll be fine."

The three shell-shocked family members start toward the door to April's room.

"Just a minute," the policeman says. "I need an address for this James person."

"I'm telling you," Debbie says, "it can't be him."

"You let us decide that," the policeman says in a flat tone.

After giving him James's address, they walk silently into April's room holding each other's hands.

Standing between August and Debbie, March feels them squeeze his hands at the same time as they react to their first glimpse of April.

"Oh no," August whispers.

When they stop, Debbie whispers to March, "We're beside her bed."

"April," August says clearly, "it's me, August. March is here, too. And so is Debbie. Can you hear me, April?"

The cadence of the beeping monitors is the only sound that tells them April is still clinging to life.

"April," March says huskily, "this is March. I'm going to put my hand on you so I can see you." After finding the rail on her bed, March next locates April's arm. He moves his hand carefully up to her shoulder, then to her neck. With a touch as light as a feather but as sensitive as a bloodhound's nose, he moves his fingers over her face. He pauses at her swollen bottom lip and he clenches his teeth. He discovers her eye swollen shut. When he touches the stitches above it, he winces involuntarily. His finger travels the length of the bandage on her nose. Tears well up in his eyes.

Beside him, he hears both August and Debbie sniffing with their own tears.

Placing both hands on the side of April's face, he bends down and kisses her forehead. As he does, his tears drip onto her. "Listen to me, baby sister. You will survive this. You hear me? You will live. Don't worry, I will find whoever did this to you. And when I do, they will regret the day they were born. That is my promise to you."

April moans and says, "James, is that you?"

"No," March says, "your family is here. It's March, August, and Debbie. You are in a safe place. Don't be afraid. James isn't here."

In a voice thick with emotion, August says, "She's gone back to sleep, March."

Straightening back up, March answers him, "She may look like she's asleep, but she could still be aware of us and what we are saying. Trust me on that one."

"April, this is Debbie. We're all here for you. We're going to take care of you. I love you."

There is a knock at the door. March hears it open.

"Can I speak to you all, please?" It is the policeman again.

In single file, they exit April's room. March takes out his handkerchief and blows his nose.

"Yes sir, Officer," August says, "what is it that you need?"

"I don't hardly know how to tell you all this. I heard some traffic over my radio and learned that the sheriff's office in Weakley County has been trying to find either you or March."

March feels a chill run through him and his heart feels as heavy as a stone. "What do they want with us?"

"Do you all know Smiley Carter?" Officer Henderson asks.

"Sure." August says, "That's my father."

"I'm sorry, sir," the policeman says, "but your father has been shot and is in critical condition."

"What?!" August screams. "What happened?"

"That's really all I know about him, but that's not all. There was a woman. They only used the name Tucker in the report."

"That's our grandmother, who raised us," March cuts in.

"Well, I'm afraid your grandmother has been kidnapped."

CHAPTER THIRTY-THREE

With her wrists duct-taped behind her and her mouth sealed with a piece of duct tape, Tucker struggles to keep her panic in check. The black hood covering her head and face make it impossible to see where her captor is taking her. The smooth roads they've been traveling tell her he has kept to the highway so far.

Her captor slows again and turns to the right. This time the road is rough and filled with potholes. The jostling of the truck, coupled with her inability to anticipate the sudden jerks, causes Tucker to be slammed against the passenger door. Her head strikes the window. Stars twinkle in the periphery of her limited vision as she almost passes out from the blow.

The driver slows to a crawl and travels several more yards before coming to a stop. "Don't run off," he laughs. "I'll be right back."

When she hears him exit the truck, Tucker pulls and tugs at her bindings, but to no avail. She rolls onto her back, lies flat in the seat, then pulls her knees to her chest.

After several moments, Tucker hears the click of the door handle on the driver's door. With both feet she kicks toward it. Her feet hit the door just as it begins to open, slamming it into her kidnapper. Her efforts are rewarded with a cry of pain from her captor. But when the air is suddenly filled with angry swearing, her hope that he has been disabled disappears.

Suddenly the passenger door is jerked open. "I'm going to kill you, old woman! I think you busted my knee cap!" the redheaded man cries. "I'm going to kill you right here! You hear me?! You are dead!" He grabs her under her arms, drags her out of the truck, and lets her fall on the ground.

Tucker lands hard on her side and all her air goes out with a whoosh. While fighting to get her breath back she hears the metallic click of the hammer on a pistol being pulled back. Suddenly the hood is jerked off her head. She's surprised to see that it's nearly dark. The smell of a body of water close by fills her nostrils. All of a sudden the duct tape is ripped off her mouth. An involuntary cry leaps out of her.

The redheaded man steps into her field of vision. The amber glow of his truck's parking lights makes both his hair and his complexion appear orange. Pointing the gun at her face, he says, "I'm going to enjoy killing you. I wanted to see your face when I pulled the trigger."

"Y' ain't gonna kill me," Tucker replies.

"Oh, I'm not, am I? And why not?"

"'Cause y' b'lieve I'm yore bait t' catch somebody else."

He stares at her and finally lets the hammer of his pistol down slowly with his thumb. "Stand up."

"I can't," Tucker says. "I need my hands cut free so's I can get up."

"I'll cut your hands loose when I'm ready to," the man snaps. "Get on your knees and I'll help you stand up."

Tucker complies with his request and he helps her to her feet. "Where are we at?" she asks.

"We're at my old stomping grounds. Where we're going, nobody will find us."

"What's yore name?"

"Not that it's any of your business, but everybody calls me Red."

"Well, y' listen t' me, Red," Tucker says through her clenched teeth. "Th' day will come when you'll beg me t' kill you. 'Cause what I aim t' do t' y' ain't like nothin' y' ever heard of. Death'll be a relief."

Red laughs. "I'm here to tell you, old woman, you're not like any woman I've ever met. I think you really must be crazy."

Tucker takes a step toward him. "Let me tell y' what kind of crazy I am. I'm th' kind of crazy that y' better be scared of."

Red raises his pistol and points it at Tucker's leg. In a calm and icy tone, he says, "You're right, I'm not going to kill you. But that doesn't mean I won't shoot you. Whether you like it or not, you're going to help me get what I want. And after I do, I'll leave you to the buzzards. Now, stand right there and wait for me." Walking back to the truck, he turns off the lights, and shuts the motor off. He closes and locks the doors. He slips a small flashlight out of his jacket pocket, turns it on, points it on the ground, and says, "Follow that path."

Tucker begins moving down the shadowy path. It meanders between giant oak and poplar trees. A little farther she spies some cypress knees crowding around the mother trunk that gave birth to them. The smell of the water becomes stronger and the ground becomes spongy with moisture. Suddenly the path disappears into black nothingness.

"Stop," Red commands. He comes around her and walks toward the end of the path.

Tucker strains her eyes as she looks past him. *Them's flashin' beacon lights out there. He's done brought me t' Reelfoot Lake.* Like a sleeping dragon that smells fresh flesh, an old memory stirs in Tucker. A chill of fear zips through her spine. The sound of splashing water brings her back to the present, allowing her to escape the coming nightmare. Looking at the scattered light from the waving flashlight, she sees Red pushing a boat into the water.

"This is an original, wooden Calhoun Reelfoot boat," Red says proudly. "It's probably one of the only wooden ones you'll find still being used around here. It was my dad's and his dad's before him. It's designed to handle all the submerged logs and stumps in the lake—a real stump jumper! And it's hard to turn over as long as you sit still and let it take all the bumps. But if you start trying to shift your weight around or move suddenly, it'll pitch you in the water. I'm telling you this so you'll behave. Because if you fall in, I'm not fishing you out. I'll find another way to get what I want. Do you understand?"

"I understand," Tucker replies. "Now cut loose m' hands so's I can git in without fallin'."

She feels the cold steel of a knife blade between her wrists.

"Just remember what I told you," Red says. With a quick pull, he slices through the duct tape.

With her hands free, she pulls the duct tape off each wrist. She walks forward, puts her hands on each side of the bow, and steps over the bow and into the boat. It rocks back and forth as she makes her way to the other end. Childhood images of a parallel incident pierce her heart. When she sits down and faces the middle of the boat, her teeth are chattering—but not because of the chill of the December night. The smell of the waking dragon's breath has her in the grip of fear.

Red pushes the boat off the bank and jumps in. Gripping the bow-facing oars, he rows farther into the inky blackness of the lake.

Backlit by the stars, bushy cypress trees are silent witnesses to the dark crime being carried out on the lake. Small waves lap against the side of the boat.

Blinking rapidly, Tucker tries to stay in the present and avoid falling into the dark rabbit hole of her past.

Red pulls the rope on the Briggs & Stratton engine in the middle of the boat and it coughs to life. As he turns the throttle, the long shaft that runs from the engine through the back of the boat to the propeller starts turning. He makes a wide turn and heads out at a slow, steady speed. An occasional thud is heard as the boat strikes a stump lying just below the surface or passes over a floating log.

After almost an hour, Red gradually slows the boat until he completely cuts the engine off. The boat coasts between wooden pylons that support a small hunting cabin. When the boat is completely underneath the floor of the cabin, Red ties it to a pylon. He switches on his flashlight and shines it on the floor over them. He stands up and pushes up a trapdoor in the floor. Reaching inside, he finds a rope ladder and lowers it into the boat. "Okay," he says to Tucker, "this is where we get out." He crawls up the ladder and disappears into the cabin.

Tucker raises her head and sees yellow light coming through the trapdoor. Keeping her body low so she won't lose her balance, she makes her way to the ladder and begins climbing up it. When her head breaks the plane of the floor, she sees Red using a match to light a kerosene lamp sitting on a crude wooden table. Four cane-bottom chairs are slid underneath the table. Another burning kerosene lamp on a wall illuminates a wood-burning cookstove below it.

Tucker's entire body is trembling as she continues crawling through the opening and finally stands inside the cabin.

"Home sweet home," Red says. He bends down in front of the stove, opens a door, and sticks a wadded-up piece of newspaper and some kindling inside. He strikes another match, lights the newspaper, and closes the door. "We'll have some heat in a few minutes." Like a tour guide in a museum, he gives a wave of his arm around the one-room cabin and says, "This place has been in my family for three generations. What do you think . . . uh . . . What should I call you anyway?"

In a childlike voice, Tucker says, "My name's Tucker."

Red walks to the far end of the room. The blackness at that end swallows him. "Well, Tucker," he says from the darkness, "this is going to be your home until this matter gets straightened out."

The sudden flare of a lit match illuminates Red's face and the far wall. He lights a kerosene lamp hanging on the wall, and the entire end of the room is revealed. Four rustic, single beds are lined in a row on the wall.

Tucker's eyes widen as she sees a small, dark-haired girl wearing a dress and lying on one of the beds. Her legs are spread unnaturally wide. Her panties hang rumpled on one foot that is hanging off the side of the bed. Tucker looks at the man standing beside the bed, zipping up his pants. It is her father.

CHAPTER THIRTY-FOUR

What are we going to do?!" August's panic-stricken voice echoes in the hospital hallway. "I've got to go and see about my dad."

"But we can't leave April," March says. "She's going to need us now more than she ever has. When she becomes fully aware of what has happened to her, I'm afraid she'll try to kill herself. I know that when I was in the place she's in, that's what I wanted to do."

Debbie slips her hand into his hand and intertwines her fingers with his. She says, "Why would anyone shoot Smiley Carter and kidnap Tucker?"

"I can't imagine a reason for either act," August replies. "My first thought was there was some kind of botched robbery attempt. But that really doesn't explain the kidnapping. Kidnapping is always about a ransom of some kind."

"Maybe someone in Dresden knows about the money Tucker received from Ella's life insurance policy, and that's what they're after," March suggests.

"March," Debbie says, "what if you and I stay here with April while August goes on to Dresden?"

"I don't like the idea of us splitting up," March answers. "I'm worried about August driving all that way by himself at this hour. What if you get sleepy and have a wreck?"

"Sleepy?!" August exclaims. "I'm so wired up right now I probably won't sleep for days."

"You say that now," March says, "but once you hit the interstate and it's quiet, all that adrenaline will be gone. You're going to need someone to keep you awake."

"Wait," Debbie says, "you've got that fancy new bag phone, don't you, August?"

"Yeah. I just haven't figured out what all it will do."

"What if you called us every hour, to check in and talk to someone for a few minutes so you won't get so sleepy?"

"Sure, I can do that. That's a good idea."

"I guess that's the best we can do," March reluctantly agrees. "And if you don't call us every hour, we'll be calling you."

"No problem," August says. "Besides, I want reports on April's progress."

Suddenly, they hear screaming from April's room. A running nurse beats them to the door. As she rushes into the room she tells the trio to wait outside.

April's screams continue.

After a moment, Debbie says, "Here comes another nurse. I think she has a syringe with her."

When the second nurse steps into the room March hears the creaking leather belts of Officer Henderson approaching them. "What's going on?" the policeman asks.

"Don't know," March says. "April just started screaming. Two nurses are with her now."

As he is speaking, April's screams cease.

"She's probably becoming more alert and aware of what's going on around her," the officer says. "That's a good sign. Maybe she can tell us more details about what happened to her."

The door to April's room opens. March detects the scent of honeysuckle he noticed when the first nurse dashed into April's room. She says, "We've given her a shot of Valium to calm her. So she's going to sleep for a while."

"Did she say anything?" the policeman asks.

"She kept repeating the name James, just like she was doing when she first arrived."

"That's it," Officer Henderson says, "I'm paying a visit to this guy's house to see what his story is."

As he walks away, Debbie says, "I just don't believe James had anything to do with this."

"You're too trusting," March says. "This guy could be some sort of sexual predator. He works with girls out at that wilderness place where he could get away with lots of things."

"Well, listen you two," August says. "I'm heading west. We'll be talking to each other."

March holds his arms open. "You be careful. I love you."

August steps into his brother's embrace. "Hey, I'm a big boy. I can take care of myself. I love you, too."

March listens as Debbie and August exchange a good-bye kiss. "We'll call if anything happens here," Debbie says.

"Okay," August says. "Bye now. Oh, by the way, when did you shave off your beard?"

Rubbing his cheek, March says, "Debbie whacked it off tonight. She likes me better clean-shaven."

"Well it makes you look younger," August says. "Keep it that way."

March and Debbie face the direction of August's retreating footsteps. When they can no longer be heard, Debbie says, "You want something to eat?"

"Nothing to eat," March answers, "but some coffee sure would be good."

"I'll be right back."

"Wait. Take me into April's room before you go. I want to hold her hand and talk to her."

Taking his hand, Debbie leads March into April's room and stops beside her bed. "I'll be back in a minute," she whispers.

March locates April's hand, picks it up, and gently holds it between his two large hands. "April, this is March. Some bad things happened to you tonight, things that you will learn about when you wake up from the dark place you've retreated into. Someone very evil has done this to you. It is not your fault that it happened. That's a truth I want you to tell yourself over and over.

"I also want you to know that what has happened to you has not affected my love, or August's or Debbie's, for you. You are still dear to us. Nothing can ever change that. What happened to you does not define who you are.

"You will have to work hard to not let what happened to you poison your heart. You are alive, April! That's the most important thing. As long as we're alive, we can find a way to overcome anything."

"March?" April's voice is hoarse and her tongue sounds thick.

"Yes, April, it's me!"

"I love you, March."

"And I love you. How do you feel?"

April doesn't reply.

Squeezing her hand, March says, "April, talk to me."

The door to the room opens and the smell of coffee wafts in.

"Debbie," March says, "come here quick. April's awake." He feels Debbie at his side.

"She doesn't look awake," Debbie says.

"She just spoke to me. She told me she loved me."

"April," Debbie says, "this is Debbie. Can you hear me? Speak to me or squeeze my hand if you hear me." There is no response from April.

"I promise, she talked to me," March says.

"I believe you. She must have just surfaced for a moment from the Valium haze they put her in. But it's a good sign that she spoke to you and knew you. Here, take your coffee."

Releasing April's hand, March waits for Debbie to press the cup of coffee into his open palm. Lifting it to his mouth, he feels the heat rising to his face. Carefully, he takes a sip. "Mmm, that's good, no matter where it came from."

"There are a couple of chairs in here that we can rest in, if you feel like sitting down. Or we can go to the waiting area," Debbie tells him.

"I'd rather stay in here. I want to be here in case April wakes up again. And we need to keep up with the time, too, so we can know when to expect a call from August."

After sitting down, they sip their coffee in silence.

Over the next couple hours they answer two phone calls from August. Nurses come in and check on April periodically. But April doesn't regain consciousness.

A little before 4:00 a.m. a knock on the door awakens March. When he doesn't hear Debbie getting up and going to the door, he finds his way to the door. When he opens it, the voice of Officer Henderson greets him. "I hope I'm not disturbing you, but I wanted to report to you what we found at James Washington's house."

March steps into the hallway and closes the door behind him. He runs his hand through his hair, stuffs his shirttail back into his pants, and says, "Thanks for coming back by to tell me. What did you find?"

"There wasn't anything about my conversation with him that made me suspicious that he did this to your sister. He seemed genuinely shocked when I told him what happened to her. However, he did shed some light onto what April's state of mind might have been. It seems he told her that she would no longer be in his employ. April got very upset about it and stormed out of the house. She had called a taxi to pick her up and told James she was going to your brother's apartment."

"Did James say why he was firing April?"

"No, he didn't say. Why do you ask?"

"It's just that April loved being there and taking care of his boys. It made her feel like she had a sense of purpose. And from everything she told us, James valued her very much. I just wonder what happened."

"Has she woken up or said anything?"

"She woke up twice. One of the times was when you were still here and she was screaming bloody murder. The other time she called me by name and told me she loved me. But that's it."

The policeman's shoes squeak on the floor as he shifts his weight. "What I'm trying to learn is what happened that prevented April from making it to your brother's apartment. We're checking with all the taxi companies to see if we can locate the one that picked her up."

"Do you think it could have been the taxi driver that did this to her?" March asks.

CHAPTER THIRTY-FIVE

The sun has barely cleared the horizon, filling the cloudless morning with its dazzling light, when August turns into Tucker's driveway. Just off the edge of the driveway, Preacher's motorcycle leans on its kickstand.

August jogs to the front door and walks in without knocking. Just as he clears the doorway, he sees movement to his left. Preacher is pointing a pistol directly at him. Throwing up his hands, August cries, "Don't shoot!"

Preacher immediately lowers the pistol and says, "August, I'm sorry. I didn't hear you drive up." He walks over to him and gives him a hug. "I didn't mean to scare you. I'm just on edge over what happened here yesterday."

Looking over Preacher's shoulder, August sees a pool of suds on the floor and a scrub brush lying in the middle of it. "How's Smiley? Where's Tucker? Who's responsible for this? What are you doing here? Why—"

"Easy, easy," Preacher says gently. "Not so fast. I'll tell you everything we know. But first, you look exhausted. Do you need some coffee and something to eat?"

August's shoulders sag. "Yes, that sounds good. It felt like I would never get here."

"Let's go into the kitchen. You can sit and relax while I see if I can find something to fix. You're by yourself?"

"Yes. March and Debbie stayed at the hospital with April."

Preacher stops and spins around to look at him. "The hospital? What's wrong with April?"

"Preacher," August says wearily, "this has been the most agonizing night of my life. April was raped and beaten and dumped at the entrance to the ER."

Preacher stares at him with his mouth open.

"Yes," August says, "it's true. She was raped every way imaginable. And her face looks like she was hit by a train."

Tears begin running down Preacher's cheeks. He tries to say something, but nothing comes out. He hugs August again. As he pats August's back, he manages to say, "I'm so, so sorry."

When Preacher releases his hold on him, August turns him around and nudges him forward. "Let's go sit at the table."

In the few seconds it takes for them to walk to the kitchen, Preacher has managed to compose himself. "Now you sit down. I'm going to cook us both some breakfast. I cannot imagine how full your head must be with thoughts chasing each other and how heavy your heart must be with worry. Let me tell you what happened here and then I want to hear about April.

"Yesterday I dropped by just to pay a visit and see how your dad and grandmother were doing. When I got here the door was open. I walked in and found Smiley on the floor with a pool of blood under his head. The living room was a wreck and the kitchen drawers had been emptied on the floor. Tucker was nowhere to be found. I called the sheriff and an ambulance. When the sheriff got here, he noticed that there was a message on Tucker's answering machine. The message was for someone named Big Country and said if he wanted to see his grandmother alive he needed to return what he'd stolen."

"Where's my dad now?" August asks.

"They took him to the hospital in Martin. I honestly don't know if he was transferred to Memphis or they kept him. We'll check on that after you eat."

"Who the heck is Big Country?"

"Sheriff Harris and I were hoping you kids could tell us because we're clueless."

"I've never heard of anyone called that. Is it possible that whoever did this came to the wrong house and all this is just a case of mistaken identity?"

"We did talk about that possibility." He sets two plates of scrambled eggs and toast on the table, then turns and gets the freshly brewed pot of coffee and pours them both a cup. "Dig in, and then tell me about April."

August takes several sips of coffee. "Ahh, that tastes wonderful." He stabs several bites of eggs and eats half of the piece of toast. "I didn't know I was so hungry."

"About April . . ." Preacher prompts him.

"Yeah, well the police got in touch with me last night and told me she was in the ER. I called March, and he and Debbie met me there. April hasn't come to yet, so no one knows for certain exactly what happened. For a while there was a suspicion that James, the man she works for, might have done it. But March told me while I was driving here that James had been interviewed by the police and was no longer a suspect."

"My gosh, this is all unbelievable. To have all these things happen to the same family in a matter of hours . . ." Preacher shakes his head.

"I'll tell you one thing," August says, "if they catch the person or persons that did this to April, they better put them in jail and keep them there because if March gets his hands on them, he'll kill them."

Nodding his head, Preacher says, "I can see why he would feel that way."

"No. I'm serious. You didn't see the look on his face or hear the tone of his voice when we were at the hospital. He will kill them if he gets a chance. I don't know if any of us, including Debbie, know everything about March's life when he was away from us. Underneath his calm, gentle exterior there's a rage I'm afraid of." He looks at Preacher and sees his eyes are glazed over, focused on something August cannot see.

After a few seconds, Preacher's gaze shifts to August's face and his eyes become alive again. "I know what it's like to live with that kind of rage inside. I hope I can help March before he does something that will ruin his life like I did mine."

August is about to ask Preacher to elaborate, but Preacher says, "You ready to go to the hospital?"

Images of Smiley fill August's mind. "Yes, let's go."

"We'll stop by the sheriff's office on the way. I'm sure Sheriff Harris would like to speak with you."

"Whatever you say," August replies.

Twenty minutes later, August parks in front of the Sheriff's Department and he and Preacher get out of his car.

At the front desk Preacher spies a deputy with the same receding hairline and frail-looking body as Barney Fife on *The Andy Griffith Show*. He catches the deputy's attention and asks, "Is Sheriff Harris in?"

"Who's asking?" the deputy replies.

"Tell him Preacher and August Tucker are here."

The deputy gets up and disappears through a door. A moment later he reappears and holds the door open. "Ya'll come ahead. The sheriff will see you."

As they pass the deputy, he says, "Third door on the right."

The door to the sheriff's office is open, so they walk on in.

Sheriff Harris stands behind his desk. Sticking out his hand, he says, "Good morning, Preacher. Good morning, August."

They both shake his hand.

"Before you start," Preacher says to Sheriff Harris, "you need to know that there's been trouble for this family in Knoxville last night, too."

The sheriff's eyebrows go up. "What do you mean?"

"You know who April is, don't you?"

"Sure I do. She's a beautiful young lady."

"Last night she was raped and beaten and dumped at a hospital."

The eyebrows that were peaked above the sheriff's eyes suddenly dart down and meet at the crease between his eyes. "How is she? Did they catch who did it?"

"She's beat up pretty bad," August says. "And she hasn't woken up enough yet for her to tell anyone what really happened. So no one's been arrested."

"I'm sure sorry," the sheriff offers. "Where is March?"

"He stayed in Knoxville with April."

"I told him about the message on the answering machine," Preacher says. "Big Country doesn't mean anything to him, either."

"Well I do have some good news about Smiley Carter," the sheriff says. "He was shot in the head but thankfully with a small caliber pistol. The bullet struck his skull at just the right angle that it sort of ricocheted and traveled under the skin and then exited without causing any serious damage. The deputy I had stationed at the hospital overnight told me this morning that Smiley is alert and can probably go home today."

"That's incredible!" August shouts. "It sounds like a miracle! I've never heard of a bullet ricocheting off someone's head." He begins to laugh and cry at the same time. "Talk about a hard head!"

Preacher puts his arm around August's shoulders. "No doubt God delivered him from death yet again." Looking at the sheriff, he says, "Did Smiley shed any light on what happened?"

Shaking his head, Sheriff Harris says, "No. He said he heard a crash in the living room. He was going to check it out but was so focused on watching where he was walking that he never looked up before getting shot. The only clue we've got is that cryptic message on the answering machine."

"If you don't need us anymore, August and I are going to run over and see Smiley."

"That's fine. You two go ahead. If Smiley remembers something that might be helpful, call me immediately. We've got to figure out where Tucker is."

CHAPTER THIRTY-SIX

Tucker opens her eyes. Lying on her side on the floor of the cabin, she notices the morning sun striking the floorboards and highlighting the film of dust covering them. Moving only her eyes, she looks at the woodpile beside the cookstove and notices that the axe and hatchet are still propped against the wall. Slowly she uncurls from the fetal position she slept in. A sharp pain in her side makes her wince. *I must of busted a rib 'r two when Red drug me outta th' truck last night.*

Behind her she hears the creaking springs in Red's bed as he shifts his weight.

All I gotta do is git t' that axe afore he wakes up.

As she begins standing, her joints play their usual morning song like a percussion ensemble, snapping and popping.

"You might have moved and snuck around like a cat when you were young," Red's voice comes from behind her, "but you've gotten too old for that now. I thought someone was knocking on the floor from underneath. I see where you're headed, so stop right there."

Tucker turns and faces him.

Stomping his feet into his cowboy boots, Red says, "What happened to you last night? I thought you had a stroke or something.

You got all glassy-eyed and acted like you couldn't hear or see anything. When you laid down on the floor and curled up like that, I decided to leave you alone. Lucky for me you didn't come to during the night, or you would have gotten that axe and made mincemeat out of me, wouldn't you have?"

With her face a mask of indifference, Tucker says, "Maybe this ain't th' first time I been here."

As he walks across the cabin, Red freezes midstride. "Huh? What did you say?"

"I said what I said," Tucker replies.

"Nobody's ever been here except family or friends of family." Red walks to the stove and begins putting some wood into it. "What makes you think you've been here before?"

"Did y' tell me y' got a woman from Dresden pregnant a long time ago?"

"What?" Red looks over his shoulder at Tucker. "What are you talking about? I asked you a question."

Folding her arms across her chest, Tucker says, "An' I asked you a question."

Red walks to the shelves stocked with canned goods and removes a can of Spam and a can of pork and beans. "Listen, old lady, I—"

"My name ain't old lady," Tucker interjects. "Call me Tucker."

Red rolls his eyes as he opens the can of Spam. Shaking the contents into the cast-iron skillet on top of the stove, he says, "Okay then, Tucker. I don't have to answer any of your questions. I'm the kidnapper here, and you're the prisoner, remember?"

"What did th' woman look like?" Tucker asks.

"Well she wasn't hard to look at, that's for sure," Red says with a smile. "She had a body that would make a man groan in his sleep and hair the color of a crow." He busies himself slicing the Spam into small bits.

"What about her eyes? What color was they?"

"Her eyes? Lord, who remembers what color a woman's eyes are? But now that you mention it, her eyes were an unusual shade of blue. They practically glowed, they were so bright."

Tucker swallows hard and squeezes her fists. "Don't y' think it's a sorry person who runs off an' leaves a woman when she's pregnant?"

Throwing his head back, Red cackles. "Who are you? My mother? Quit your preaching and sit down at the table."

As she moves to the table, Tucker looks out the windows and sees that the cabin is surrounded by water. She slides one of the chairs out from under the table and sits down. Once again her eyes fall on the axe.

Red bangs two metal plates on the table and scrapes food out of the skillet onto each of them.

"This looks like dog food," Tucker says. "What is it?"

"It's Spam and pork and beans mixed together. It's good! Don't insult my cooking. You better get used to it because that's going to be your staple while you're here."

"Don't I git a fork t' eat with?"

Red holds her stare. "Here's the deal, Tucker. There's no end to the number of things in this cabin that you could use as a weapon. But none of them are going to do you any good because I'm not staying here. After I eat this plateful, I'm heading back to shore. If you'll promise me that you'll not use it to attack me, I'll give you a fork."

"What makes y' think y' can trust me?"

"Because I believe you're old-school. You're one of those people who won't break a promise."

Reaching toward him, Tucker says, "Give me th' fork."

Red jerks it out of her reach. "Not until you say you promise."

Without looking at him, Tucker says, "I promise."

Once she gets her fork, she quickly shoves several bites in her mouth. Red does the same.

As they eat, they shoot quick glances at each other like two dogs that are on guard against the other trying to get their food.

After a few minutes, Tucker says, "Why are y' doin' this?"

Between bites, Red says, "I've told you. Big Country stole something from me, and I want it back."

"I don't know nobody named Big Country."

"So you know him by his real name. I showed you the picture with him in it, so I know he's your kin. I'm guessing you're his grandmother."

"You're wrong," Tucker says. "He ain't th' kind t' steal from folks."

"Whatever you say," Red replies dismissively. He scrapes together the last fragments on his plate and forks them into his mouth. Picking up his empty plate, he stands up.

"I'm thirsty," Tucker says.

"You can pour you some of that Jim Beam on the shelf, or you can fix you some coffee after I'm gone."

"I don't see no water fer makin' coffee."

"Use the lake water. That's what we always use. And when you have to use the bathroom, use the trapdoor in the floor. Now, I've got to get a move on." Red slips on his coat and gloves. He raises the trapdoor, then drops the rope ladder through it. "I'll be back. When I come, you will open this door and let the ladder down. Then you will go to that back wall and stand there until I get inside. So that I'll know where you are, you will keep a steady tapping on the floor with your foot. Understand?"

"What I understand," Tucker replies, "is that you is a dead man. Y' just don't know it yet. When y' come back, I'll be waitin' on y'. I promise y' that."

Shaking his head, Red says, "*Crazy* is the only word I can think of to describe you. You just do like I said." He climbs down the ladder to the waiting boat.

Tucker listens to the fading sound of the boat's motor as Red heads to shore. Silence fills the cabin. A piece of hickory pops loudly inside the stove as the fire converts the wood to gas and then ash. Looking over at the row of beds, Tucker sees her pa sleeping on his back. She rubs her eyes and he disappears.

Walking over to the stack of firewood, she grabs the axe. *I ain't puttin' up with this nightmare no more.* In quick steps, she walks to the bed. She raises the axe over her head and slams it down into the wooden frame. The sharp edge buries itself three inches deep. Tucker rocks the axe back and forth to free it. Again she raises the axe and slams it into the frame, six inches from the previous spot. When it strikes, a large chip of wood flies into the air. *Yes!*

Thirty minutes later, the mattress lies on the floor and the bed frame has been reduced to splinters, chunks, and pieces that are one to two feet long. Breathing heavily, Tucker wipes sweat from her reddened face. She squats down and gathers an armload of the wooden debris. She opens the door of the stove and pitches the wood into the eager flames. "Stay hungry, fire," she says aloud, "'cause I'm gonna be needin' y' t' help me git rid of Red."

CHAPTER THIRTY-SEVEN

March?"

Standing on the edge of a cliff, March hears a woman call his name. Someone squeezes his hand. Looking to his left, he sees a small girl with long blonde hair standing beside him.

"March, is that you?" she asks.

Suddenly, he recognizes that the girl is April.

"April," he says, "where have you been? Are you okay?"

"April, how do you feel?" another woman's voice says.

Realization dawns on March that the other woman's voice belongs to Debbie, and, like a spoonful of sugar stirred into a hot cup of coffee, the elements of his dream dissolve. He feels the hard stainless steel rail of April's hospital bed against the side of his head and the soft blanket underneath the back of his hand. A small hand squeezes and shakes his hand.

"March, wake up and talk to me."

Returning the squeeze, March says, "I'm awake, April. I'm right here. Gosh, it's good to hear your voice."

"You fell asleep holding her hand," Debbie says.

"What time is it?" March asks.

"It's a little past 7:00 in the morning," Debbie replies.

Letting go of April's hand, March stands up and stretches out the kinks from having slept in a chair for the last several hours.

"Where is your beard?" April says. "I wasn't sure that was you. It kind of scared me when I woke up and saw a strange man holding my hand."

March rubs his cheek, which produces a sound like sandpaper rubbing against a board. "Debbie cut it off last night."

"I like it," April says.

"How do you feel this morning?" Debbie asks.

"Like I was used as a tackling dummy by a college football team," April replies. "I hurt all over. How long have I been here?"

"You were brought here last night."

"Brought here? By who? What happened to me?"

March puts his hand on the bed and locates April's hand. Holding it between his hands, he says, "Don't you remember what happened last night?"

"Last . . . night . . ." April says slowly. "Last night . . ."

Keeping hold of April's hand with one of his, March lays his other hand gently against the side of her face. "If you don't remember, it's okay. You don't have to do that right now."

"Oh no," April says.

She grips his hand and he feels warm tears running down the side of her face.

Debbie puts her arms around March's waist and rests her head on his arm.

In a choked voice, April says, "I remember. I remember what happened. It was James."

"James did this to you?" March asks. He feels blood rushing to his head.

"No. That's not it," April says. "James fired me last night."

"Oh, April," Debbie says sympathetically. "I'm so sorry. Why did he do that?"

"Because he's a prick!" April spits the words out. "He's just like every other man in the world, only concerned about himself. He used me."

"Used you how?" March asks.

"He just wanted me to take care of his kids until his wife died. Now he's through with me and tossed me away like a piece of garbage."

"But I thought you and he were—" Debbie says.

"Ha! So did I," April cuts her off. "Obviously he was just playing me so I'd stick around. Telling me he loved me and giving me that kiss were just part of his plan; it didn't really mean anything."

"Do you want to talk about what happened last night?" March asks.

There's a knock on the door.

March turns his head and says, "Come in."

The door pushes open. "Good morning," a woman says, "I'm Detective Katherine Sullivan." Approaching the bed, she asks, "How is everyone this morning? You must be the brother?"

Extending his hand, March says, "Yes. My name is March and this is my fiancée, Debbie."

"You all can call me Kate. Hi, April. I'm with the sexual assault division and was hoping you could talk with me and tell me what happened last night. Do you feel up to it?"

"Yes," April replies.

"March, would you and Debbie mind stepping outside while I talk with April?"

"No!" April says. "I want them in here."

"Are you sure?" Kate asks. "Because I'm going to want lots of details that you might not want to share in front of them."

"Yes, it's okay," April says. "I was just about to tell them anyway."

Kate flips open the pages of a notebook. "You were at James's last night, correct?"

"Yes."

"Why don't you start there and tell us your story."

"I've grown very close to James since I've been a nanny for the kids," April begins. "Actually, I love him, and I thought he loved me the same way. But last night he blew all that up. He told me I didn't need to be there anymore. I begged and pleaded with him, but he wouldn't change his mind. That's when I got mad. After treating me special, and being kind and loving toward me, he just kicked me to the curb! He's nothing but an SOB. I called a cab to come get me. My plan was to go to August's."

"Who's August?" Kate asks.

"That's my other brother. He lives here in Knoxville, too. I packed a suitcase with as much as I could cram into it and went outside to wait for the cab. James told me not to leave angry, that I could wait until tomorrow to leave. But I wasn't going to stay there another second. When the cab came, I got in and gave him August's address. On the way there, we passed by a bar, and I had the sudden urge to get drunk. I made the cab stop, and I got out and went in."

"Do you remember the name of the bar?" Kate inquires.

"It's called T-time, like the *T* in UT. Lots of kids from campus go there, including some of the athletes."

"You've been there before?"

"Yeah, a couple of times."

"Do you usually get drunk when you drink?"

"No, not at all. I bet I've only been drunk a couple of times in my life. Usually I just drink a beer or maybe two."

"But this time you intended to get drunk?"

"Yes I did! I was angry and felt humiliated by James. All I cared about was forgetting everything, and I figured alcohol was the quickest, surest way to make that happen."

"That all checks out," Kate says. "We've talked to the cab driver and recovered the suitcase you left in the cab."

"Oh?" April says. "I guess I was so upset I didn't even think about that."

"So, what happened when you went into the bar?" Kate asks.

"I grabbed a stool at the bar and told the bartender to start setting me up shots of whiskey and not to stop until I passed out. He looked at me kind of funny and then laughed. I guess he thought I was joking. I don't know how many I downed before the room started spinning and my stomach felt queasy. I suddenly felt like I was going to throw up and headed toward the bathroom. More than once I stumbled and people steadied me. Then this one guy, a really big guy, put his arm around my waist and lifted me off the floor. I started gagging, and he rushed me to the bathroom and shoved me through the door.

"After I threw up in the toilet, I splashed some water on my face and walked out of the bathroom. This same guy was waiting for me. He acted really concerned and said I reminded him of his little sister and asked if I needed a ride somewhere. I really don't remember what I said, but the next thing I knew I was in a car and he was driving. I just wanted to sleep, so I closed my eyes."

"Can you describe the man to me?" Detective Sullivan asks.

"He was tall."

"How tall? Tall like your brother here?"

"Maybe even taller," April replies. "And he was big, too. He had on a letterman jacket like the UT football players wear."

"What do you remember about his face and hair?"

April frowns as she searches her memory. "His hair was cut short and I think it was brown. He had fat cheeks. I remember that for some reason. And his nose was sort of crooked, like maybe it had been broken."

"What color were his eyes?"

"I don't remember except that they were dark."

"Okay then," Kate says, "you went to the bar and got drunk. Then you're in the car with this guy who sounds like he is an athlete. What happened next?"

April is quiet for several moments. She grabs March's hand and squeezes it.

"It's okay, April," March says. "We're here with you. You're in a safe place here. As long as I'm beside you, no one is going to hurt you. Take a deep breath."

April begins whimpering. In a trembling voice, she says, "I guess I passed out in the car. When I came to I was lying on a bed with no clothes on. It was a dorm room. The guy who picked me up was in there but so were two other guys. Music was playing really loud. They were laughing and drinking beer. They all flipped a coin and one of the other guys said, 'I get her first!' He came at me unzipping his pants. When he took his cock out, he told me to spread my legs. I screamed and he clapped his hand over my mouth and told me to shut up. I bit his finger hard enough that I tasted blood. He jerked his hand away and I screamed again. That's when he hit me. All I could see was stars. I thought I was going to pass out." April's words are choked off. In a whisper she says, "I wish I had."

March bends down, kisses her hand and holds it against his tear-stained cheek. "My sweet baby sister," he says softly.

"The guy shoved my legs apart and entered me. He rammed me over and over until I felt like I was being broken into pieces. Then suddenly he was done and got off of me. The guy who drove me there came to the bed and told me to roll over. When I didn't move, he flipped me over like a ragdoll. I didn't know what was going on until all of a sudden he entered me from behind. Oh my god!" April suddenly screams.

Debbie bursts into tears and cries out April's name.

"Isn't this enough?" March says angrily to Kate.

"I'm sorry," Kate says evenly, "but this is what I have to hear, and I have to hear it all."

April says, "I'm okay. I can do this. When he entered me from behind I felt like he was ripping me in two. I screamed and screamed. Someone hit me in my side and I lost my breath. When he finally got off of me, I laid there. I thought I was dying. I could feel fluid coming out of me and didn't know if it was my blood or their semen or both. They were all three laughing and congratulating each other. I thought they were done with me. But I was wrong because the next thing I knew I was jerked up and shoved onto my knees on the floor. The third guy stuck his cock in my face and said, 'Do it!' When I refused to open my mouth, he slapped me. I tried to stop it from happening, but I couldn't."

Suddenly her story dissolves into convulsive crying.

March puts his arms around and underneath her and hugs her. Rocking her gently, he whispers into her ear, "April, April, April . . . I love you, sweet sister. Whoever did this is going to pay. That is my promise to you."

As March releases April and straightens back up, there is a knock at the door.

CHAPTER THIRTY-EIGHT

Turning toward the door of April's hospital room, March says, "Come in."

When the door opens, Debbie gasps. "It's James!" she whispers to March.

James's footsteps are tentative as he enters the room. "Is it okay if I come in?"

Like a bull charging a matador, March lowers his shoulder and rushes toward the sound of James's voice. "This is all your fault!" he yells. In spite of his blindness, March's aim is perfect. His shoulder strikes James in the chest and they crash into the wall.

"March!" Debbie screams.

March grabs James's neck and begins choking him. "If you hadn't kicked April out, none of this would have happened!"

Debbie and Detective Sullivan grab March's arms. "March!" Debbie yells, "Stop it! Let him go!"

"Sir!" the detective says firmly, "release him, or else I am going to have to hurt you."

Slowly, March relaxes his vicelike grip on James's neck and allows Debbie and Kate to pull him off of James.

In a deft and practiced move, Kate handcuffs March's hands behind his back. In a terse tone, she says to Debbie, "Get him out of here."

Debbie grasps the front of March's shirt and begins pulling him toward the door.

As they pass through the opening and step into the hallway, a voice farther down the hallway says, "What's going on?"

"It's April's doctor," Debbie says to March. "Doctor Oliver."

The doctor's soft-soled shoes make little noise as she quickly approaches them. "What happened? What's going on?"

The door to April's room opens and she can be heard screaming, "Get him out of here!"

The detective guides James out of the room as she says, "It's best if you leave, sir. The family doesn't want you here right now."

Straining at his handcuffs, March barks, "The family doesn't ever want to see you again!"

As James moves down the hallway with Kate, he feebly calls out, "I just wanted to say I was sorry."

"You got that right," March growls.

Doctor Oliver hurriedly disappears into April's room.

"March Tucker!" Debbie snaps at him. Putting her hand on his heaving chest, she says, "Have you lost your mind? Your sister has been traumatized enough without seeing you act like a crazed maniac. What were you going to do, kill James right there in front of her? Really, March, you've got to get a grip."

As the flow of adrenaline begins subsiding, March's breathing and heart rate slow. Instead of seeing red, he returns to his black world. "But if James hadn't fired her—"

"Stop right there," Debbie cuts him off. "This is not James's fault. I told you that April was attracted to him. She told me she loved him. But I think she used fairy-tale thinking and made their relationship something it wasn't. I don't know why he let her go, but he has a right to do that. It's an employer/employee relationship. April just made a bad choice when she decided to react to things by getting drunk. It's the guys who raped her that deserve our rage, not James."

Debbie's reasoned words find their way through the heat of March's anger. He takes a deep, ragged breath and says, "You're right. I just want to do something to take away April's pain. I feel so helpless."

"Yes, I understand that. I feel the same way."

"Have you calmed down?" the voice of the approaching detective says.

"Yes, ma'am," March replies apologetically. "I lost my head. It was a foolish thing to do, and I'm sorry. I'm okay now, though."

"Well, turn around and let me unlock your handcuffs. I don't blame you for being angry and upset, but based on the story April told me, James is not the person you need to be angry with."

"Yes, ma'am. You're right." With his hands free, March puts his arm around Debbie's shoulders and pulls her to him.

She pats him on the chest.

"I've gotten most all the information I need from your sister," Kate says. "I'll go to the bar and ask around. Maybe somebody saw her there and can give me the name of the guy she left with. Here's my card. You all can call me anytime. If April thinks of any more details, please let me know."

"We will," Debbie says.

As Kate walks away, Doctor Oliver rejoins them in the hallway. "We're going to discharge April."

"So soon?" Debbie says.

"Yeah, I know," the doctor says. "It seems unfair, doesn't it? But insurance companies dictate what kind of care people receive nowadays. Physically April is going to be okay. She will be extremely sore for a bit. I gave her a prescription for hydrocodone that she can take for pain. She can follow up with her regular physician. I also gave her the name of a really good therapist who can help, because she's going to need help to recover from what happened to her."

March extends his hand. "Thank you for your help, Doctor."

"You're welcome."

March and Debbie stand silently in the hallway for a few moments, trying to process all the drama of the night and morning. Finally, March says, "I've got to tell her about Tucker and Smiley Carter."

"Oh my god, I completely forgot," Debbie says. "The news is really going to upset her. You know that, don't you?"

"Yes I do. But she'll be mad if I try to keep it from her. Besides, I feel myself being pulled to go to Dresden to see what's going on. It's hard being so far away."

"Why don't we take her to your apartment and tell her?"

"That's a good idea."

They turn and walk into April's room.

"Where's James?" April asks.

"He's gone," Debbie says.

"Are you in trouble, March, for what just happened?" April asks.

"Luckily, the detective cut me some slack," March answers her. "I don't know what happened to me. When Debbie told me he was walking into your room, everything turned red. I hardly even remember what happened. I'm sorry if I scared you or upset you."

"The only thing I wish is that they hadn't pulled you off of him and you'd killed him."

Debbie says, "You don't mean that, April. You're just upset about everything."

"Yes I do mean it," April snaps at her. "My world was just coming together when he shattered everything. I'll never forgive him."

"Well, look," March cuts in, "The doctor says you're discharged and ready to leave. We're going to go to my apartment, if that's okay with you."

"Does August know what happened?" April asks. "Where is he? Why isn't he here?"

"Yes, he knows about everything," March says. "But an emergency situation came up and he had to go somewhere. I'll tell you all about it when we get to the apartment."

"Where are your clothes, April?" Debbie asks.

"I really don't know. But wherever they are you might as well burn them because I'm never wearing them again."

"You want to leave in your hospital gown?"

"Yes. I'm fine. Let's get out of here."

"Grab my coat," March says to Debbie. "She can wear that."

"And my toboggan," Debbie says.

At that moment an aide comes through the door pushing a wheelchair. "Here's your chariot," the man says. "I hear you're leaving us."

"Help me get up," April says.

March reaches for her and she grasps his forearm and begins pulling herself to the edge of the bed.

"Ow! Ow! Ow!" April cries. "It hurts."

"Let me help," the aide says.

"Don't you touch me!" April snarls. "My brother will take care of me."

"Let me just pick you up and put you in the chair," March says. Checking to be sure where the chair is, he carefully scoops her up and places her in it.

When the trio arrives at March's apartment, March opens his passenger door, gets out, and opens April's door. "Come on, sis, let's go inside."

April takes a few steps and stops. "Oh, Debbie, it hurts to walk. Oh my gosh, it hurts."

Debbie rushes to her side. "Put your arms around my and March's shoulders," she says. "That way we'll bear most of your weight."

Slowly they make their way up the sidewalk to the front door. Once inside Debbie asks, "How about a long hot shower or bath?"

"That sounds wonderful," April replies.

"And I'll find you some clothes of mine to wear," Debbie offers.

The two women disappear into the bathroom.

Once he hears the bath water running, March goes into the kitchen and puts on a pot of coffee to brew. He sits at the table, places his clasped hands on top, and rests his forehead on them. *Dear God in heaven, how much more are you going to put on our family? How much more can we take? I don't know why you allowed this awful thing to happen to April, but I'm depending on you to deliver her from the demons that are sure to possess her. Don't let her become consumed with anger and shame. Guard her heart. I don't know where Tucker is or even if she is alive, but if she is, let her know that I'm coming for her. I will find her, and I will rescue her.*

A hand touches his shoulder. He lifts his head.

"It's me," Debbie says. "I thought you'd fallen asleep. You want me to pour the coffee?"

"Sure."

"April let me help her into the shower. March, I don't care what the doctor said, April's body is broken, inside I mean. She has terrible, ugly bruises in places a woman shouldn't have bruises. It's—" She loses her voice as she begins to cry.

March stands up and wraps his arms around her.

She collapses into his chest. Her body convulses as she cries.

The sympathetic vibrations of March's heart trigger his own tears, and they trickle onto Debbie's head.

Like two survivors of a shipwreck clutching a single life preserver, they hold each other tightly, hoping to avoid drowning in the sea of emotions. After several minutes, their tears dry and they loosen their grip on each other.

"How about that coffee?" Debbie says. "You sit down while I fix it."

Twenty minutes later, April walks slowly out of the bathroom and into the kitchen.

"April!" Debbie says with alarm. "Your hair!"

"Yeah," April says, "I hope you don't mind. I found some scissors in the bathroom. It looks bad, doesn't it?"

"I didn't mean to sound so shocked," Debbie says. "It will just take some getting used to. I've never seen you with hair that short."

"Is there any more coffee left?" April asks.

"Absolutely," March answers her. "Sit down here beside me. Debbie was going to fix us something to eat, but we thought we'd wait to see what you wanted."

April gingerly lowers herself onto the chair. "I'm not very hungry."

"Fix us some scrambled eggs and toast," March says to Debbie. "I'll get her to eat." Smiling, he adds, "She can't resist my charming ways."

"Somebody help me before I gag," Debbie says, laughing.

As April lifts her last bite of eggs to her mouth, Debbie says, "Good job, April. You ate all those eggs."

"Don't you feel better now?" March asks.

"Maybe a little," Aprils says.

March clears his throat and says, "There's something I've got to tell you, April. And there's no easy way or easy time to do it. So here goes. Last night while August and Debbie and I were at the hospital with you, we got word that Smiley Carter had been shot and Tucker had been kidnapped. That's where August is. He went to Dresden. Smiley is going to be okay but no one knows where Tucker is."

"Shot? Kidnapped?" April says slowly. "How? Why?"

"That's what everyone is asking," March says, "but nobody has any answers."

Sniffing back her tears, April says, "Well, we've got to go to Dresden. Now!"

"But are you in any kind of shape to make the trip?" Debbie asks.

"If I lost both my legs and didn't have crutches," April says, "I would crawl on my stumps for Tucker and Smiley Carter. You two get your things together and take me to Dresden."

CHAPTER THIRTY-NINE

With August and Preacher on either side of him, Smiley Carter walks slowly toward the front porch of Tucker's house.

"Take your time, Pop," August says.

"I'm trying to," Smiley replies. "Slow is about the only speed I've had since my stroke, but that doesn't mean I like it."

"Here we are at the steps," Preacher says. "Let's take them one at a time."

Using them for support, Smiley makes his way onto the porch.

August opens the front door and steps inside. He quickly turns around to help his dad through the door. "Do you want to sit here in the living room? Or do you want to go on back to your bedroom and lie down?"

Smiley looks at Tucker's empty recliner and shakes his head. "I just can't believe Tucker's been kidnapped, and no one knows where she is. Help me to the couch and I'll rest there." With Preacher and August's assistance, he backs up to the couch and sits down.

"How about a cup of real coffee with chicory in it?" Preacher asks.

Clapping his hands together, Smiley says, "Now that would really hit the spot. What they give you in the hospital tastes like stump water. You know where everything is, don't you?"

Preacher walks toward the kitchen and says, "Yeah, I think so."

Sitting down beside Smiley, August puts his arm around his father's shoulders and says, "I'm glad you're home. When I heard last night what happened to you, I wasn't sure I would ever see you alive again. I'm not ready to give you up just yet."

Smiley claps his hand on August's thigh. "And the only thing what saved me was the good Lord and my hard head." He laughs. Just as quickly his expression turns somber. "And when you told me this morning what had happened to April, I thought my heart was going to break. My sweet, little April . . ." Twin tears roll down his cheeks, leaving shiny tracks. "For someone to do that to her shows how depraved a man can become if he gives his soul over to the Evil One. But there will be a judgment day for those who did that to her. Maybe not here on earth, but God will settle the score and there will be no mercy given."

"Don't count out them getting what they deserve while they are still living," August says. "I believe March will try to find them and, if he does, it won't be pretty what he does to them."

"Vengeance is mine, saith the Lord," Preacher intones as he walks into the living room. "I just heard the end of what you said, but we all need to be careful about wanting to settle scores. All that does is lead to bloodshed and unending resentments that are passed from generation to generation. Prisons are full of people who have tried to settle scores. It just never works."

"I believe you, Preacher," August says. "It's March you're going to have to convince. They should be home any time now. I even thought they might beat us here."

"How did March say April was doing?" Preacher asks.

"He said she's really, really sore, but insisted they come right away. She wanted to see you, Dad."

"I used to pitch that girl in the air and catch her," Smiley replies. "I just wonder if I can somehow help heal her heart from this awful thing that has happened to her."

About that time, footsteps and voices are heard on the porch.

Springing to his feet, August says, "That must be them."

The door opens before he can get there, and Debbie steps inside. She gives him a weak smile and hugs him. "August," she whispers in his ear, "I feel like I've been traveling with an open container of gasoline and a lit match in the car. Your brother and sister are in a bad, dark place."

August squeezes her and says, "We're all going to stick together and come through this somehow."

Debbie releases him and, seeing Smiley, says, "Oh, Smiley, how wonderful to see you here." She hurries to him.

"Come here, pretty lady," Smiley says. They embrace on the couch.

March enters the front door, holding April's hand and leading her inside.

April stands close beside March. Her chopped-off hair sticks out at odd angles. Her pale complexion looks even paler against the red and purple bruising on her face. Debbie's borrowed clothes hang loosely on her thin body.

August steps up to April and puts his arms around her. "April, I'm so sorry."

April's arms hang at her side like the arms of a marionette whose strings have been severed.

August steps back and looks at her, but she doesn't return his gaze. Giving March a quick hug, he says, "I'm glad you all got here safely."

Smiley tries to stand up but sags back onto the couch. Opening his arms, he says, "Come here, my baby April. Let ol' Smiley hold you."

April doesn't move. Her eyes begin to redden and then tears begin flowing down her face—but the blank facial expression she wore when she walked into the house doesn't change.

When March doesn't feel her move away from him and toward Smiley, he leans over and starts to say something to her.

Suddenly April wipes the tears off her face with the palms of her hands. Fire dances in her eyes and her nostrils flare. "Okay, everyone, I was raped. Not by one man, but by three. So it happened and it's over with. All right? So, I'm fine now. Really. Once these bruises disappear, no one will be able to see any difference in me. Don't treat me like I'm fragile or something, because I'm not. I'm fine. You hear me?! I'm fine!"

Everyone stares at her.

"And quit staring at me like I've got three heads or something!"

Turning her face so April can't see her, Debbie wipes away fresh tears.

August bites his bottom lip and sits down beside Smiley.

Clearing his throat, March steps past April, finds a chair and sits down. "What I want to hear about is what is known about Tucker's kidnappers. What's being done about it?"

"The only clue there is to work with," Preacher says, "is the recording the kidnapper made on Tucker's answering machine. It's so cryptic that we're not even sure that Tucker is who he meant to kidnap. Nobody can make any sense of it. The FBI is supposed to be coming in this evening. Anytime there's a kidnapping they are involved. Maybe they'll be able to notice something that we're missing."

"What kind of deadline has the kidnapper put on his demands?"

"That's one of the things that doesn't make sense," August says. "He didn't put any kind of deadline on it. He just said he wants what was taken from him returned to where it was stolen from."

"What was stolen?" March asks.

Shaking his head, Preacher says, "Nobody knows. That's why this is so hard to figure out. The kidnapper even addresses his remarks to someone none of us has ever heard of."

Cocking his head to one side, March asks, "Who does he address his remarks to?"

August says, "It's someone called Big Country."

CHAPTER FORTY

Squatting in front of the wood cookstove, Tucker opens the fire door and stirs the ashes and burning embers until there is a red glow. She lays two pieces of firewood onto the exposed hot coals and positions a third piece of firewood at a forty-five degree angle on top. She shuts the door and stands up with a grunt. "It's a good thing I know somethin' about makin' a fire or I'd freeze t' death out here."

She lumbers across the cabin to the shelf-lined wall. Eyeing her choices of food, she says, "Can't say much about th' options fer food 'round here—pork an' beans, Spam, beanie weenies, an' Vienna sausage. All them people on TV that talks about cholesterol would prob'ly condemn this place on account of there bein' so much processed meat." She selects a can of beanie weenies and walks to the table.

She pulls out a chair, sits down, and tries to lift the metal ring on top of the can to open it. "I don't know why they make things s' hard t' open. My fingernails ain't long enough an' my fingers is too thick t' git this stupid ring up." She grabs her fork and uses the handle to slide underneath the ring and pry it up. Then she grips the ring and pulls open the top of the can. "Ain't no sense in somethin' bein' s' hard t' git open."

Tucker makes short work of the contents of the can. She glances at the trapdoor in the floor of the cabin. Sitting beside the trapdoor is the stack of small pieces of wood and the axe propped against them that she placed there earlier. "Come on back, Red. Ol' Tucker's got a s'prise waitin' on y'."

A beam of yellow light suddenly spotlights the stack of wood. Turning her head to find the source of the light, Tucker sees that the setting sun has dropped low enough to shine through one of the windows. Getting out of her chair, she walks to the window and gazes across the blue water of Reelfoot Lake. She watches as a pair of bald eagles dive and snatch an evening meal of fish out of the water. A small breeze creates ripples on the lake. The top of each ripple catches the rays of the golden sun, making it look like the lake is covered in glittery flakes of gold.

Tucker rests her forearms on the high windowsill. "I can't b'lieve that a place that is filled with th' beauty of God's creation can also hold s' many scary mem'ries fer me. I can't figure out th' connection b'tween my pa an' Red's family that owns this place. An' I never dreamed I'd come back here one day an' this'd be where I found out who March's daddy is. What am I s'pposed t' do with that informa-tion? Would it hurt more than it'd help March? That's why I never told Maisy that m' pa was her father; it would've undone her more than she was already. But March ain't like Maisy—not by a long shot. Lord, I need y' t' give me some kind of sign on this one. Let me know what I oughta do."

As the sun sends out its final rays before dipping behind the horizon, the sparkling water turns midnight blue. Then suddenly it turns black when the sun's flames are extinguished. Tucker carefully finds her way across the dark cabin and lights a lamp on the table. Soft yellow light illuminates a small circle around her.

Suddenly, in the distance she hears the sound of a small engine approaching the cabin. A grim smile creases Tucker's features. "Come t' judgment, Red." Moving to the stack of wood now lying in the shadows beside the trapdoor, she picks up the axe and grips it firmly.

When the boat is approximately twenty feet from the cabin, the engine is shut off. Coasting, the boat bumps against the pylons as it glides underneath the cabin.

"Knock, knock, knock," Red says with a laugh. "Is Tucker home?" When Tucker doesn't answer, he says, "Speak up, old woman. I told you how this was going to work when I came back."

"I'm here," Tucker says.

"I want to hear you walk over to the stove."

Stooping over, Tucker picks up several pieces of wood. She tosses them one at a time, making sure that each one lands closer to the stove than the previous one.

"Very good," Red says. "Now walk across the cabin to the beds."

Not expecting Red to ask her to move around so much, Tucker looks anxiously at the few remaining sticks. She picks them up and repeats her previous procedure, throwing the lone remaining stick at the foot of a bed.

"That's what I like," Red says from under the floor, "someone who follows orders. Now walk over to the grocery shelves."

Tucker's heart hammers against her chest and she looks helplessly toward the shelves. "I'm tired of walkin' 'round. Y' can either come on in or not. I don't care."

"Why does your voice sound like it's right over me instead of on the other side of the cabin? Old woman, you better not be playing games with me."

Sweat beads up on Tucker's face. Quietly, she sits down on the floor and starts unlacing her boots.

"Step away from the door, Tucker," Red says menacingly.

Pulling off her shoes, Tucker stands up. "Alright then!" she says, and tosses her shoes one at a time, then tosses the axe. As she'd hoped, the axe bounces and lands twice, finally resting against the shelves.

"That's better," Red says.

The trapdoor flips open and bangs against the floor.

Holding her breath, Tucker listens to the creaking rope ladder as Red climbs up it. When his hips clear the opening she lunges from the shadows and falls on him. Grabbing him in a bear hug, she rolls across the floor with him. When their momentum stops, Red is underneath her on his face. Something like the roar of a bear comes from his mouth. Tucker grabs his neck and tries to grind his face into the floor.

Red manages to get his hands underneath his chest and suddenly pushes up while twisting his body. The move throws Tucker off balance and she falls off him. Quick as a cat, Red springs to his feet and grabs Tucker by the hair. He slams the side of her head against the floor.

Tucker sees stars briefly, then loses consciousness.

When Tucker comes to she is sitting on the floor with her back resting against one of the cabin's center posts. Her hands are bound behind her and around the post. Her feet are also bound. When she moves her head a searing pain shoots through her temple. She winces.

"Hurts like hell, don't it?" Red says. "Well good!"

Tucker opens her eyes and sees him sitting at the table and holding a cloth against his forehead.

"Nobody, man or woman, lays a hand on me without paying a price," he says angrily. "And where in the hell is the other bed?! I found the mattress, but where's the bed frame?"

He takes the cloth off his forehead and Tucker sees a bright-red abrasion where she pushed him against the floor. "Looks like somebody else has a headache," Tucker says.

Red flings the wet cloth at her, but it lands harmlessly on the floor. Red drags his chair in front of Tucker, sits down, and says, "I want some answers to some questions."

"An' so do I," Tucker replies.

"Shut up! I'm asking the questions. I'm the kidnapper here, and you're the prisoner. You seem to have a difficult time grasping that concept. I want to know what you did with the other bed."

"I got rid of it."

"I know that! I'm asking you what you did with it."

"I put it in th' stove an' burned it up."

Red stares at her openmouthed. "You did what?"

"I didn't stutter."

"How in the world did you do it?"

Nodding toward the axe lying across the room, Tucker says, "I chopped it up an' fed it a piece at a time."

Red shakes his head in disbelief. "What possessed you to do that?"

"What's yer last name?" Tucker asks.

"My last name? What has that got to do with anything?"

"I been in this here cabin b'fore, when I was a little girl."

Red waves at her assertion. "There's no way that can be true. Only people that's been here is family for three generations."

Tucker gives him a direct stare.

After a few moments, Red says, "What's your last name?"

"Tucker."

"I said what's your last name, not your first name."

"Tucker is m' family's last name, but it's also what I've been called m' whole life."

248

With widening eyes, Red says, "Your last name is Tucker? And you're from Dresden? What was your pa's name?"

"Raymond. Raymond Tucker."

Keeping his eyes on Tucker, Red gets up out of his chair and walks to the stove. He opens the door and stirs the coals. "My mama's last name was Tucker. Her daddy had an older brother who lived in Dresden. I never knew him. The story was that he just went missing and was never found. It's a good thing he went missing because if he'd been around when I was growing up, I'd have killed him."

Raising her eyebrows inquisitively, Tucker says, "Oh? Why's that?"

"Mama said he molested her when she was a little girl."

"That'd be my pa," Tucker says in a flat tone.

Red looks at her and then over at the beds on the wall. "You mean to tell me that when you were brought here as a little girl it was to—"

"That's what I'm sayin'," Tucker finishes his sentence.

Turning his back on her, Red walks to the stack of firewood and selects two pieces. He walks back to the open door of the stove, pitches them in, and slams the door shut. Rubbing the scar on the side of his face, he continues looking at the stove and says, "That's messed up. That's totally messed up! I admit I'm mean and that I'd kill a man over a quarter, but messing with little girls . . . Prison is where those kinds of people belong so they'll get what they deserve. Inmates have a way of doling out justice on perverts." Facing Tucker, he says, "I'm sorry that happened to you. Is that why you chopped and burned the bed?"

Tucker nods her head slowly.

"Then good riddance to it," Red says. "Look, if I untie you, will you promise to behave yourself?"

Once again Tucker nods.

"That's not good enough," Red says. "I want you to say you'll behave."

"I'll behave," Tucker says.

Red steps behind her and unties her wrists. Then he moves to her feet and unties them, too.

Tucker rolls onto her hands and knees, grasps the center pole she was tied to, and pulls herself to a standing position.

Red goes and gets a bottle of whiskey off the shelf and sits down at the table. He pours some of the amber liquid into two coffee cups, then says, "Come sit down."

Tucker joins him and sits across the table. Staring into her cup, she says, "Th' one y' call Big Country, his real name is March. He's th' middle child of my daughter's three children. All of 'em had different fathers. I've raised 'em all. My daughter's dead." She pauses and raises her gaze to find Red listening intently to her. Holding his eyes with hers, she says, "My daughter's name was Amazing Tucker."

CHAPTER FORTY-ONE

March jerks his head as if he's been slapped. The color drains from his face. His palms start sweating and his throat goes dry.

"Are you okay?" August asks. "Do you know this guy called Big Country?"

Nodding slowly, March says, "Yes I do. I am Big Country." He hears a collective gasp from the group. "And I know who shot Smiley and kidnapped Tucker."

"What are you talking about?" Debbie asks. "I've never heard you refer to yourself as Big Country."

March detects a tone of disappointment in Debbie's voice, perhaps because she's upset that there is something about him that he hasn't revealed to her. Looking toward her, he says, "I've told you everything there is to know about me, except for one period of time. I was hoping it would stay buried in the past and I wouldn't have to deal with it." Biting his bottom lip, he bows his head, then adds, "Clearly I was wrong about that."

March feels a hand on his arm. Preacher says, "Son, are you sure of what you're talking about?"

"Yes sir, I am. And I guess I'm going to have to tell you all the story."

"Wait just a minute," Preacher says. "I know you all are tired from your trip, and it's close to suppertime. Why don't I run to town and get a bunch of burgers and fries for all of us? April, you can make us some tea while I'm gone. Is that okay with everyone?"

Everyone, except April, gives verbal assent to Preacher's plan.

"What about it, April?" Preacher asks. "Or would you like to ride on my motorcycle with me to go get the food? Someone else can fix the tea for us."

Her voice devoid of emotion, April says, "Sure, I'll go with you." She turns and heads out the front door.

Moving to catch up with her, Preacher says, "We'll be back shortly."

March stands up and says, "I think I'm going to take a quick shower while we wait on them."

Debbie moves to take his hand. "Come on, I'll help you find what you need."

When Preacher arrives at his motorcycle, April is standing beside it and eyeing the seat.

"I didn't think about having to get on," she says. "I'm so sore I don't think I can raise my leg high enough to get it over the seat."

"Well, let's try it a different way," Preacher says. "You know, women in the old days didn't ride horses by straddling them. They rode sidesaddle. You ever heard of that?"

"No."

"It's really simple. They kept both legs on the same side of the horse. There was a specially made saddle that gave them something to hold on to. You can just hold on to me. Want to try?"

"Sure."

"Let me get on first." Preacher quickly straddles his bike. "Now you back up here and sit down sideways behind me."

April backs up to the Harley and eases herself onto the seat.

"Now hold on to me," Preacher encourages her.

Tentatively, April grips his jacket.

"That's fine," Preacher says, "or you can hold on to my waist, whichever makes you feel most comfortable and safe." He raises the motorcycle off its kickstand and starts the engine. Over the low rumble, he says, "If it's okay with you, I'd like to drive over to Tucker's barn first before we go into town. There's something I'd like to show you. But I want you to feel okay about that."

"Whatever you want to do," April replies.

Squeezing the clutch, Preacher puts the bike into gear and drives the short distance to Tucker's barn. He shuts off the engine and leans the motorcycle onto its kickstand. Getting off, he says, "You can just sit there because this won't take but a minute."

Preacher takes off his jacket and lays it across the seat. "Nobody in your family has ever seen what I'm about to show you. Truth is no one's seen it for years now. But I've got to take my shirt off to show you. Are you okay with that?"

A cloud passes over April's expression and a fleeting look of fear touches her eyes. She folds her arms across her abdomen.

"April, I promise I'm not going to do anything to you. God just put it on my heart to share with you part of my past."

The fear in her eyes disappears and April says, "Go ahead. I'm just sort of jumpy I guess."

Preacher unbuttons his shirt and removes it, exposing his tattoo-covered torso.

April slides slowly off the motorcycle and approaches. Dozens of demonic-looking characters stare at her from Preacher's chest and abdomen. Images of flames dance around the demons.

Preacher turns and exposes his back to her.

April stares wide-eyed. "It reminds me of Gustave Doré's illustrations of Dante's *Inferno*, but more macabre."

Turning to face her, Preacher says, "I don't know who those people are, but I want you to look closer here." He touches a spot four inches above and to the right of his belly button.

April puts her face closer to his abdomen. "It looks like some kind of ugly face with all kinds of folds on— Wait! It's a scar of some kind, isn't it?" She looks up at Preacher.

"You're right," he answers. Touching just below his shoulder, he says, "And here." He turns back around, reaches behind him, and touches two places on his back.

"What is all this?" April asks.

Preacher puts his shirt back on. As he buttons it, he says, "Those scars are from being shot and stabbed."

Frowning, April says, "I don't understand."

"My brother and I were in a fight with some guys and a man ended up getting killed. When the sheriff finally showed up, I was the only person there with the dead man."

"Where was your brother?"

"He ran away, and, even though he was the one who killed the man, I took the rap for him." Preacher slips his jacket back on. "Here's what I want to tell you, April. All those ugly, disgusting tattoos were done while I was in prison. Some of the scars are from knife fights I had in prison. I was angry and resentful about what had happened to me. I was filled with burning hatred toward my brother. For years, I strutted around that prison with a chip on my shoulder, ready to fight anyone who looked at me wrong."

"I just can't believe this," April says. "You're such a gentle, kind man—a man of God."

"I haven't always been the man I am today. I would have eventually died a violent death in prison, I have no doubt. But one day an old man who was in prison for life came to me and told me something that changed my life. He said, 'Son, you're mad because you think you got a raw deal and you don't belong here, aren't you?

Well so does everyone else who walks into this prison. But this place is only a prison if you let it be. I know a man who was beat with a whip until he lost so much blood that he nearly died. Then the ones who whipped him took giant spikes and hammered them through his hands and his feet. People all around spat on him, slapped him, made fun of him, and called him names. All because they was scared of him. They was scared of him because they couldn't break him. He never hurt no one, never robbed no one, never broke no laws. No sir, he didn't deserve what they did to him. And you know what he did after they nailed him on them pieces of wood and left him to die? He asked God to forgive them.'"

Tears have begun to run down Preacher's flushed cheeks. "'Why would he do that?' I asked the old man. 'He done it for you.' 'Why me?' 'Because he knew you would need it one day.' 'Need it? Need what?' 'Forgiveness, that's what.'"

April's body begins to tremble, and when she blinks, tears splash.

"I looked at that old man like I didn't know what he was talking about. He squinted one eye, tapped me on the chest, and said, 'You are a lost man. Lost in all your anger and hatred. You've built your own prison and only God can save you.'" Preacher sniffs and wipes the tears off his face. "I began a journey that very day, April, that led me to the foot of the Cross. But to get there I had to forgive lots of people who had wronged me. I don't mean to make it sound that simple, either. Some days the anger and resentment felt as fresh as the day I was wronged, but I kept trying. Each morning I prayed to God that he would help me have a forgiving heart just for that one day."

Taking a step toward April, Preacher waits for her to give him a sign that it's okay.

She drops her head and her tears drip off the end of her nose. Then she takes a small, hesitant step toward him, then another.

Preacher opens his arms and she falls into them.

She puts her face into his chest and screams and cries. She pounds his chest with her small fists.

"Let it out, April," he says calmly. "Let it out."

After a minute, April's cries die out and she rests her cheek against Preacher.

"What happened to you," he says, "is perhaps the most awful thing one human being can do to another. But you must not make the mistake I did and waste your life filling it with bitterness and hatred because it will destroy you from the inside out. You're going to survive this and be okay. It will be a long journey for you, but God will be with you every step of the way. And your family will be here, and I'll be here."

In a ragged voice, April says, "But I don't know how."

Patting her, Preacher says, "Today you don't have to know how. Today all you've got to do is go with me to get some hamburgers and fries. Are you ready to ride?"

April looks up at him and gives a weak smile. "I love you."

"And I love you, April. I love all your family. You are some of the most awe-inspiring people I've ever known. Now come on, let me help you back on my bike, and let's go get supper."

CHAPTER FORTY-TWO

Red stares at Tucker with his mouth agape. "That girl, Amazing, was your daughter?"

"Yep," Tucker says.

"How do I know you're not lying?"

Folding her arms across her chest, Tucker replies, "Y' couldn't figure out two plus two."

"What the hell is that supposed to mean?"

"Don't be cussing at me," Tucker says in a curt tone. "Mind yer manners."

Red slams his fist on the table and yells, "Quit telling me what to do!"

Turning her face away, Tucker says, "Yellin' ain't gonna git y' nowhere."

Red runs his hand through his shock of red hair. "Lord, give me patience before I kill this woman."

As quick as a rattlesnake's strike, Tucker slaps him across the face. "Don't use th' Lord's name in vain around me. That's one thing I can't abide."

Red jumps out of his chair, grabs the edge of the table, and flips it end over end. The two cups and the whiskey bottle careen across the floor, spilling alcohol in their wake. The kerosene lantern shatters when it hits the floor. Suddenly the spilled alcohol and kerosene burst into flames. Rivulets of the burning liquid snake across the cabin floor.

Red dashes and picks up the water bucket. At the trapdoor, he lowers the bucket by means of the rope tied to its handle into the lake water below.

As he strains to lift it, Tucker walks casually over to the frameless bed mattress and lifts it off the floor. Stepping over to the flames, she lowers it and smothers the fire, putting it out.

When Red finally has the full water bucket in his hand, he looks dumbly at Tucker. "What happened?" he asks.

"I put th' fire out," Tucker replies. "You was gonna make it worse by pourin' water on it. All that'd done is scatter th' fire all over th' cabin floor an' prob'ly ended up burnin' th' place down. Y' ain't got much sense, do y'? Ever'body knows y' don't put out that kind of fire with water." Shaking her head, Tucker sits the table back on its legs. "Git that extra lantern off the shelves an' bring it over here. Y' need t' come have a seat an' calm down."

Red sets the dripping bucket on the floor, drops the trapdoor back into place, and retrieves the lantern from the shelves.

Tucker puts the chairs back in place. When Red lights the lantern, she says, "I'm gonna make us some coffee." Opening the door to the stove, she stirs the coals, and pitches in some more wood. She carries the coffee pot over to the water bucket and fills it. Walking back to the stove, she says, "Y' hungry?"

"I could eat some Spam," Red answers her.

"Then bring me a can over here," Tucker instructs him.

Like a dutiful child, Red does as he is told.

After a few minutes the smell of coffee and cooking meat fills the one-room cabin.

Looking over her shoulder, Tucker sees Red staring at the lantern on the table. She turns back to the skillet of meat and turns the slices over. A loud hiss and sizzle is the response. She picks up the steak knife she used to slice the Spam and slides it underneath the cuff of her long-sleeve shirt. "Have y' got all th' dots connected yet?" she asks.

"Huh? What?" Red says.

"I said, have y' got all th' dots connected yet?" The hot skillet in one hand and the pot of coffee in the other, Tucker lumbers over to the table and sets them on the rough-hewn planks of the table top. She forks a couple pieces onto her and Red's plates, then pours some coffee.

Red cuts himself a bite of Spam, chews, and says, "I know there's more to all this than I realized. Your pa was my great-uncle."

"Which means that you an' me is kin."

Shaking his head slowly, Red says, "Yeah, I know. We're some sort of cousins I guess."

"An' my daughter's name was Amazing, but we always called 'er Maisy. Yore description fit 'er to a T."

"But she was a beautiful woman and you're—"

"Yeah, I ain't. I know that. She had my height and bone structure, but she had her father's features."

"Where's her father?" Red asks.

"Dead an' gone." Tucker says, then swallows a gulp of coffee.

"Who was her father?"

"Your great-uncle."

Red's fork stops midway between his plate and his mouth. "But I thought you said my great-uncle was your pa."

"I did."

"You mean—? Your pa was—" Red drops his fork onto his plate. "My Go—I mean gosh, Tucker, your pa was the father of your daughter?"

Tucker looks down at her plate and pushes around the half-eaten slice of Spam.

The scar on Red's face turns crimson and his jaw muscles flex. "That's the most messed-up, complicated thing I've ever heard of."

Lifting her head to look at him, Tucker says, "It gits more complicated. Yer th' father of Maisy's boy."

Like mercury draining out of a broken thermometer, the blood drains from Red's face. His complexion turns pasty white. "What boy?"

"March, the one you call Big Country."

"How do you know that?"

"'Cause before Maisy died she left me a letter with th' identity of all three of 'er children's fathers. She give th' names of two of 'em, but she said March's father was a man she met who worked fer a travelin' carnival an' she wasn't sure 'bout his name. You's th' one what told me you is that man."

Red cannot return Tucker's direct gaze. "Man, this is getting all messed up. Big Country can't be my son."

"Just 'cause y' say that don't change th' truth," Tucker says. "He's yore boy, but he took on his mama's features."

Red finally looks at her. "You mean that a boy born in Tennessee ends up in Las Vegas where I find him on the street and that boy is my son? You couldn't sell that story to a publishing house because they would say it's too far-fetched."

"That may be, but th' truth is th' truth. What I'm wonderin' is what is it that March is supposed t' have stolen from y'? What do you two have t' do with each other?"

"He stole money and drugs," Red replies, "and lots of both. Then he set me up so the Feds busted me and sent me to prison. He can't ever give me those years back, but he can at least give me back the money."

"You're wrong 'bout that," Tucker says matter-of-factly.

Red gives a derisive laugh. "Your little grandson has done lots of things you don't know about."

"You mean, yore son."

"Uh . . . yeah . . . right," Red mutters. "Anyway, he worked for me as sort of a deliveryman or sometimes as an enforcer, if I needed one. The last job I sent him on he simply disappeared. Never heard a word from him. I've had a recent conversation with the two men who were supposed to be with him on that last job and they didn't know the answers to any of my questions."

"How do y' know they didn't lie t' y'?"

"Let's just say that my interrogation techniques don't leave any room for lying. They would have done anything to know the answers I was looking for. So Big Country has to be the one. I took that starving boy off the street and took care of him. Gave him food and clothes and a place to live. He would have died if it wasn't for me." Red gets out of his chair and starts pacing. "And this is how he repaid me. He stabbed me in the back." His voice rises.

Suddenly he turns and stomps toward the table. Slamming both fists on the table, he leans over and shoves his face within a foot of Tucker's face. The yellow light from the lantern dances in the irises of his eyes. He twists his face into a malevolent expression. "I see what you're trying to do. You play the dumb country bumpkin, but you're smart like a fox. This fantastic yarn you've spun is supposed to get in my head. You think I'm going to feel sorry for you and your grandson." Droplets of his spit land on Tucker's glasses. "Well here is my truth. Your grandson is nothing but a dirty little snitch and there's only one thing to do to a snitch and that's to kill him! I don't care if he is my son. He's going to give me what I want. Then I'm going to kill you and then I'm going to kill him."

CHAPTER FORTY-THREE

March steps out of the shower and towels himself off. He finds the sink and stands naked facing the mirror. *Are you really ready to do this? To stand naked in front of your family? Because telling them this part of your story is going to be like that.*

Suddenly he hears the voice of Dr. Sydney, his therapist and psychiatrist from when he was at Patricia Neal Rehabilitation Hospital, echoing in his memory, "March, you must quit hiding behind your blindness. You use it to block people from getting to know you. There is a little book that was written by John Powell that is titled *Why Am I Afraid to Tell You Who I Am?* The basic premise of his book is this: If I tell you who I really am, and you don't like me, then what am I to do with myself? Therefore I will be who you want me to be rather than being my real self.

"Your past is your past, March. It is part of you. That doesn't mean it defines you, but it certainly has something to do with the person you are today. The only way to live in the light and feel comfortable with yourself is to be open and honest with people about your journey. If they don't embrace you, then you don't need them in your life."

March takes a deep breath of the humid air in the bathroom and lets it out slowly. *Okay, big boy, this is the crossroads. Quit being afraid of your past and of people knowing about it. Remember Dr. Sydney's mantra, "That was then, this is now." Who you were is not who you are.*

There is a soft tap on the bathroom door. Debbie's hushed voice says, "Are you all right, March?"

"Yeah," he replies. "I'm getting dressed. Come on in if you want to."

The doorknob clicks and March feels cool air on his feet as Debbie comes inside. "You've been in here a long time. I just thought I'd check on you."

March feels for and finds his clothes, steps into his underwear, and pulls on his T-shirt. "I've been sorting through things in my mind while taking a journey into the past." Just saying it out loud gives him a tight feeling in his chest and fear rings a bell of alarm in the back of his brain.

"Whatever this is," she says, "you don't have to talk about it with everyone, if you don't want to. I can tell you're nervous about it."

That old feeling from his dreams of standing on the edge of a cliff sweeps over him. "Will you catch me if I fall?"

"I don't know what you mean."

An overpowering urge to run out of the bathroom and out of the house hits March. With a tremor in his voice, he says, "This part of my past that I'm going to tell everyone—what if people hate me because of it? What if it changes how they think of me?"

"March, this is your family you're talking about. I don't believe any of that will happen. But suppose it does. Let's say they do hate you and don't think of you the same way. What then?"

March hesitates and feels tears stinging his eyes. In a hoarse whisper, he says, "Will you still be there for me?"

In a tone filled with tenderness, Debbie answers, "Oh, March."

March feels her press her warm body against his. She wraps her arms around him.

"I will always be here for you, March. I will catch you if you fall." Her hand gripping his chin, she pulls his head down and kisses him.

The instant their lips touch, March feels warmth fill his chest. He puts his hands on her sides, just above her hips, and lifts her off the floor.

Debbie wraps her legs around his waist and he slides his hands under her hips.

He pulls back from their kiss and feels her hot breath. Their lips barely touch as he says, "Do you know how much I love you?"

"Yes, but tell me anyway."

"There was a song I used to love hearing Miss Ella sing. I don't know why, but I've never forgotten the lyrics. It went like this:

Just at the close of a bright summer day
Just as the twilight had faded away
Soft on the breeze like the coo of a dove
Someone was singing an old song of love
Tell me you love me and say you'll be true
I love nobody in this world but you
Your heart and my heart in love will entwine
Give me your love and I'll give you mine
Come along with me to the quiet shady nook
Where flowers bloom at the side of the brook
Nature is sleeping, the birds are at rest
I'll place a wild rose on your beautiful breast
I've something to ask you while you're by my side
A question of love, of groom and of bride
But if you refuse me my heart it will pine
Give me your love and I'll give you mine

Tell me you love me and say you'll be true
I love nobody in this world but you
Your heart and my heart in love will entwine
Give me your love and I'll give you mine

"That's how I feel about you," March concludes.

"You have got to be the sweetest man I have ever known," Debbie says. "And you are either going to have to get dressed so we can walk out of here now, or we're going to have sex right here, right now."

Laughing, March says, "Only because I don't want to try and explain your cries of pleasure to my family, I think I'll get dressed."

Debbie slaps his shoulder playfully, "My cries of pleasure?! I'm not the one who sounds like a howler monkey when we have sex."

After March gets dressed, he opens the door and walks toward the living room. Just as he does, the front door opens and April and Preacher enter.

"Who's hungry for supper?" Preacher asks. There's the rattle of paper sacks and the squeak of Styrofoam cups as they begin taking everything out and putting it on the table.

Smiley Carter claps his hands together. "Man, I do love the smell of greasy hamburgers and fresh French fries! Help me up before March gets in there 'cause I've seen that boy do serious damage to a stack of burgers before."

"Hey," March calls out, "I'm still a growing boy!"

Everyone laughs.

"But one of these days," Smiley says, "you're gonna start growing out and not up. Not many people can age like Preacher here and keep their slim physique."

"Give me your hand, Pop," August says, "and I'll pull you off that couch. Although I may have to call in reinforcements to help me."

Again, everyone laughs.

"Ya'll go ahead," Smiley says, "make fun of the old, crippled black man. I swear, I thought my days of persecution were over with." He gives a loud grunt as August pulls him to his feet.

They all make their way to the kitchen and find a seat around the table. August passes out the burgers like a card dealer while Preacher makes sure everyone gets a drink. As if on cue, silence settles on the room.

"Preacher," August says, "will you offer thanks for our food?"

"Be glad to, August," Preacher replies. "Dear merciful and loving God, our father in heaven, we are thankful to you for this simple meal before us. So many in the world today will go hungry. Help us to remember to be grateful for the simple things that we so often take for granted. Bless this dear family in their time of crisis. Strengthen their hearts and calm their fears. And especially bless Tucker wherever she is. In Jesus's name, Amen."

"And amen, Preacher," Smiley echoes. "Thank you for those good words."

"Let's dig in," March says.

For the next several minutes, the only sounds heard are of everyone hungrily devouring the food.

"From the sounds of it," Debbie says, "I'd say we were all starving. I didn't know I was so hungry."

"Whew, that was good," August says.

"Let me get a trash bag," April says, "and we can get rid of all this trash."

The noise of the paper wrappers and sacks being wadded up reminds March of the sound of applause before a performer on stage begins singing. Like small ocean waves striking him, tiny waves of tension pulse in his chest. As the noise of cleanup dies down, March senses everyone looking at him. Underneath the table, Debbie lays her hand on his thigh.

Clearing his throat, March says, "What I am going to tell you all is a chapter in my life that I had hoped I could run away from. Unfortunately it has come looking for me, or, as Tucker might say, my chickens have come home to roost. You all know about all my travels when I ran away. Different ones of you know different pieces of that story. But this is the whole story.

"When I arrived in Las Vegas I was nearly starved to death. It was cold on the streets. I ate out of garbage cans behind restaurants. One night, when I thought I couldn't go on living anymore, a man gave me food and a warm place to stay. I have never been so grateful in my entire life. I felt like I owed him my life. And he played on that gratitude. He told me I owed him and needed to pay him back by doing favors for him. Because I didn't know what he had in mind, I was willing to hold up my end of the bargain." March pauses and takes a drink of his Coke. "That night I was introduced to the world of child prostitution and doing things I had never even heard of."

"Dear God," Smiley says.

"When you're living that kind of life," March continues, "time ceases to exist. Days and months mean nothing, so I really don't know how long I did that for him. But once I hit my growth spurt, I wasn't the young, innocent-looking boy that perverts wanted. That's when my job description started changing. This guy who basically owned me was a major drug dealer, not just in Las Vegas, but across the country, too. Lots of drugs and money flowed through his hands. But he was very careful to keep himself distanced from all the traffic. And that's where I came in. I became his courier. Whether it was delivering drugs or picking up payments, I did it all.

"He started taking me to the gym regularly to lift weights and I really bulked up. That was when I got the nickname Big Country. I grew my beard, too, so it would enhance my menacing appearance. I learned how to handle a pistol. He used me to ride herd on other guys in his entourage because I was the only one he trusted. My very last job for him was when the two guys I was trying to keep in line jumped me and threw me off that bridge in East Tennessee, thinking it would kill me.

"It's my guess now that those two guys stole the money and drugs and set this man up. That he's come calling for me tells me that more than likely those two guys are dead and didn't give him what he wanted. I know exactly where his cabin is in the mountains. Most likely that's where he has holed up with Tucker. All I need is for someone to take me there. I have an old score to settle with this man and a new score, too, after what he did to Smiley and Tucker."

"I'm going with you," August says. "I have a personal score to settle with this guy, too."

"Whoa, whoa, now," Preacher says. "Let's hold on just a minute. We need to get the law enforcement people involved and let them handle things."

"I appreciate what you're saying, Preacher," March replies, "but this is the most sadistic and dangerous man I've ever known. If he even smells the police, he will without a doubt kill Tucker. And August, I don't need someone to help me kill this man. I'll do that myself. Your anger will get in the way and cause you to mess things up."

A chorus of protests, led by Debbie, rises up in shock at March's assertion he will kill the man.

March listens patiently until their cries die down. "You've all had your say. You have to believe me, though. I know this man like nobody else does. I'll be able to walk right up to him. He won't suspect anything from a blind man. And killing him is the only way to deal with him."

"This man you're talking about," Preacher says, "What does he look like? Does he have a name?"

"He has red hair and a jagged red scar on his neck. The only name I ever heard him called by was Red."

CHAPTER FORTY-FOUR

Jumping out of his chair as if it were on fire, Preacher says, "What did you say?"

March turns toward Preacher's voice. "Everyone called him Red. I don't know what his real name is."

"And you're certain about the scar?" Preacher asks.

Cocking his head to one side, March says, "Of course I am. You couldn't miss it."

"No, no, no," Preacher moans, "it just can't be. Lord help us all."

"What's the matter, Preacher?" Smiley Carter asks. "I've never seen you affected so."

Slowly, Preacher returns to his chair. He draws a deep breath and says, "I can tell you that I now know how Red found you, March."

"Please do," March says.

"This is going to be as hard for you all to swallow as it is for me to tell you." He pauses, then says, "The man you call Red is my brother."

There is a collective gasp from everyone at the table.

"I know this is shocking news," Preacher continues, "but that's because there's a lot about me you don't know. I've told different people around here pieces of my story, but no one's heard the whole of it. I guess if anyone deserves to hear the truth, it's you all.

"I grew up over around Reelfoot Lake, moving back and forth between Tiptonville and Samburg. During the time I was growing up, and for generations before that, Reelfoot was a rough place. My mother's father and his brothers, my grandfather and uncles, were part of an organization called the Night Riders. They more or less ran things back then, dispensing justice and enforcing whatever they considered to be the law. Outsiders were not allowed to move into the area to live. It was okay if they spent money hiring fishing and hunting guides, but if they decided to buy a place and live there, their car might have its tires slashed or rocks would be thrown through their windows. If that didn't convince them to move away, any women might be raped or the house might be burned down."

"And a black man might be strung up with fish hooks," Smiley interjects.

"I heard stories about that," Preacher says. "They gave me nightmares at night when I was little."

"They wasn't just stories," Smiley says. "It really happened."

"My mother was an alcoholic," Preacher continues. "She had a parade of men through her life while I was growing up. Some of them she was married to and others she just shacked up with. Red and I had different fathers. He was two years younger than me. We pretty much raised ourselves. Mom was always more interested in whatever man was in her life at the time than she was in being a parent. I was cooking meals for me and Red when I was seven or eight years old. We used to lay in bed at night listening to our grandfather and uncles telling stories about the Night Riders. The way they told it, it made them sound like heroes. I couldn't wait to become one of them. By the time I was twelve I was slashing tires and breaking out people's windows for the Night Riders.

"It was when I was in my late teens that it started bothering me to scare and intimidate people. I began to see that it wasn't right. But not Red. He didn't seem to have a conscience. He got off on people begging him to leave them alone or in seeing that scared look on their face. I once caught him trying to kill our dog by hanging him."

"Oh my god," April says softly. "What kind of person does things like that?"

"A sociopath," August replies bluntly.

"Yes, you're right," Preacher agrees. "But because I'd practically raised him, I felt responsible for Red. My role in life became trying to bail him out of trouble or to protect him from someone bigger than him that he'd decided to pick a fight with. One night, when I was a senior in high school, a carload of guys from Union City came looking for trouble. People from Union City thought they were better than we were and called us river rats. Well, that night me, Red, and Ron Dale were hanging out at one of the picnic pavilions at the state park. This car pulled up and six guys got out. I knew right away what was coming, and I tried to get Red and Ron to leave. But Red was eager to fight.

"Even though there were six of them, the three of us held our own. Then suddenly one of them pulled out a switchblade. That just seemed to make Red even more excited. He charged the boy. They hit the ground and rolled. When Red jumped up, the knife was buried in the chest of the boy, and he was dead. Someone must have seen us fighting because just then the sound of a siren came from down the highway. The boys from Union City jumped in their car and tore out of there. Red, Ron, and I started running. A spotlight from a squad car hit our backs and an officer hollered at us to stop. I told Ron and Red to keep running, and I turned around to face the spotlight.

"I told them I'd killed the boy. As a matter of fact, I told that story so many times that there were times when I'd get confused over who did the killing. I even told Tucker one time that I had murdered a man. The sheriff wanted the names of Red and Ron, but I refused to give them to him. Because I was eighteen at the time, I was charged as an adult, found guilty, and sent to prison." Preacher sags back in his chair, exhausted from the telling.

Preacher's stunned audience sits in silence.

March finally speaks, "So, when did you figure out the connection between me and your brother? Did you tell him about me being Tucker's grandson? Are you the reason he kidnapped her?" March's fists clench. "Because if you are, then you and I are going to have trouble."

"No," Preacher says quickly, "nothing like that. I have rarely spoken to my brother since I got out of prison, and I've seen him even less. But a little over a week ago, he showed up at my place out of the clear blue. He said he'd made a visit to our old stomping grounds. He must have seen you and Tucker together somewhere and recognized you."

"Boyette's," Debbie says.

"Huh?" Preacher says.

"We all went to Boyette's a little over a week ago. As impossible as it seems, we must have crossed paths with Red and not known it."

"If I still had my eyesight, I would have seen him," March says, "and none of this would have ever happened."

"Woulda, coulda, shoulda," August says. "There's no sense in everyone trying to figure out who's to blame for what. We've got to talk to the law about all this so we can find Tucker and get her out safely."

"First of all," Preacher says, "what March said earlier about my brother is true. He is crazy. He's just as likely to kill Tucker as not."

"But won't he lose his leverage if he kills her?" August asks.

"That's the way a normal kidnapper might think," Preacher answers. "But Red is anything but normal. The truth is Tucker may already be dead."

"Blessed Jesus, no," Smiley says.

"I'm sorry. I know how that must have sounded. But we've all got to look at the cold hard facts. The other thing is that I don't think Red is in East Tennessee."

"Then where is he?" March asks.

"There is an old family cabin that has been in our family for generations. It sits up on pylons out in the lake in an area called Black Bayou. It's used with permission by duck hunters or fishermen. I'd put money on the fact that he has Tucker in that cabin."

CHAPTER FORTY-FIVE

Tucker blinks as Red's spit peppers her face. His bloodshot eyes are bulging and the scar on his neck looks like it could start bleeding any moment.

"You hear me?!" he screams. "I'm going to kill you all!"

Dropping her arm to her side, Tucker feels the handle of the steak knife slip out of her shirtsleeve and into the palm of her hand. She pulls the blade free from her sleeve and grips the handle. Continuing to look at Red without changing her expression, she swings her hand up from under the table and drives the knife through the back of Red's left hand and into the board underneath his palm, pinning it to the table.

Like the calm before a storm, Red stares dumbly at the knife sticking out of his hand. Then a scream of pain mixed with rage erupts from his mouth. "You said you wouldn't do anything if I turned you loose!"

"I lied!" Tucker yells. She stands up quickly, pulls the wooden chair out from under her, and lifts it into the air.

Red has grabbed the handle of the knife and is trying to pull it free from the table. Looking up, he sees the chair descending on him like an avalanche. Just before the chair strikes him the table releases the knife, and he jerks it out of his hand. Blood pours out of both sides of his hand.

The chair strikes Red before he can stand up straight and jump out of the way. The rails and stiles splinter across his back. Swearing at the top of his lungs, Red grabs for Tucker, but she steps back just out of his reach.

Moving as fast as she can, Tucker heads toward the woodpile in the corner of the cabin. Behind her she hears the table thundering to the floor as Red flips it in frustration.

"Oh no you don't!" Red cries, and he lunges toward Tucker. His feet get tangled in the remains of the chair and he falls. Stretching as far as he can, he grabs Tucker's ankle just as he hits the floor.

Like a clapper striking a church bell, terror strikes Tucker's heart as she feels Red's hand on her ankle. His grip throws her off balance, and she falls like a tree across the stack of wood. Keeping her eyes riveted on her goal as she falls, she reaches for the axe resting in the corner. When she lands, all the air gushes out of her lungs and her chin strikes a piece of wood, causing her to bite her tongue. The metallic taste of blood fills her mouth. Her hand lies inches short of the axe. She has a fleeting memory of reaching for her pa's hatchet the night she murdered him.

Tucker kicks against Red's hand on her ankle, but she is unable to free herself. She stretches again for the axe and her fingertips brush against the handle. Gathering her strength, she pulls against Red and drags him toward her. This time when she reaches for the axe, her hand falls squarely on the handle. Twisting herself onto her back so she can see Red, she swings the axe at him.

The axe strikes a glancing blow against the right side of Red's head, partially severing his ear. Crying out in pain, Red lets go of Tucker's ankle and grabs the side of his head. He rolls across the floor and finally stands up.

Keeping her grip on the axe, Tucker scrambles to her feet. She spits a mouthful of blood onto the floor. As she tries to take a deep breath, searing pain shoots through her side. For a moment darkness closes in on her vision and she feels her knees giving way. But she shakes her head and everything comes back into focus.

Red stands ten feet away from her. His left arm is hanging at his side, and blood drips down his fingertips. His right hand is holding the side of his head while blood runs down his face and neck. Grinning, he says, "You're going to die a slow death, and I'm going to enjoy watching it."

Ignoring his grim threat, Tucker holds the axe in two hands and charges toward him. Just as she swings the axe at him, Red steps to the side and sticks his foot out, tripping her. Tucker falls hard onto the floor. The searing pain in her side stabs her again.

Expecting Red to pounce on her, she rolls onto her back to block him. But Red is standing right where he was and still grinning.

"Olé!" Red says. He takes his hand off the side of his head.

Tucker sees his ear hanging halfway off.

Motioning at her, he says, "Come on."

Tucker rolls onto her knees and then stands up. Unable to take a deep breath, she pants openmouthed like a hunting dog after a long hunt. Holding her axe in a wood chopping position, she takes deliberate steps toward Red.

In a relaxed tone, Red says, "Keep on coming."

When she's four feet away from him, Tucker swings the axe toward his head.

Red sidesteps the axe and, using her forward momentum against her, shoves the back of Tucker's shoulder.

Tucker lands on her knees and loses her grip on the axe. She watches helplessly as it slides across the floor.

From behind her, Red says, "Go ahead. Pick it up."

On all fours, Tucker crawls toward the instrument she has repeatedly wielded during her life both for her own salvation and to dispense justice. Using it like a cane, she manages to get off the floor and stand up. Her back is no longer straight but bent in response to the pain in her side. The blood-smeared visage of Red swims in her field of vision.

"Olé, el toro," Red says. He gives her a cunning look and motions for her to approach him. "Come on. You can do this. Come and kill me. You know you want to. Did you know I made your grandson a child prostitute when he was in Las Vegas?"

Red's words barely penetrate Tucker's fog of pain and fatigue. But at the mention of March, she says hoarsely, "You what?"

"You heard me. I was March's pimp when he was a kid. Too bad he didn't stay a small kid because I made lots of money off of him."

The last bit of adrenaline left in Tucker surges and she lumbers toward Red like the dying bull he has reduced her to. Fatigue and lack of oxygen has rendered her impotent. She stumbles past him without ever raising the axe.

Once again Red trips her as she passes and she falls on her face. This time she is unable to rise.

"Are you done?" Red asks. When there is no response, Red says, "Then it's my turn."

Tucker hears his approaching footsteps stop beside her head. She sees the mud-encased soles of his boots. Suddenly she feels him grip her hair and begin pulling her across the floor. If she could get a breath she would have cried out, but she can only whimper in pain.

Red drags her to one of the center posts and pulls her to a sitting position. Squatting in front of her, he grabs her chin and forces her to look at him. "Do you know what the children of Israel used to do to their enemies so they wouldn't be a problem for them anymore?"

Tucker blinks slowly in response.

"Surprised I know the Bible? Prison gives you lots of reading time. Those Old Testament stories of genocide were intriguing to me. The Israelites would cut the hamstrings of their enemies and of their horses. No surgery back then to fix that, was there?" He laughs. "It was actually a pretty ingenious tactic."

Tucker continues to look at him mutely.

Red grabs the boot on her right foot and begins untying it. Once it is loose enough, he pulls it off and tosses it aside. He reaches in his pocket and takes out a knife. When he pushes a button on the side, a bright blade jumps out of the handle. Red twists it and turns it to catch the yellow light from the kerosene lanterns. "This," he says, "is my best friend. It has never failed me and has always done what I asked it to do." He slips Tucker's sock off. "Don't worry, I'm not going to hamstring you. That might make you bleed to death, and I'm not ready for that. But I am going to make sure you don't chase me around this cabin anymore." In a quick motion, he slips the blade of the knife under her Achilles tendon and slices it in two.

Tucker looks at her foot as if it belongs to someone else. The pain never registers before she passes out.

CHAPTER FORTY-SIX

Shifting in his chair to face Preacher, March says, "How do you propose to find out if Red has Tucker at the cabin without tipping him off?"

"I'd do some surveillance," Preacher replies. "Using a high-powered telescope, I could set it up on the shoreline and watch the cabin. Or I could get in touch with a friend of mine who is a commercial fisherman on Reelfoot and ask him to drive his boat by there. If that is where they are, there should be smoke coming from the stovepipe and a boat should be tied up underneath the cabin."

"That sounds risky," March says.

"Yeah," August agrees. "What if Red sees you on the shoreline or thinks the guy in the boat is the sheriff or something? Couldn't that trigger him to do something rash?"

Preacher is silent.

"Well?" March says. "Could that happen?"

Debbie leans closer to March and whispers, "He's thinking. Give him a minute."

Finally, Preacher says, "Yes it could. But the truth is anything could set Red off."

"So, what if you do find him?" April says. "What is your plan after that?"

"I haven't thought that far into it," Preacher replies. "But someone has to get inside that cabin."

Smiley lets out a loud yawn. "When I was in the Army, the first sergeant made sure we got a good night's sleep before an important mission. All ya'll have got to be tired. Why don't everybody bed down. You too, Preacher. Why don't you just stay here tonight? No sense in going back to your place."

"That's an awfully fine gesture, but I don't want to impose on you good people."

Placing her hand on his, April says, "I wish you would stay. I feel safer when you're near. You can sleep in Tucker's bed, March and Debbie will take the spare bedroom, and August and I will sleep here in the living room."

"Now wait a minute," Preacher says, "I'm not going to sleep in a bed while you have to sleep on a couch. You take Tucker's bed and I'll take the couch. Those are the only conditions that I'll agree to spend the night here. Trust me, after sleeping on the beds in prison I can sleep anywhere."

"I think Preacher's made himself heard plenty plain," Smiley says. "Ain't no sense in arguing. With that settled, I'm heading to bed." He grunts as he gets to his feet.

"I don't want to make anyone uncomfortable," Preacher says, "but I feel moved to do something, if you all will go along with it."

"I'm in," March says.

"Me, too," Debbie agrees.

"I'm game for whatever," August chimes in.

"You know I'll agree to it," April says.

"Preacher," Smiley says, "sounds like the entire congregation is at your disposal."

They all laugh.

Standing up, Preacher says, "Let's go in the living room."

Everyone dutifully follows him.

"Now get in a circle and hold hands," Preacher instructs them.

April slips one hand in his and her other hand into March's. March takes Debbie's hand, and she takes August's hand. August grasps Smiley's hand. And Smiley completes the circle when he takes hold of Preacher's hand.

"There were many nights while I was in prison," Preacher begins, "that a small group of men, who had given their lives to Jesus, would stand in a circle just like this and hold hands. We were lost men who had regained our lives through the power of the Cross. But we needed each other's strength to get through the evil and darkness of prison life. Right now we five people need each other because we don't know what the future holds. But even with our combined strength we still need the strength of our God in heaven."

"Amen, Lord," Smiley says softly. "Bless you, sweet Jesus."

"The Lord is my shepherd," Preacher says, "I shall not want. He maketh me to lie down in green pastures. He leadeth me beside the still waters."

Smiley lends his voice to Preacher's recitation, and the two of them continue. "He restoreth my soul. He leadeth me in the paths of righteousness for his name's sake. Yea, though I walk through the valley of death."

April joins in the refrain. "I will fear no evil for thou art with me; thy rod and thy staff they comfort me. Thou preparest a table before me in the presence of mine enemies. Thou anointest my head with oil; my cup runneth over. Surely goodness and mercy shall follow me all the days of my life: and I will dwell in the house of the Lord forever. Amen."

"And amen," Smiley says.

Hugging Preacher's arm, April says, "That was sweet. Thank you."

Patting her head, Preacher says, "Sure. Glad to do it."

"Goodnight, everybody," Smiley announces as he heads down the hallway to his bedroom.

A chorus of goodnights ushers him along.

Debbie pulls March down so she can whisper in his ear. "Why don't we ask Preacher to perform our wedding ceremony? What do you think?"

He nods his head, and a broad smile spreads across March's face. "Go ahead and ask him."

"Preacher," Debbie says, "March and I have something we want to ask of you."

"What's that?" Preacher asks.

"We've decided to get married and we want you to perform the wedding ceremony for us. Will you?"

"Oh my gosh!" August exclaims. "What a cool idea."

"I'm really honored by your request and even more excited that the two of you are getting married," Preacher says. "I'd be delighted to do it."

March sticks his hand out. "Thank you, Preacher. You're the best."

Shaking March's hand, Preacher asks, "Have you set a date yet?"

"We were thinking about New Year's Day," Debbie says.

"I like that," Preacher says. "It's about new beginnings and starting fresh. Lots of symbolism in your choice of date."

"I'm going to grab us some pillows and covers," August says to Preacher.

"I hope it won't offend you, Preacher, that Debbie and I will be sleeping together, even though we're not married."

"No offense taken. I learned a long time ago that I can love and appreciate people even if I don't agree with everything they do. You kids run along."

CHAPTER FORTY-SEVEN

Tucker? Is that you?"

The voice of Mama Mattie startles Tucker. "Mama Mattie? Where are you?"

"I'm here, child. I'm always here."

Tucker looks around but cannot see anything in the inky blackness.

"Shut up, and come help me feed the animals!"

At the sound of her pa's voice Tucker feels a chill run through her. She feels like she is six years old. "Please don't," she pleads.

"Just do what I tell you," Pa says.

A shiny hatchet drifts across Tucker's field of vision.

"Why do you hate me, Mama?"

Maisy's cry unnerves Tucker even further.

"Don't be afraid, Tucker. It's all going to be okay."

When Ella's voice touches Tucker's ears, Tucker immediately begins to cry. "Ella, I need y' so bad. I miss you."

Suddenly Tucker regains consciousness and her nightmare evaporates like fog burned off by the sun. She tries to open her tear-moistened eyes, but only manages to open one of them. The dim light of dawn is kissing the windows of the cabin. Without warning pain from her leg shoots through her. Her ankle lies in a reddish-brown circle of dried blood. Reflexively she tries to reach for her wounded Achilles and discovers her hands are tied behind her—and they are numb. Her swollen tongue fills her mouth. When she leans her head back against the post she is tied to, she feels a knot on the back of her head and winces. That movement pulls against her scalp, sending a new pain ripping across the top of her head.

Behind her she hears the sounds of Red getting out of bed and putting his boots on. He walks past her toward the stove, and she notices his hand is wrapped in a blood-stained rag.

Red opens the door to the firebox, sticks the poker in, and stirs the ashes and embers. Then he walks over to the woodpile, picks up an armload of wood, and carries it to the open door. One at a time he carefully lays the wood on the hungry, glowing embers. Next he turns his attention to filling the coffeepot with water from the bucket and scoops coffee into the basket. All the pieces in place, he places it on top of the stove.

He drags a chair from the table and sits down beside Tucker. "I see you survived the night. How are you feeling?"

Tucker tries to speak, but her parched throat and swollen tongue prevent anything intelligible from coming out of her mouth.

"What's the matter?" Red taunts her, "Cat got your tongue?" His maniacal laugh echoes against the walls of the cabin. "I'll bet you're thirsty, aren't you?"

Tucker gives a tiny nod.

"Well, I'm not sure if I'm going to give you anything to drink or not. Because if the idea is for me to watch you slowly die, then I don't need to do anything that will keep you alive. See my line of reasoning? My goals and your goals are not the same, except that we both want the other dead. I suppose I could cut your hands loose since you aren't going to be running off anywhere." The shrill laugh of an unbalanced mind precedes him as he walks behind Tucker.

Released from the tether, Tucker's arms and hands hang uselessly at her side. Like a thousand tiny pinpricks, the return of the blood flow tingles her hands. It reminds her of holding the bloom from a thistle plant.

Red strides over to the shelves and grabs a can of Spam. Holding the can over his head, he says, "The breakfast, lunch, and supper of champions!" The unwashed skillet from the night before is warming on the stove, the white, coagulated grease turning clear and small bits of Spam creating bubbles. Red opens the can, dumps the meat into the waiting skillet, then cuts it into thick slices. The slices sizzle. Red pours himself a cup of the black coffee and returns to sitting in front of Tucker.

"Smells good, don't it?" he asks. He takes a careful sip of the hot coffee. "Mmmm, that's good, if I do say so myself. You can tell a lot about coffee just by the way it smells. Did you know that? Here, see for yourself." He holds the coffee under Tucker's nose.

Tucker's stomach replies by giving an involuntary growl.

"You might not say it smells good, but your stomach does," Red says with a grin. "You want some? I'll tell you what I'll do. I'll set this cup on the floor over here, and if you can get to it, you can drink all you want. See? I can have a kind side, too." Turning up the cup and drinking some first, he takes five steps and sets the mug on the floor, then returns to his skillet of Spam.

Tucker stares at the mug of coffee sitting ten feet away. Her stomach growls again, imploring her to put something in it. She opens and closes her fists, testing them to be sure her fingers still work. Slowly she rolls onto her side and begins pulling herself along the floor with her forearm. Like the cannons firing at the end of Tchaikovsky's *1812 Overture*, pain thunders from every quarter of her body. Stars float in her peripheral vision and the light in the room dims. Tucker lies down and closes her eye as a wave of nausea passes through her.

"Oh come on, Tucker," Red says, "you can do better than that. You're just not trying. It's not much farther."

Opening her eye, Tucker gets a sideways view of the coffee mug sitting five feet away. Lying on her stomach, she reaches forward with both arms and finds she is able to stick the tips of her fingers between the wooden floorboards. She strains to pull herself across the floor. The edge of the floorboards bite into her fingertips. She is only able to move a couple feet before she lets go of the boards. She rolls onto her back and inspects her stinging fingertips.

Red sits down at the table with the skillet of hot Spam in front of him. He takes a piece out of the skillet and eats it. With his mouth still full, he says, "You know, I think you did better when you were on your side, don't you? It's all about physics, Tucker. On your side you have half the drag as you do when you're on your stomach. Of course, if you laid on your back and pushed yourself with your feet—oops! I forgot. You can't use both your feet, can you? Then it looks like it's back on your side, if you still want that coffee. But you need to hurry up or it's going to be cold."

Tucker shifts onto her side and begins pulling herself again with her forearm—one, two, three feet. She's close enough to see the drips on the side of the cup where Red had taken a drink earlier. Reaching as far as she can, she slips her fingers into the handle on the cup.

"Hooray!" Red exclaims and claps his hands. "I knew you could do it."

Tucker slowly pulls the cup across the floor toward her. She turns onto her stomach, lifts the cup to her mouth, and tips it up. But the cup is empty.

"Oh, I'm sorry," Red says, "I didn't realize I'd already drunk all the coffee. That wasn't very nice of me. Sometimes I'm just not a very nice man."

Tucker flings the mug in his direction. It lands impotently five feet away from him.

"Ol' gal, I think you are about out of gas. But I don't have time to play cat and mouse games with you right now. I've got to run and make a phone call to find out if Big Country has returned to me what was mine. I'll be back before dark. Until then you're free to eat or drink anything you can get to. Enjoy yourself and have a nice day." Red throws the trapdoor open and crawls down the rope to his waiting boat.

CHAPTER FORTY-EIGHT

Opening his eyes, Preacher sees the gray light of dawn filtering through the curtains in the living room of Tucker's house. The only sounds are August's soft, regular breathing and the purring of the refrigerator compressor in the kitchen. He sits up, picks his boots up off the floor, and walks in his stocking feet to the front door. He takes his leather jacket off the coat rack and silently steps outside.

The cold December air has the effect of a slap in the face. His head jerks back and his eyes blink rapidly. *Whoa! Now that's a wake-up call if there ever was one.* He sits down on the porch steps and slips on his boots. He walks to his motorcycle while putting on his jacket.

Lifting the motorcycle from its leaning position to an upright position, he pushes up the kickstand with his foot. After shifting the transmission into neutral, he begins pushing the motorcycle down the driveway and onto the road. He continues pushing the eight hundred-pound machine down the road for almost half a mile. Panting, he finally stops and rests the bike on its kickstand. *That's one way to get your morning exercise*, he reflects as he leans against the bike. A trickle of sweat makes its way down to the small of his back.

Once his breathing slows, Preacher turns to his motorcycle and says, "Now you can open your mouth and bark all you want." Sitting astride the bike, he hits the starter, and the powerful engine roars to life. After letting it idle for a few moments, Preacher puts his Harley in gear and heads toward his trailer.

Forty minutes later, Preacher is cruising down Highway 22 toward Reelfoot Lake. A bungee strap holds his telescope securely on the back of the seat behind him. In his saddlebags are a sandwich and some drinks—and his nine millimeter pistol.

At nine o'clock Preacher eases through the communities of Samburg and Tiptonville, which are perched on the edge of the lake. He follows the road that hugs the irregular shoreline of Reelfoot. Once he passes Big Ronaldson Slough he pulls off the road and eases through the tall grass and trees. Preacher stops when he sees the ground getting spongy.

He shuts off his motorcycle, unstraps the telescope, and walks carefully toward the edge of the lake. He locates two large bald cypress trees that have grown together at the base of their trunks but continue separately from a height of five feet to their arching tops thirty feet in the air. "This is perfect," Preacher says. "I'll be able to see you, but you won't be able to see me."

After unfolding the telescope stand, he secures the instrument on top. Leaning over, he looks through the eyepiece. He turns the dial of the focuser as he slowly sweeps the telescope back and forth. Suddenly he stops. "There you are." Turning the focuser a tiny bit more, he says, "The old place just never changes. Sort of like this lake." He looks more closely at the details of the cabin. "There's smoke rolling out of the stovepipe, just like I figured there would be. That's a good sign. But no signs of a boat." A frown creases his face.

Straightening back up, he says, "Maybe I was wrong, but I don't think so. Someone's been there, that's for certain. Could be Red has left Tucker out there by herself. Or maybe they were both there and now he's taken her somewhere else. And maybe Red's only left the cabin for a little bit and will be back. Good thing I brought something to eat and drink because it looks like I may be here for a while."

Five hours later Preacher has taken a break from looking through the telescope and is instead sitting on the ground resting his back against one of the cypress trees. A sound incongruent with all the nature sounds around him pricks his ear. Jumping to his feet, he looks through the telescope, and spies a boat approaching the cabin. "Yes! I knew I was right. Turn and look this way so I'll be sure."

As if the driver of the boat is an actor taking instructions from a director, he looks directly at Preacher. The move startles Preacher. "What's wrong with me? He can't see me inside these trees." Looking closely, he sees the red shock of hair on the head of his brother. He continues watching as Red guides the boat underneath the cabin and ties it off, then disappears through the trapdoor in the floor of the cabin.

"That's all I needed to know," Preacher says. He takes the telescope apart and carries it to his motorcycle. Giving a second look around to be sure he hasn't left any trash, he mounts his Harley and begins the journey back to Dresden.

By the time he reaches Tucker's house Preacher is driving by headlight. Switching off the engine, he steps off the bike and stretches his back with a groan. He looks up at the stars blinking between breaks in the clouds and sees a full moon embarking on its nightly passage across the sky.

He knocks on the front door and says, "It's Preacher."

A voice inside calls out, "Come on in."

When he steps inside everyone is standing and looking at him.

"Where have you been?!" March demands.

"How could you have left without telling anyone where you were going?" August asks.

"I was worried about you," April says.

"We've been on pins and needles all day," Debbie says.

"You gave us all a scare," Smiley says.

Unzipping his leather jacket, Preacher says, "I'm so sorry I upset you all. It's been so long since I've had to answer to anyone or had anyone to notice my comings and goings, I just took off without leaving a note for you all. It's the consequence of my living alone for all these years." He turns and hangs his coat on the rack. Turning back to face them, he says, "Where I've been is to Reelfoot."

"Let's all go sit down," Smiley says, "and then you tell us what you found."

Everyone makes their way into the living room and finds a spot to sit.

Once everyone is settled, Preacher says, "Red is at the cabin."

"Did you see Tucker?" Smiley asks.

"No I didn't. But someone was there, or at least had been there, because there was smoke coming out of the stovepipe. When I first got there I didn't see a boat. But later this afternoon I saw Red driving a boat to the cabin and going inside. There's no way to be positive Tucker is at the cabin, but I can't think of any reason Red would be there unless she was."

"So, what's the plan for rescuing Tucker?" August asks.

Preacher opens his mouth to speak, but March answers first. "I've been thinking about it since last night, and I have a plan. We know it won't be safe to approach the cabin in the daytime because Red is likely to kill Tucker at first sign of trouble. So this has to be done under the cover of darkness. Who in this room is most familiar with moving around in the dark?"

The strangeness of the question gives them all pause.

"I am. I've been living in darkness for the past several years. Darkness doesn't influence my movements or intimidate me. Preacher, you've got to get me to that cabin in silence and I'll get inside and take care of Red. I've been looking forward to that for a long time."

Debbie cries out, "March, you can't!"

"I hope you rip his heart out!" April says.

Everyone is startled at April's venomous words.

"Wait, wait, wait," Preacher says. "Everyone is running ahead of themselves. March, I realize you have no difficulty getting around with your blindness, but you've never been in this cabin and don't know anything about the inside of it."

"But you do," March says. "All I need you to do is lay it out for me so that I can see it in my mind's eye. Debbie does this for me all the time. Once I've seen it in my head, it's locked in."

Grabbing March's hand, Debbie says, "But March—"

March pats her hand. "I'll be fine. I know I'm big, but I can move like a cat. Red will never know I'm there before I grab him."

"I hate to say it," Smiley says, "but it's a good idea. Sounds like the best idea, unless somebody else has a better one."

Shaking his head, Preacher says, "I don't like putting people in harm's way. I'd rather do it myself."

"You're not putting anyone in harm's way," March retorts. "I'm placing myself there because I want to. I want to rescue my grandmother and get my hands on Red."

"If you're firm on that," Preacher says, "then we need to do it tonight. The longer this drags on, the greater the chance of harm to Tucker. Let's go to the dining table. I'll set up the interior of the cabin on it."

CHAPTER FORTY-NINE

It's eleven o'clock," Preacher says. "We better get going."

March feels Debbie's body tense beside him. He puts his hand on her knee and squeezes. "I'll be fine."

Debbie kisses him on the cheek. "I love you. Come back to me."

As March stands up, August says, "Come here, brother." They embrace. "Bring Tucker back with you."

April sniffs back a tear. "Be safe, March."

"God be with you," Smiley says.

Turning to Preacher, March says, "Let's get this done."

Preacher places his elbow into March's outstretched hand and leads the way out of the house. They walk to the back and crawl inside Tucker's pickup truck. "Maybe driving Tucker's truck will give us good luck," Preacher says.

"Maybe," March says.

For the next ninety minutes the two men ride in silence.

Finally Preacher pulls off the road and stops at a boat dock. He shuts off the engine and says, "Do I need to go over the interior of the cabin again?"

"Not necessary," March answers. "I've got it memorized and I see it as clearly as a photograph."

"All right, then. My buddy, Ezra, said I could borrow his Reelfoot boat. We'll run the motor until we're about a half mile from the cabin, then I'll row us the rest of the way. I don't want to take a chance on the sound of the motor waking Red up."

"Good idea," March says. "Sound carries a long way on the water."

March listens as Preacher exits the truck. A few seconds later his passenger door opens and Preacher grips his arm. "Let's go."

Following closely behind Preacher, March feels the change under his feet when they transfer from solid ground and step on the floating dock. For a second he loses his balance.

Preacher grabs him. "Steady there. You okay?"

"Yeah. The transition just threw me a little. I'm okay now."

"We're almost to Ezra's boat slip," Preacher says as he walks more slowly. A few more steps and he says, "Here it is. I'm going to help you in first. Remember, these boats will throw you out in a second if you don't keep your center of gravity low. So always squat or kneel."

March makes it into the boat with no difficulty. "Whew!" he says, "This was one part of our plan that I was nervous about. Not having something solid to put my foot on when I went from the dock to the boat . . . I wasn't sure I'd be able to do that."

The boat rocks side to side as Preacher steps in.

A soft breeze on March's face tells him Preacher is pushing the boat out of its slip. Suddenly the small engine jumps to life, and the gentle breeze becomes a small wind as the boat slips free of the cove and enters the open water of Reelfoot Lake.

Preacher opens the throttle and March pulls his jacket tighter around his neck in an effort to keep the cold December air at bay. As they speed across the lake, more than once their trajectory suddenly changes when they hit a submerged log or stump. But Preacher always resets their course.

Finally, Preacher cuts the engine. The only sounds are the small waves lapping against the side of the boat, the pinging sound of the engine cooling down, and the chattering of ducks on the water in the distance.

"Now I'm going to find out how old and out of shape I really am," Preacher says. "It's been a long time since I rowed one of these babies."

"Why don't we take turns?" March asks.

Preacher grunts as he begins rowing and replies, "Because I want you to have all your strength when we get to the cabin."

"How are you going to find the cabin without using some kind of spotlight or flashlight?"

"I know the general direction. But I'm hoping that the full moon up there will break through the clouds at just the right time for me to see the cabin."

Once again the two men lapse into silence as Preacher focuses on rowing steadily and March tries to envision what he will find in the cabin.

Some time later, Preacher whispers between gasps of air, "I see it."

"How far away?" March whispers back.

"About a hundred yards."

In his mind's eye March pictures the pale-blue light of the moon spotlighting the darkened cabin and reflecting off the tips of the waves, giving the surface of the lake the appearance of scattered aquamarine gemstones.

Preacher dips the paddles of the oars soundlessly in and out of the water as he slowly rows closer to their rendezvous with evil. "Fifty yards," he whispers.

Snapshots of the first time he met Red flash through March's mind, as do images of what his life became under Red's control. He squeezes his fists tightly.

"We're almost there," Preacher whispers. "Thirty feet . . . Twenty feet . . ."

A few seconds later, March feels the boat come to a stop. He imagines Preacher holding on to the pylons and easing the boat underneath the cabin, being careful not to let the edges of the boat bump against the wooden posts. March hears Preacher secure the boat with the rope they brought with them. Then Preacher pats him twice on top of his shoulder.

March slips off his boots and socks, then removes his coat, sweatshirt, and T-shirt. He unfastens his jeans and slips them off, too. It had been his idea to strip down to keep any noise, even the rustle of clothing, from waking Red. It would also make it harder for Red to get hold of him.

Preacher takes March's right hand, and, stretching it over the side of the boat, places it on Red's boat, which is parked beside them underneath the trapdoor.

Trusting that Preacher has placed him as they had planned, March squats and steps into Red's boat. Standing up slowly, he reaches overhead and finds that the trapdoor has been left open. He grips two sides of the opening and slowly pulls himself up. As his head passes through the opening, he feels heat from the woodstove to his left.

Holding himself suspended in air, he listens for any sounds in the cabin. His shoulder muscles are taut. Hearing nothing, he eases up through the opening until he finally pulls his legs into the cabin and sits on the floor. A thin sheen of sweat covers his body.

Walking on his hands and feet like a giant crab, March slowly moves toward the row of beds to his right. After covering eight feet, he stops and reaches out in front of him. Just as Preacher had told him it would, his hand makes contact with one of the chairs at the table. Moving sideways, he makes it around the end of the table.

Slowly, he begins creeping across the ten feet of space between him and the beds. All of a sudden the back of his hand bumps into something on the floor. He freezes and holds his breath while at the same time trying to figure out what the "something" felt like. *Something covered in cloth.* In movements so slow they could barely have been noticed, he reaches out and finds the object again.

Keeping his touch light as a feather, he traces the length of it and estimates it to be six feet long. His sweat-drenched features are creased with a frown of puzzlement. Then, like a bolt of lightning, it hits him—*It's a body! But who?! Is it the dead body of Tucker, or is it Red passed out drunk on the floor?* March's heart beats so rapidly it thunders in his ears.

A mixture of emotions courses through his veins—fear that he may have discovered his dead grandmother and excitement that the object of his revenge may lie helpless in front of him. Moving to one end of the body, he discovers one of the feet doesn't have a shoe on it. Carefully he makes his way to the head. Afraid to touch it, he leans closer and sniffs to see if he can smell alcohol. When no smell registers, he turns his head so that his ear is facing down. He detects no sounds of breathing.

Immediately tears well up in his eyes. It takes all his self-control not to scream out Tucker's name. He lays his hand on her head and strokes her short hair. *I'm so sorry, Tucker. I'm sorry I didn't get here sooner. But don't worry, that instrument of Satan lying in the bed over there is about to face Judgment.*

Pivoting on the balls of his feet toward the beds, March wipes the stinging tears from his eyes. Suddenly Red mumbles from one of the beds. The bed creaks as he rolls over, then silence fills the cabin again. Every sinew in every muscle of March's body is coiled like a cheetah stalking its prey. Like that great cat of the savanna, he silently approaches the bed Red is lying in.

His stealth is quickly rewarded when he makes contact with the end of the bed. Creeping along the rail, he comes to the head of the bed. The smell of whiskey drifts up from the covers. Following the scent, March inches his face closer and closer to the source. When he can feel the warmth of Red's breath on his face, he says, "Hello, Red. Welcome to hell."

March flings the covers off of Red and grabs the chest of his shirt with one hand and the crotch of his pants with the other. With a loud roar he stands up and lifts the startled and swearing Red over his head and slams him onto the floor. As all the air whooshes out of Red, March falls toward him, intending to drive his knee into his chest. But Red has rolled out of the way, and March lands hard on the floor.

"Who are you, and what do you want?" Red calls out.

"I am the judge and the jury that's come to make you pay for all you've done," March answers.

"Big Country, is that you?"

March doesn't answer but slowly moves toward Red's voice.

"Now, you're not going to hold grudges are you, Big Country? Let's let bygones be by—"

Red's voice is stopped when March drives a fist into Red's face and another into his ribs.

Red scurries backward. "You've got me at a distinct disadvantage, don't you think? I'm not used to stumbling in the dark like—"

Again Red isn't allowed to finish his sentence as March's fist finds its mark.

Red falls backward until the wall of the cabin stops him. He starts sliding toward the woodpile in the corner. "Now listen to me," he says, "you and I can make a deal. I can still use a smart guy like you. In my line of work your blindness won't necessarily be a handicap." His foot hits the edge of the woodpile. He reaches out and searches for the axe.

Out of the darkness March says, "Looking for this?" He swings the axe and buries it in the center of Red's chest.

CHAPTER FIFTY

New Year's Day dawns clear, revealing the brilliant white snow left behind as the old year passed away the night before.

August shakes March's foot. "Wake up, big guy! Today's your special day."

Propping himself up on one elbow, March says, "I still don't see why you and I and Smiley had to spend the night here in Smiley's house."

"Everyone told you it's bad luck for the groom to see the bride before the wedding."

Waving his hand in front of his face, March says, "But I'm blind. Don't you all get it?!"

August laughs. "I guess it's just the principle of the thing, then. It was an argument you couldn't win. Come on, Pop has got breakfast going."

March slips out from under the covers, and, touching his brother's elbow, follows August into the kitchen.

"Here comes the groom, here comes the groom," Smiley sings.

"Pop, I think that's supposed to be sung about the bride," August says.

"I knows that," Smiley says. "But there ain't no bride here. But we sure do have us a groom. How do you feel, March, on your last hours of freedom before you get that ol' ball and chain fastened to your ankle?"

"Huh?" March says.

"Ignore him," August says. "It's some kind of expression he uses from the old days."

"Those are the only kinds of expressions I know," Smiley says with a broad grin.

March gives the air an audible sniff. "Homemade sausage—heavy on the sage—maple syrup, which means pancakes, and black coffee with chicory. How close am I?"

"Son," Smiley says, "if I could teach you to smell raccoons the way you smell food, I could sell you for a high price to some coon hunter. You hit the menu right on the head!"

Taking March's hand and placing it on the back of a chair, August says, "Have a seat and dig in."

There is a scraping of chairs on the floor as all three find a place at the table.

March is about to find his fork, when he feels the large, warm hand of Smiley on the back of his hand.

"Before we eat," Smiley says, "let's hold hands and have a blessing."

March takes Smiley's hand and reaches for August, who grasps his hand.

"Sweet Jesus," Smiley says in somber tones, "you have marked the paths of all of us. You've been by our side in good times and in dark times. Whether we were on the mountaintop of joy or lying on our belly in the valley of despair, you were there. Today is a very special day for your servant, March. You know he's a good boy with a good heart. He has come through the fire more than once and lived to tell about it. If anyone deserves your special blessing, it's this boy.

He's about to begin a new chapter with his beautiful bride-to-be, Debbie. May he dip his pen in the inkwell of your heart as he begins writing this chapter, so that you will be present in every chapter, every page, every sentence, and every word. Bless this day, Lord. And bless this food. In the blessed name of Jesus we pray. Amen."

March keeps his grip on Smiley's and August's hands even after the echo of the amen has left the room. He squeezes them and gives them a shake. In a voice choked with emotion, he says, "And amen." He clears his throat and says, "Now get out of my way because I'm fixing to eat like there's no tomorrow."

In what looks like choreographed moves the three men fork pancakes and sausages off the serving plate in the middle of the table without anyone getting stabbed in the process.

Smiley fills their coffee cups from the pot sitting beside him.

August pours syrup on March's pancakes. "Your plate's ready," he tells his brother.

Quickly March forks in a bite of sausage and a bite of pancakes dripping with syrup. "Mmmm, that is heaven." He washes the food down with a gulp of coffee before attacking the stack of pancakes again.

"I know I've said it before," August says, "but it's practically a miracle that you're alive today to get married. I mean, how many times can one person cheat death?"

"It's the hand of God. That's what it is," Smiley says. "Don't let anybody call it luck or chance. God has a powerful plan for March's life and so delivered him from the lion's den on more than one occasion."

"You don't have to convince me," March says. "That night in the cabin when I killed Red, there were any number of ways things could have turned and he killed me."

"Even you killing him could have turned out bad," August says. "But because there was such a stack of charges pending against

Red, plus Preacher's statement that it was self-defense, you weren't charged with a crime."

"You wielded God's sword of judgment and punished the evil doer," Smiley says. "Punishment swift and certain—more of that is needed today."

"Maybe I shouldn't say this," March says, "but I'm not sorry I killed him. He deserved to die."

"Hey," August interjects in a light tone, "that's all over and done with. This is a happy day, a joy-filled day. Eat up. Noon will be here before you know it. We'll have to start getting ready before too long."

At 11:30 the three men pull into the gravel parking lot of the church.

"I've always liked this church building," Smiley says. "It's been here a long time; since the early 1900s. I think it was a Cumberland Presbyterian church first. But it's been used by several groups since—Primitive Baptist, Missionary Baptist, even a C.M.E. church met here for a while. Now Preacher is pastoring a Church of Christ group here. I'm glad all the groups preserved the clapboard siding on the building and didn't cover it with brick or that aluminum siding stuff. There's something warm and inviting about an old wooden church building."

"Is Debbie here?" March asks.

"She and April said they weren't coming to the church until the last minute," August answers. "They wanted to get completely ready at Tucker's house."

"Is anyone else here?"

"There's a few cars, including the sheriff's," August says.

"What's he doing here?"

"Sheriff Harris has been involved with this family ever since he came into office," Smiley answers. "I'm sure he's happy to see something good finally happening to you all."

The three of them exit the truck and make their way toward the church.

A man pushing a small woman in a wheelchair approaches them. "March?" the woman says.

March freezes. A rush of strong emotions fills his chest and his eyes immediately tear up. Turning to face the woman, he says, "Dr. Sydney, can it really be you?"

"The one and only," Dr. Sydney replies.

"But what are you doing here?"

"I heard there was a wedding taking place. You didn't think you could pull this off without me hearing about it, did you?"

March kneels on one knee beside the wheelchair and takes Dr. Sydney's hand. "I can't believe you drove all the way here, but I'm so glad you did. It means the world to me. Debbie is going to be so surprised."

"March," Dr. Sydney says, "I wouldn't have missed it for the world. I'm incredibly happy for you."

"If it hadn't been for you," March says, "I don't think this day would have ever come. You helped save me."

"Oh hush, hush now. Let's not get into all that. This day is about you and Debbie. Now get on inside. You've got a wedding to attend."

A few minutes before noon, Preacher, March, and August are standing at the front of the auditorium. There is a commotion at the back, where the front door of the church is.

"Will y' watch where yer a-goin'?! You're gonna put m' other leg in a cast, Shady Green." Tucker's voice echoes in the small, wood-lined auditorium. With Shady Green behind her pushing the wheelchair, they bang and scrape their way through the doorway. The white cast covering the lower half of Tucker's leg and foot sticks out below the dress she is wearing. "Watch whatcher doin'," she fusses at Shady.

"I twyin', Tucker," Shady replies. The oversized knot in his necktie is off-center and the perpetual cowlick on the back of his head is sticking straight up. The tongue-and-groove wood floor creaks as he slowly pushes Tucker toward the front of the auditorium.

Smiling, August leans toward March and whispers in his ear, "She actually wore the dress after all the protests that she wouldn't."

March smiles at the news.

"Here comes April," August whispers.

March listens to April's approaching steps and hears her as she sits down on the front pew and unbuckles the case of her Autoharp. She strums an introduction and then sings:

I'm just a poor wayfarin' stranger
Travelin' through this world of woe
Yet there's no sickness, toil, or danger
In that bright world to which I go
I'm going there to see my father
I'm going there no more to roam
I'm just a-going over Jordan
Just a-going over home
I know dark clouds will gather round me
I know my way is rough and steep
Yet beauteous fields lie just before me
Where God's redeemed their vigils keep
I'm going there to see my mother
She said she'd meet me when I come
I'm just a-going over Jordan
Just a-going over home
I want to wear a crown of glory
When I get home to that good land

I want to shout salvation's story
In concert with the blood-washed band
I'm going there to see my Savior
To sing His praise forever more
I'm just a-going over Jordan
Just a-going over home

As April's clear soprano voice finishes the last note, people can be heard sniffing back tears. Smiley Carter blows his nose.

Tucker says, "Y' sing like an angel, April. Sing us another one."

April strums for several moments and then sings:

Some lovers like the summertime when they can stroll about
Spooning in the meadows may be grand without a doubt
But give me the wintertime, for the girl I have made mine
Was captured while the snow was on the ground
I traced her little footprints in the snow
I found her little footprints in the snow, Lord
I bless that happy day that Nellie lost her way
I found her when the snow was on the ground
I called to see the girl I love one winter's afternoon
That she had gone out walking, they informed me very soon
They said she had strolled away, but where they could not say
So I started off to find her in the snow
I saw her little footprint just outside the cottage door
I traced it down a country lane, I traced it to the moor
I found she'd lost her way, there she stood in blank dismay
Not knowing where to steer for in the snow
I called her, she saw me, and as we were walking home
She promised me that never more without me would she roam
I'm happy now for life, for her I've made my wife
Whose footmarks I traced plainly in the snow

Preacher waits for the music to come back from the rafters and settle onto everyone's heart. When everything is quiet, he says to the audience, "Will everyone stand please?"

There is a rustle of clothing and a creaking of wooden pews as the audience stands to witness Debbie's entrance.

On cue, April sings:

You are my flower that's blooming in the mountain for me
You are my flower, that's blooming there for me
The grass is just as green, the sky is just as blue
The day is just as bright, the birds are singing, too
The air is just as pure, the sunlight just as free
And nature seems to say, it's all for you and me
When summertime is gone and snow begins to fall
You can sing this song and say to one and all
So wear a happy smile and life will be worthwhile
Forget your tears but don't forget to smile

During the last lines of the song Debbie takes March's hand and pulls him to her side.

"Be seated please," Preacher tells the audience. "Welcome to everyone and thank you for coming. We are all gathered today as friends and family who are interested in the future of Debbie and March and as witnesses of the marital union they are forming.

"Marriage is the very first bond of society, established in the Garden of Eden. The ancient Genesis record reads, 'for this reason a man will leave his father and mother and be united to his wife, and the two shall become one flesh.' When Jesus makes commentary on this, thousands of years after the creation, he says, 'Therefore what God has joined together, let man not separate.'

"Listen to this wedding ceremony described in the Song of Solomon. 'Daughters of kings are among your honored women; at your right hand is the royal bride. Listen, O daughter, consider and give ear: forget your people and your father's house. The king is enthralled by your beauty; honor him, for he is your lord. All glorious is the princess; her gown is interwoven with gold. In embroidered garments she is led to the king.'

"I know there was a time when you two thought you would never find someone who would want you for a mate. It is my sincere hope and prayer that God used his angels to bring you two together and that your marriage is the accomplishing of his Will. If you steadfastly endeavor to do the will of God, your life will be full of joy, and the home that you are establishing will abide in peace.

"Let me ask you to join hands please."

March and Debbie turn to face each other and hold each other's hands.

"I've never seen you more handsome," Debbie whispers.

"And I've never seen you more beautiful," March whispers back.

"March," Preacher says, "repeat after me. Debbie, you have stolen my heart. I am yours, and you are mine. Place me like a seal over your heart. My love is as strong as death. Many waters cannot quench my love; rivers cannot wash it away. This love I pledge to you."

In call-and-response style, March repeats each phrase.

Turning to Debbie, Preacher says, "Now Debbie, it's your turn." In the same manner, Debbie echoes the exact words that March has pledged to her.

Preacher reaches into his coat pocket and extracts the wedding bands. "These rings are made from the precious metal gold. But its present perfect shape did not happen naturally or accidentally. The gold had to be extracted from the earth that concealed it. It had to be subjected to the refining process of extreme heat. And then a skilled craftsman brought it to its current shape. Each time you two look at your ring or feel its presence on your finger, remember that true, lasting love doesn't happen accidentally. You must constantly work on refining and crafting it.

"March, place this ring on Debbie's finger, hold it there, and repeat after me."

There is a pause as March takes Debbie's small ring and slides it onto her ring finger.

Preacher continues, "As a token . . . of the vows we have made . . . with this ring . . . I thee wed." March dutifully repeats each phrase.

"Now, Debbie," Preacher says, "place this ring on March's finger, hold it there, and repeat after me."

There are several moments of silence as Debbie has to work hard to get March's wedding ring past his large knuckle.

"Take your time," Preacher whispers to her. "You're doing fine." When she finally gets the ring in place, Preacher says, "As a token . . . of the vows we have made . . . with this ring . . . I thee wed." Debbie solemnly repeats the phrases.

"As you have agreed together in these vows and sealed them with these rings, as a minister of the gospel and by the authority of your license, I declare you husband and wife. May the Lord bless and keep you; may the Lord make His face to shine upon you and be gracious unto you; may the Lord lift up his countenance upon you and give you peace.

"March, you may kiss your new bride."

With tears streaming down his face, March leans down. He takes Debbie's face between his hands and feels her warm tears on her cheeks. Rubbing them aside with his thumbs, he says, "I love you, Debbie Tucker."

Placing one hand on the side of March's face, Debbie says, "I love you, March Tucker."

She waits as his face moves toward her in slow motion.

When March feels her warm breath on his lips, he hesitates for a second, then covers her mouth with his.

ACKNOWLEDGMENTS

I was blessed to have some great teachers who, in their own ways, helped me to become the writer I am today. I'm indebted to them all!

Mrs. Julia Rich, my eleventh-grade English teacher. She taught me how to conjugate verbs and to think for myself.

Mrs. V. J. Shanklin, my twelfth-grade English teacher. She taught me the importance of good punctuation.

Dr. Porter King, who taught my English literature classes in my freshman and sophomore college years. He helped me understand form and simplicity in writing.

Author Sylvie Kurtz, who was my instructor a few years ago when I took a course in writing from the Long Ridge Writers Group. She showed me how to make my stories feel more immediate and how to make the reader feel they are in the story.

I owe my editor, Danielle Marshall, a true, Southern "Bless your heart" for her steady hand guiding me through the process of preparing four books at once for publication. She encouraged me when I was frustrated, gave guidance when I couldn't find my way, and challenged me to be better. The journey of editing four books was one that I dreaded. But Danielle made it seem like it was nothing. Thanks for being the leader of my team!

ABOUT THE AUTHOR

David Johnson has worked in the helping professions for over thirty-five years. He is a licensed marriage and family therapist with a master's degree in social work and over a decade of experience as a minister. In addition to the four novels comprising the Tucker series, he has authored several nonfiction books, including *Navigating the Passages of Marriage* and *Real People, Real Problems,* and has published numerous articles in national and local media. David also maintains an active blog at www.thefrontwindow.wordpress.com. When he's not writing, he is likely making music as the conductor of the David Johnson Chorus.